MISCHIEF IN MOROCCO

THE CONTINENTAL CAPERS OF MELODY CHESTERTON

BOOK TWO

SARAH F. NOEL

Also By Sarah F. Noel

The Continental Capers of Melody Chesterson

A Venetian Escapade

The Amsterdam Enigma

Tabitha & Wolf Historical Mystery Series

A Proud Woman

A Singular Woman

An Independent Woman

An Inexplicable Woman

An Audacious Woman

A Discerning Woman

An Indomitable Woman

An Intrepid Woman

A Patient Woman

An Enigmatic Woman

Acknowledgements

I want to thank my wonderful editor, Kieran Devaney and the eagle-eyed Patricia Goulden and the members of my amazing ARC team for doing a final check of the manuscript, particularly Olita, Amanda, and Wendy.

To the best group of former strangers I could have wished to tour Morocco with: Brett, Olivia, Fiona, Raymond, Kim, Judy and our fantastic tour guides, Lahcen and Hakima. Finally, our driver Omar and the wonderful Mansour, who made our night with his pipe playing.

FOREWORD

This book is written using British English spelling. e.g. dishonour instead of dishonor, realise instead of realize.

British spelling aside, while every effort has been made to proofread this thoroughly, typos do creep in. If you find any, I'd greatly appreciate a quick email to report them at sarahfnoelauthor@gmail.com

CHAPTER 1

June 1, 1911 - Morocco

D*ear Diary, I'm dusty, exhausted, hungry and bored. But more than any of those things, I am irritated beyond belief*

Melody found that, in fact, she was too irritated to write anymore and put her diary aside. As much as she tried to hide it, she was fuming. Melody had spent multiple train and boat rides, to say nothing of some very uncomfortable, bumpy carriage rides, trying to maintain her composure around Alessandro. As she usually did when confronted with a challenging situation, Melody had done her best to channel Granny, the Dowager Countess of Pembroke. There was no doubt that Granny would never have given Alessandro the satisfaction of knowing how much he had hurt her.

Once Melody had realised that all of the charming Conte Foscari's supposed romantic interest was nothing more than an attempt to get closer to her brother, Rat, in order to monitor his progress as a newly minted British Secret Service agent, she had determined to be as aloof with him as possible. This would have been far easier if they hadn't all been in very close quarters for the many days that it had taken them to travel from Venice to Casablanca. What was most galling was that Alessandro seemed not even to notice her stiff formality. Despite his initial reservations about Alessandro, Rat now seemed to be utterly in the man's thrall. He was happy to use the long journey to pick the brain of the more seasoned British operative. The two men had quickly formed an easy camaraderie, with Alessandro taking the role of mentor to the younger man.

The resolution of the intrigue they had stumbled upon in Venice had only fed Rat's insecurities about his readiness for assignments in the field. There was no doubt that he would never have solved the murder of Antonio Graziano without the help of Melody, his little sister. If this was not galling enough, discovering that Alessandro had been ordered to oversee his progress by some nameless sceptic in the British Secret Service Bureau had only added to these self-doubts.

While a lesser man might have allowed these doubts to fester into resentment towards the man sent to monitor him, Rat was too eager to learn and too modest to do anything other than be grateful for the guidance of the older, wiser operative. He and Alessandro seemed to spend the entire trip discussing arcane details of European politics and British foreign policy.

Melody was determined to prove herself a worthy member of the Moroccan expedition and spent the first day trying to keep up with the conversation and feigning interest. Still, once they started comparing the relative weaknesses of the various European heads of state and how those might affect the behaviour of their relative governments, Melody could no longer stifle her yawns nor even pretend to care. Instead, she took up a book and reread Tabby Cat's favourite novel, *Pride and Prejudice*. Stealing secret glances at Alessandro's handsome face, Melody considered Elizabeth Bennet's initial distaste towards the proud Mr Darcy. Of course, that comedy of errors had ended up with the star-crossed lovers in each other's arms. Real life was never that simple.

If she was honest with herself, everything about their stay in Venice had left her discombobulated. Melody had always considered herself a good judge of character. Yet her inability to spot what a scoundrel Xander Ashby was, and to be so taken in by Alessandro's romantic overtures, had disarmed her. While Melody had cause to question her intuitions about character, she also felt proud and buoyed by her significant contributions towards discovering Signor Graziano's killer. Even Rat had admitted that he would never have solved the case if not for her help.

While she enjoyed the sense of pride she felt in her brother's acknowledgement of her contribution, Melody couldn't overlook the fact that, even so, his preference had been to leave her behind in Venice when he was called to Morocco to help deal with a crisis. He had only agreed to her joining him on the trip under sufferance. Though, she acknowledged to herself wryly, if he had mentioned that Alessandro was joining their party, Rat might have had a far easier time persuading Melody to stay behind in Venice.

Despite all the very dull talk of the various European powers' jostling for power and influence in North Africa, Melody still had no real idea why Rat and Alessandro had been summoned to Morocco. She had heard enough to understand that the major power battle was between France and Germany. Britain's interests were primarily in monitoring the situation and ensuring that it didn't spiral out of control. Perhaps if she hadn't become bored and stopped paying attention she might have learned more. As she had this thought, Melody realised that she had missed what might be the only opportunity she would have to learn the political context of whatever they were about to encounter. Chagrined at her easy willingness to tune out the critical conversation going on in front of her, Melody sat up a little straighter and was determined to take advantage of however much of the journey they had left to soak up whatever knowledge she could.

"Of course, the Germans did not need to be quite so provocative," Alessandro was saying. "One would think it would be obvious how the French would react. After the crisis of 1905, there could be little doubt how such a move would be interpreted."

"Indeed," Rat agreed. "And so, what can we conclude from such a deliberate provocation?"

Alessandro shook his head, "I am not sure. And more to the point, neither is the British Government. Hence, our orders to travel to Morocco. While there are certainly those who consider war as inevitable at some point, I do not believe that anyone wishes us to stumble into it because of some minor skirmish."

"Could this really be the match that starts a broader conflagration?" Rat asked, eager for the other man's insights.

Alessandro considered the question. "From a distance, and indeed if one were only to read the more populist London broadsheets, there is no question that Germany is our enemy and France our ally. However, many voices in the government would argue quite the opposite. Indeed, Britain's history with both powers is complicated, to say the least. For the most part, our government's primary interest is in maintaining the political status quo in the region and ensuring that no single European power can monopolise Morocco's trade. However, British interests go beyond securing trade for British merchants and businesses in Morocco; whoever controls this country controls the Straits of Gibraltar, which is a maritime choke point for travel to India and beyond."

Alessandro's words made perfect sense and yet they seemed to sit uneasily with Rat. Melody knew her brother too well not to sense his anxiety. His chewing on his bottom lip told her all she needed to know. Yet, he seemed hesitant to vocalise whatever was on his mind. Finally, Melody became too impatient with her brother's hemming and hawing and said, rather more sharply than she might have wished, "Conte Foscari, this lesson in international relations is all very well, but what is the mission that you and my brother are tasked with?"

If there was any doubt as to how inappropriate this question was, the daggers that Rat was shooting at her with his eyes left no doubt.

For his part, Alessandro merely looked amused. In a tone so patronising that it set Melody's teeth on edge, the conte took on the look and tone of indulgence that one might with a precocious yet truculent child and replied, "Miss Chesterton, you cannot imagine that is something that I am able to reveal, however charming the questioner. I suggest you return to your book and not worry yourself about such matters."

Melody was so infuriated by this answer that she didn't reply for fear that she would be unable to control her emotions. Hence, the silent fuming. But then she thought again about what Granny would do; she would never let anyone, certainly not a man, talk down to her.

Taking a calming breath, Melody sat up a bit straighter and, channeling the dowager as best she could, replied, "Conte Foscari, I realise that you believe that your secret mission is somehow beyond my capacity either to understand or to be sufficiently discreet about. However, I assure you that if someone who spends as much time worrying about the best tie of his cravat, as you seem to, can grasp the concepts, then I can as well."

Alessandro said nothing, but the smirk he gave her made Melody want to slap that handsome face. As hard as it was to believe, Rat seemed oblivious to the tension between his new friend and his sister. He pulled Alessandro's attention back to discussing arcane points of official and unofficial British policy towards its European allies and foes.

Melody turned away from their conversation and looked out of the carriage window. There was something quite mesmerising about the countryside they were driving through. While there were some cultivated plots of land, and trees that she couldn't identify were dotted throughout the fields, the minimal greenery threw the otherwise golden-brown of the rest of the vista into stark relief. Most of the landscape was arid, hardy, often dusty, land, with some scrubby vegetation at best. It was like nothing she had ever seen.

Occasionally, Melody would see a small cluster of stone dwellings making up a village. They passed farmers and herders tending to their flocks of goats and lambs. Sometimes, someone would pass them, riding a donkey or a horse. As Melody continued to stare out of the window, she started to notice the landscape changing. Now, there were increasing signs of trade and commerce with groupings of roadside stalls selling fruit and vegetables or other goods, including pottery. The owners of the stalls would look up as their carriage passed, calling out in an exotic-sounding language that Melody couldn't understand. Sometimes, they passed beggars who cried out to them for alms. Nothing in Melody's eighteen-sheltered years had prepared her for the sights, sounds, and smells of Morocco.

CHAPTER 2

At some point, lulled by boredom at the conversation and the movement of the carriage, Melody fell asleep on Mary's shoulder. When the carriage hit a particularly large bump in the dirt road, she was jolted from her nap. Awakening with a start, it took her a moment to remember where she was. Lifting her head, she looked out of the window and realised that they must be in Casablanca. In place of the countryside that they seemed to have been driving through endlessly, now they were in the thick of a bustling city.

Various odours, some pleasant, some not so much, wafted through the carriage windows. Melody smelled fresh bread, and her stomach gurgled, reminding her that they hadn't eaten in a while. Embarrassed by such an unladylike sound, particularly in front of Alessandro, Melody could only hope that they were almost at their destination and that there would be food waiting for them there.

The streets were so narrow and so filled with vendors and their customers that Melody wasn't entirely sure how they were managing to make their way through. Indeed, the going was slow, and at one point, they came to a complete standstill. There was a lot of shouting coming from up ahead. After they had been standing in the same spot for some minutes, Alessandro opened the carriage door and stepped out.

Returning a few moments later, he explained, "There was some kind of altercation up ahead. Apparently, a boy tried to steal a loaf of bread. The shopkeeper had him by the arm and was screaming for the authorities while the boy swore he was planning to pay. However, this alone is not what has slowed us down. It seems that everyone else on the street took this as an opportunity for entertainment, and all other activity has ceased while people weighed in on what they saw, berated the boy, or in some cases, the shopkeeper for his lack of charity."

As Alessandro finished his explanation, the carriage began moving again. "What will happen to the boy?" Melody asked.

"I paid for his bread, and the shopkeeper let him go," Alessandro said nonchalantly, shrugging his shoulders as if the gesture was no more than a practical solution to a problem in front of him.

If Melody had been less angry at the man, she might have been inclined to attribute to him a compassion that he seemed reluctant to acknowledge. However, she was not in the mood to consider the conte as anything but a heartless monster and was determined to ignore anything that might muddy that narrative.

Melody had no idea where they were staying in Casablanca. While she assumed they would all be in the same place, Melody could only hope that it was large enough that she could keep her distance from her former beau. The trip had been long and tiring, and having to share such close quarters with Alessandro for many days had Melody at the very end of her tether.

Finally, they seemed to be leaving the narrow, winding streets of what Alessandro had said was the Medina. They had emerged onto a wide, palm-tree-lined boulevard with a very European feel to it—well, European, but with a distinctly local twist. The grandeur of the buildings with their wrought-iron balconies and railings and stucco exterior made it clear that they were entering the heavily European-influenced part of Casablanca; many of these buildings wouldn't have been out of place in Paris.

"This is Anfa," Alessandro said as the emerging neighbourhood began to look, sound and smell as if they were as far away from the Medina, even in London or Paris. Melody even caught sight of a charming cafe from which she caught a waft of the delicious intermingling scents of coffee and pastries. The cafe's patrons would not have looked out of place in a major European city, dressed in the height of fashion.

"Anfa is one of the more upscale Casablanca neighbourhoods and is where we will be staying," Alessandro explained.

"Yes, thank you for making all these arrangements, Foscari," Rat said in a tone that Melody found quite nauseating. It was only the week before that her brother had hated the man, and now he was fawning all over him. Not for the first time on that trip, she wondered if she should have stayed behind in Venice. As much as she wished to assert her independence and prove her usefulness, was it worth it in the end? She had to hope it would be.

Finally, the carriage pulled up to a villa that, even by the standards of its grand neighbours, was opulent. It was three storeys high, with tall windows framed by ornate stone carvings and with highly decorative wrought iron balconies and railings. The oak front door was set into a large archway and flanked on each side with marble pillars. The one feature that suggested this wasn't a home on the Rue de Rivoli was the terracotta-tiled roof. The house was set in a large, lush garden, filled with exotic foliage and flowers whose heady perfume filled Melody's nose almost as aggressively as the fish had in the Medina.

Whose house was this? Melody knew so little about Alessandro except for the few details that he had shared in Venice, and she had no idea how much truth there had been to those. Perhaps everything he had told her had been part of the elaborate web he had spun in order to use her to get close to Rat. As soon as she had this thought, she felt herself in danger of her eyes welling up with tears.

Biting on the inside of her cheek to get herself back under control, Melody swore to herself that she would never again allow thoughts of Alessandro to upset her. If anything, she should consider the brief and ultimately insincere romantic interlude to be a valuable life lesson.

Granny had tried so hard to instil in Melody the importance of always being in control of any given situation. Now, Melody understood better what the steely old woman had meant. She had allowed herself to lose control and had given in to a girlish, romantic fantasy—just as Alessandro had known she would. He read her naivety entirely correctly, and perhaps that was what she most hated him for; he had exploited her wide-eyed innocence, and she knew she could never get it back. Alessandro would always be the first man who broke her heart, and she would never be that open or trusting again.

Following Alessandro out of the carriage and into the villa's grounds, it did occur to Melody that perhaps this *was* his house. She knew, or thought she knew, that he only spent part of the year in Italy. She had assumed that he spent the rest in London, but perhaps that wasn't the case. A swarthy, middle-aged man opened the solid oak front door. He had a well-groomed beard and was wearing a long robe—she thought it was called a djellaba—that wasn't unlike the ones that the men had worn in the Medina. The only difference was that this one was made of a fine fabric and had elaborate embroidery on the wrists and neckline.

Despite his rather grand outfit, it did seem as if this man was some kind of butler, or whatever the Moroccan equivalent was. Whoever the man was, he seemed to know Alessandro and was expecting him. Putting his hands together as if in prayer, he bowed. "Omarh ybarek fik, Sidi," the man intoned almost reverently.

Alessandro inclined his head slightly in response, "As-salaam alaykum, Ahmed." He then started speaking quickly to Ahmed in what Melody assumed was Arabic. She was tempted to roll her eyes; of course, Alessandro spoke the language fluently. She should have expected nothing less.

Apparently, he had shared a joke with the servant because they both chuckled. Then, he gestured towards her and said something. She heard her name and then Rat's but had no idea what was being said. The men laughed again. What was he saying about her?

Finally, the servant, Ahmed, bowed in her direction and said in perfect, if heavily accented English, "Lalla Melody, welcome to Casablanca." Then he turned towards Rat, bowed yet again, and said, "Sidi Matthew, it is an honour. You must all be eager to wash off the dust of the road. Let me show you to your rooms and then Lalla Fatima is waiting for you in the salon with refreshments."

Given the rumbling that Melody's stomach had been doing increasingly, she hoped these refreshments were more than beverages. Ahmed led the way up a grand, pink marble staircase. Her room was the first they came to. Melody opened the door into a large, airy room whose huge picture window looked out onto the gardens. The room was decorated with restrained taste, with a feminine touch. There were freshly cut flowers in a crystal vase on a charming table with a mosaic top, and the bedding and curtains were silk in various pastel colours.

Melody was charmed with the room and couldn't help but exclaim in delight, "Oh, it is lovely." In truth, after days of discomfort during the trip from Venice, she would have been happy to lay her head on any fabric that was on a moderately comfortable mattress and pillow. Still, the prettiness of the room was an added pleasure, and she couldn't help sighing with relief at what looked to be an adjoining bathroom. Looking into the room at the large, claw-footed tub, she wondered whether she would have time for a bath. Then Melody considered that, apparently, they were awaited by the lady of the house and realised with reluctance that she would have to be satisfied with washing her hands and face.

Ahmed left her and Mary to explore the room while he carried on with Rat and Alessandro. Mary had learned how to serve Melody from Ginny, Tabby Cat's own maid. One of Ginny's most cherished tenets was that a good lady's maid never had to wait to fully unpack in order to allow her mistress an appropriate change of clothes on arrival at a new residence. This was a rule that Mary had taken to heart. She now began to unpack a carpet bag she was holding and retrieved a fresh shirtwaist, a hairbrush, and a few other necessities that enabled Melody to leave her bedroom a short while later looking and feeling refreshed.

While Mary had brushed and re-pinned her hair, Melody considered who this Lalla Fatima might be. Finally, for no particular reason, she decided that there was something about the name that suggested a woman of advanced years. Of course, even as she thought this, Melody realised how illogical such a thought was. However old Fatima was, she had been young once, with the same name. As Melody was being readied, she took the chance to write in her diary.

Dear Diary, I wish that Mary would hurry up. Does it really matter if I have some hair out of place? I am sure that some sweet old lady will hardly notice, let alone care what I look like. And I know that Alessandro will not care.

I do not know much about Lalla Fatima, and of course, I could hardly question Conte Foscari. Perhaps she is an elderly woman whose husband was an acquaintance of Alessandro's father. Yes, I believe that would make total sense.

As she wrote, Melody was increasingly convinced that she was going to enter the salon to find a woman of advanced years, resting on her cane and squinting at her guests with eyes dimmed by age.

CHAPTER 3

M ary had taken long enough with Melody's hair and change of
clothing that by the time she descended the staircase, she was able
to locate the salon by following the sound of Rat and Alessandro's voices,
who were already there ahead of her. She could hear the murmur of a soft,
feminine voice in reply.

If she had paused for a moment and considered what she was hearing,
Melody would have realised that the dulcet tones she was hearing were not
coming from a woman of seventy or eighty. Even so, she could barely
contain her surprise when she walked into the room and came face to face
with the most beautiful woman she had ever seen. The embodiment of
grace and sophistication in front of her was obviously their hostess, Lalla
Fatima.

Melody had never thought of herself as particularly large, yet when
Fatima rose to greet her, she felt thickset and ungainly next to the petite,
delicate woman. Fatima had large, brown, almond-shaped eyes that were
framed by long, thick eyelashes. She had a heart-shaped face with high
cheekbones and full lips that curved into a welcoming, if somewhat insincere, smile. Fatima's very long, almost black hair was only pinned up at the
front and otherwise flowed down her back in a glossy stream.

If Melody had to guess, she would have said that Fatima was a few years older than she was, but that wasn't because there was anything aged about the woman's perfect skin. Instead, it was a somewhat knowing look in those huge eyes that quickly took in everything about Melody and seemed to judge her no competition. This feeling of being assessed and found wanting was not something Melody could have rationally explained, but rather a strong intuition based on the very slight raise of one eyebrow and a quirk of Fatima's beautiful mouth. Melody had seen Granny make a very similar expression on many occasions when the dowager was judging and dismissing the people she aimed it at.

Holding out a tiny hand, Fatima said in slightly accented but otherwise perfect English, "Welcome. You must be Miss Chesterton. Sandro has told me all about you. Please, take a seat."

Sandro? Whoever this woman was, it was obvious that she and Conte Foscari were well acquainted.

"Then you have the advantage, Lalla Fatima," Melody replied in what she hoped was a polite, easy tone that in no way conveyed her true feelings.

"Please, just Fatima and I hope that I may call you Melody," the woman said in an affable tone, but with a gleam in her eye and another quirk of her lips that made Melody suspect that her own tone had been a little less insouciant than she had intended.

Was it possible that Fatima knew or at least suspected Melody's brief but mortifyingly embarrassing history with Alessandro? Just the thought of it caused Melody to flush with shame. If Fatima noticed this, she was either kind enough, or more likely clever enough, to pretend to ignore it.

Fatima continued, "Sandro and I are very old friends." Again, there was something underlying the seeming innocence of her words that led Melody to conclude that they were, or had been, more than old friends. She also suspected that such an implication on Fatima's part was no accident.

Melody had always considered herself intelligent. After fourteen years of learning at the dowager's feet, she felt herself more than able to participate in the thrust and parry of multi-layered society conversation. Even in her short time out in society, Melody had been perfectly able to navigate even the most forked-tongued banter nimbly, and to hold her own against the aristocracy's most arch matrons. Yet, she had a suspicion that she might have before her a woman who was a formidable sparring partner. Perhaps a woman who would even be a worthy adversary for Granny!

Whatever Alessandro might have intuited about the layers of meaning replete in the slight conversation between the two women, Rat was oblivious to it being anything other than the casual chitchat of new acquaintances.

He said with an eagerness that immediately made Melody suspicious, "Fatima was just telling me that her father was Moroccan and was the ambassador to France in the 1890s, which is where he met her mother. Fatima grew up in Paris and briefly in London, which is where she and Alessandro first met." Rat said all this with the eagerness of a puppy dog and Melody's heart sank at the realisation that her brother was already in thrall to the beautiful Lalla Fatima.

Searching her head for a safe topic of conversation that wouldn't expose her any more than she had already managed, Melody remarked, "Your English is flawless, Fatima."

"Merci beaucoup. When I first arrived in Britain, my English was so bad. But Sandro was a wonderful teacher, and we spent so much time together, and now you hear the result."

So much for a safe topic, Melody mused.

Fatima continued, "Do you speak French, Melody?" Reluctantly, Melody had to admit that, while it was better than her Italian, her French was not all it should be after many years of lessons.

"No matter," Fatima said in a tone that barely concealed her condescension. "I will help you when you visit the modiste."

Melody wasn't sure whether this was supposed to insult her clothes or her capacity to involve herself in anything more serious than her wardrobe; perhaps it was a double-handed insult.

Again, all of the hidden meaning beneath their hostess' words was utterly lost on Rat. "Fatima, how widely is French used in Morocco?"

"Well Matthew, at least in the regions under French influence, such as Casablanca, French is spoken by the Moroccan elites, and of course between those of us of French origin."

So, it seemed that everyone was on first-name terms already. For his part, Rat seemed delighted by Fatima's use of his given name,

"What language is spoken most commonly by Moroccans?" he asked.

"In Casablanca, you will usually find people speaking Arabic, though there are some Berber languages spoken here. If you have cause to go out into the countryside, you are more likely to encounter a range of Berber dialects. Luckily, I have a man who can aid you, Omar. He speaks many languages."

It was one of Melody's great regrets that, for all her intelligence and education, she spoke no other language with any real fluency. Granny had always harped on the importance of learning foreign languages, well, at least Italian and German. She had always been less enthusiastic about French. Rat's theory was that the highly opinionated old woman had never forgiven the French for executing their aristocracy during the French Revolution. Despite the dowager holding this opinion, at Tabby Cat's insistence, Melody had suffered through many years of French lessons. Yet she would be hard-pressed to carry on any conversation that was more complicated than ordering some food in a restaurant. She was always impressed by anyone fluent in even one other language, let alone many of them. She was intrigued by this Omar already.

"Ah yes, Omar," Alessandro chimed in. "He was extremely helpful during the crisis in '05. I am glad that he is still willing to be of assistance."

1905? What had happened in 1905? Melody tried to remember. She had a vague memory of it being one of the things that Rat and Alessandro had droned on about during the interminable carriage ride from Tangier to Casablanca. She thought that it was something about the Germans challenging French influence in Morocco. Why did they do that again? Now that she thought about it, she did remember Alessandro explaining that this incident greatly strained France's relationship with Germany and caused Britain to view Germany as a growing threat. Was that it? Or was it the other way around? No, she really did remember it being Germany who challenged France. Though she had no idea why anyone cared what happened so many miles from Europe, at the tip of North Africa.

As if her thoughts had been expressed out loud, Fatima asked, "Do you believe that we are in danger of another such crisis now?"

As they continued to discuss the precarious current situation, Melody wondered at the wisdom of Alessandro including Fatima in the conversation. She was half-French and had been raised in Paris. Surely, her allegiance was not with the British Government. Whatever her history with

Alessandro, how could he trust her enough to disclose sensitive intelligence? Rat had described the conte as a seasoned intelligence operative. However, this seemed like the kind of slip of the tongue that a man of Alessandro's supposed experience would know better than to let happen.

Melody had no idea what the mission was that Rat had spoken of, but she assumed it had something to do with this new crisis. Though, why did the British care that France had antagonised Spain and Germany? And now that she thought about it, why were they staying in the home of a French citizen? After being thrust into a murder investigation when they were in Venice, Rat had considered Alessandro a suspect almost until the end. At the time, Melody had hotly defended him, unable to believe that the handsome, charming man flirting with her could be a cold-hearted killer.

Of course, Alessandro had turned out to be innocent of the murder and had been instrumental in saving Rat and Melody from being the killers' latest victims. Nevertheless, now that Alessandro's behaviour towards her had been exposed as a charade, she found herself questioning his motives and loyalty towards Britain. In Venice, it had been Rat who had pointed out that only one of the conte's parents had been British, while his father had been Italian. Thanks to the seemingly sweet and harmless Xander Ashby and his revealed hostility towards Britain and willingness to spy for Austria-Hungary, they had come to realise that someone of dual citizenship could have surprising loyalties.

Rat's current feelings towards Alessandro couldn't be further from his initial suspicious wariness, but was it possible that he had been right all along? Her brother had told Melody very little about their supposed mission in Morocco. Perhaps if she had paid more attention to their conversations, Melody might have gleaned more. Now, it occurred to her to wonder just how much Rat really did know. Of course, she couldn't imagine what nefarious motives Alessandro might have that would necessitate him bringing Rat along with him. However, as Melody was learning, her inability to conceive of something didn't make it less likely to be the case.

Melody determined that as soon as she was able to get Rat alone, she would press him to share more information with her and alert him to her concerns about staying in Lalla Fatima's house. Even as she thought this,

Melody observed the look of devotion that was shining from her brother's eyes and realised that this wouldn't be an easy conversation.

His newfound admiration for Alessandro would be hard enough to counter, but this new infatuation with Fatima was going to make Rat even less persuadable. Of course, she didn't know that there was anything to be concerned about. However, Melody wanted to put him on his guard. Melody doubted that Rat would be open to hearing her concerns, at least at first. Still, she had to try. Her brother was a highly intelligent, thoughtful young man. Melody was sure that once she had expressed her worries, her brother would be more aware of any irregularities with Alessandro and Fatima, whether or not he wanted to be.

CHAPTER 4

As far as Melody was concerned, the evening had been too long, even though they had all been too exhausted for anything but an early dinner followed by bed.

Dear Diary, I know that Granny would say that I should rise above such things, but this Fatima woman irritates me so. There is just something about the way she smirks at me that makes me want to be entirely childish and stick out my tongue at her. Everything is made so much worse because Rat looks at her with this silly, adoring look on his face. I have no idea how long we are to stay in this house, but I am not sure that I will be able to tolerate more than a few days at the most.

Melody's last thought before she closed her eyes and surrendered to slumber was that she wasn't sure how long she could bear Fatima's sly insults, Rat's adoration of the woman, and Alessandro's disregard towards herself. Of course, she had no idea what her alternative options might be. The trip from Venice had been long and arduous, and she could neither imagine making it again so quickly nor doing it alone with only Mary by her side. Anyway, she couldn't imagine Rat being happy if she were to suggest it.

The following morning, Melody's spirits were no higher. As Mary brushed and pinned her hair, Melody considered what she had hoped to achieve by forcing Rat to bring her with him. Working together with her brother to uncover Antonio Graziano's killer in Venice, she had felt useful. More than useful, she had felt purposeful.

Ever since Melody had come into the fortune set aside for her by Granny, she had considered what she wanted to do with her life. The dowager had surprised everyone when she had set the trust up for Melody almost fourteen years earlier. Most surprising was that she hadn't stipulated it should be used as a dowry. In addition, the dowager hadn't insisted on Melody being much older to gain control of her fortune and hadn't put it under the control of a male guardian. Of course, Melody would rely on Uncle Maxie and Wolfie to help guide her investments, but she need not if she chose otherwise.

Wolfie had suggested that she might use the money to help fund her further education. However, as much as Melody admired Cousin Lily for her devotion to her botanical studies, education and research, Melody knew that more academic study was not what she craved. It had been Granny who had first suggested that Melody use some of the money to travel. Still, even though it had been barely a month since she had left London, Melody could already tell that drifting aimlessly through the major cities of Europe from one museum to another was not going to satisfy her.

Melody knew that returning to England wasn't the answer; she had cut her season short and had absolutely no desire to return until it was well and truly over. If there was any downside to being a wealthy heiress, it was that, regardless of the circumstances of her birth and early years living as a homeless waif on the streets of Whitechapel, she was still the object of every wastrel third son who needed a wealthy bride.

As Mary put the finishing touches to her hair and chose some tasteful pearl earrings for her to wear, Melody made a decision: she had to find a way to persuade Rat to include her in whatever this mission was. Melody knew that she was a good investigator, and she also believed that, however reluctant he had been to collaborate with her initially, Rat knew it too. Of course, the fact that he was now working in partnership with Alessandro complicated matters, but surely there was a way around that.

Melody was filled with a new energy and determination; one way or another, she would be part of whatever it was that had brought Rat and

Alessandro to Morocco. But first, she had to persuade Rat to tell her what exactly that was.

Descending the stairs, Melody was greeted by Ahmed. "Salem alaykum, Lalla Melody. Would you like some breakfast?"

Melody found that she was hungrier than she had thought. During their trip from Tangier, they had limited opportunities to sample much Moroccan food. Most of what she'd eaten was bread, cheese, and a lot of dates. She was interested to see what a wealthy Moroccan household served for breakfast.

"Lalla Melody, Sidi Alessandro and Sidi Matthew left some time ago, and Lalla Fatima rarely partakes of food until past midday." Of course she didn't, Melody thought sourly. The man continued, "Might I suggest that you take your meal in the garden? It is quite beautiful this time of year."

Indicating that the garden sounded lovely, Melody followed the man through the house and out some French windows. The garden was even lovelier than she expected. There was a heady scent of roses permeating the air, and as she looked around, it was apparent why: there were roses everywhere. Different colours, different size flowers, each more glorious than the next. In the middle of all these rose bushes was a paved area with a beautiful mosaic-topped table surrounded by wrought-iron chairs.

Ahmed indicated that Melody should take a seat, and a few minutes later, he returned with a tray laden with dates, fruit, pastries, and what looked like cake. He set everything down on the table and laid out cutlery. He left again and then returned with mint tea. Melody had tried some mint tea once during their travels, but this tea looked and smelled much more appetising. Along with the pastries, there was a pot with what turned out to be honey in it.

After Ahmed had left, Melody helped herself to an array of the baked goods. Biting into one of the pastries, she was surprised to find that it was savoury and was filled with a tasty filling of minced peppers and onions. There was what looked like a pancake, but it didn't taste anything like the pancakes she'd had in London. She tried spreading a little honey on it and found that it was very tasty. The cake was unusual in that it wasn't particularly sweet.

The mint tea was as delicious as it had smelled. Melody wasn't sure she'd ever had fresh mint before and decided that she would be happy to have mint tea every morning for their stay. Unlike the cake, the tea was very sweet. Melody ate more than she should have, but it was all so appetising and interesting, and she wanted to try a little of everything.

As she ate, she wondered where Rat and Alessandro had gone. She had brought her diary down with her, and as she sipped her tea, she wrote.

Dear Diary, Did Rat leave without me because I was asleep or was it just an indication that he has no intention of involving me in whatever this is? I would like to think that if it were left to him, he would choose to include me and that it was Alessandro who dissuaded him. I would at least like to think that. Am I being foolish even to believe that? I do realise that I did not help my cause by not paying sufficient attention during the trip to Casablanca. I am not sure what my next move should be, but I need to talk with Rat. If nothing else, I must make him aware of my concerns about Fatima and perhaps even Alessandro. Though I cannot imagine that he will take my worries seriously.

Melody was so absorbed in her writing that she didn't hear the footsteps approaching. Finally, realising someone was almost upon her, Melody looked up in surprise at Alessandro.

Assuming he had come upon her by mistake, Melody hurried to assure him, "I am almost finished. Let me just have another sip of tea, and I will leave you in peace."

"Miss Chesterton, Melody, there is no need to leave. In fact, I came here hoping to find you."

Melody hated how her heart skipped at these words. Treacherous heart.

Stealing herself against a flirtatious assault, Melody said coldly, "Me? What can you possibly want with me, Conte Foscari?"

Alessandro sat down, sighed, and replied, "This. This is what I want to discuss with you. This cold formality. Will it ever end, Melody?"

She had to take a very deep breath before answering. Even then, she could hear how strangled her voice was. "Excuse me, sir. But do you not think I have cause?"

"Do you? Why? Yes, I let things go too far in the gondola; I acknowledge that. In fact, I believe I said so at the time. But if that is the cause, then let me apologise again. I let myself get carried away that night, and that was wrong, and I am sorry."

Melody wanted to scream; he still didn't understand. Instead of screaming, she said in as calm a voice as possible, "It was not that evening, or not just that evening. You flirted with me each time you saw me and allowed me to believe, no, encouraged me to believe that you had a romantic interest in me when your only interest was in getting close enough to me to keep an eye on my brother. You knew that you were dealing with a young, innocent woman and could not have been in any doubt as to how your actions would be viewed and your flirtations received."

As she spoke, Melody watched his face. Was there any contrition? She wasn't sure. As she spoke the last sentence, she saw him pursing his lips a little, and his eyes dart back and forth as he was unable to maintain eye contact with her. Yes, Melody decided. He knew what he had done and to hear it said out loud made him uncomfortable. Would he acknowledge that discomfort? Melody suddenly realised that she could only stay in Morocco and continue in Alessandro's presence if, at the very least, he could admit what he had done. Because if he conceded his ill use of her, then Melody was no longer the silly girl who got carried away with a fantasy she had entirely concocted in her imagination.

She waited. And then she waited. The silence stretched on until it was in danger of becoming very awkward. Finally, Alessandro said in a genuinely apologetic voice, "You are entirely right. I behaved in a manner that was neither gentlemanly nor kind, and I apologise. You deserved far, far better than to have a man seduce you with ulterior motives."

Melody let out the breath she hadn't realised she'd been holding. "Thank you, Alessandro." She might have said more, but she didn't feel that he deserved total absolution. At least not yet. Melody's first instinct was to consider the matter resolved and continue with casual chitchat until she had finished her breakfast. Then, she thought about how Granny had taught her to always go on the offensive when one had the upper hand and had taken command of the battlefield.

Taking one more sip of her tea, she peered at Alessandro across the rim of her glass. There was no point in being anything other than direct; certainly, that is what Granny would do. "I wish to be involved in whatever work you and Rat have been sent to Morocco to do."

Alessandro had an initial instinct of his own, which seemed to be to laugh in astonishment at such a brazen demand. However, he quickly schooled his face and said, "Melody, as contrite as I am, you cannot possibly believe that I can compensate for my behaviour in Venice by allowing you, an untrained young woman, to meddle in foreign espionage? Morocco is a political powder keg at the moment and the stakes are very high if Matthew and I cannot help to defuse the situation."

"As I now know, you watched our actions closely in Venice. If that is the case, then you know the aid that I provided to my brother. I do not believe it is hyperbole to state that he would not have uncovered Xander Ashby's nefarious scheme without my help and certainly would not have solved the murders of Antonio Graziano and Silvio Verdi. Can you deny that?"

While it looked as if Alessandro would have loved to deny it, he instead nodded his head and acknowledged, "You were undoubtedly of great service to Matthew. However, he was then working alone. Now, he and I are working in partnership." Melody's feelings must have been written plainly on her face because Alessandro then added, "While we cannot share all the details of this mission with you, there may be some times and places where you might be of service."

Melody was concerned that these words were merely to placate her. Nevertheless, she realised that this might be the best concession she would get for now, and so she decided to take this opening and make what she could of it. "Wonderful. So, why do you not start by sharing where you and my brother went this morning."

Alessandro shook his head sadly. "Alas, that falls under the category of things I cannot share with you. However, we will be visiting the Medina shortly to meet with Omar. Perhaps you can join us." He paused and then added nonchalantly, "However, I must warn you that the Medina is not for the faint of heart."

Melody narrowed her eyes; she knew well enough what Alessandro was doing. While she had been a child when the dowager had first started forcibly inserting herself in Tabitha and Wolf's investigations, Melody remembered well enough conversations that no one thought she was listening to. During these conversations, it was evident that they would attempt to fob the dowager off with an aspect of the investigation that they hoped would both satisfy her need for involvement yet also dissuade her from continuing. Sometimes, it even worked.

If Melody wasn't mistaken, this was precisely the move that Alessandro was attempting. He had no idea who he was dealing with. She would go with them to the Medina, and they wouldn't hear a squeak of complaint out of her. Whatever fear or distaste she felt would be kept to herself.

"I would love to join you. What time should I be ready?"

If Alessandro had expected her to say otherwise, he did an excellent job of hiding it. Perhaps he had expected her to agree but still believed that she would be deterred after this one outing. Instead, he remarked, "I will ask Fatima to loan you a headscarf, unless you have something appropriate. While it is not expected that foreign women show the same modesty in their dress as the locals do, nevertheless, we should be respectful and do not need to draw undue attention to ourselves."

Melody assured him that she had a headscarf that would suffice. For some reason, she couldn't bear the thought of being any more beholden to Fatima than she already was by accepting her hospitality.

CHAPTER 5

An hour later, they were in Fatima's carriage and headed away from the new, European-style neighbourhood. Fatima's carriage was significantly more comfortable than the one they had rented in Tangier. Still, Melody was far too on edge about their expedition to relax back into the velvet cushions. Apart from any nervousness she felt about their trip to the Medina, Rat was glaring at her for the entire journey. Melody had no idea what Alessandro had told him about why she was joining them, but it was evident that Rat was not happy at her inclusion in the party.

It was not a long drive to the outskirts of the Medina, and Melody spent most of it looking out of the window and trying to avoid catching Rat's eye. Melody knew she had done nothing wrong and had no reason to feel guilty, but she also knew how insecure her brother was about his new role as a Secret Service Bureau operative. As much as he was grateful for her helping solve the investigation in Venice, the fact that he needed that help only helped feed his lack of confidence in his abilities.

When the carriage stopped, Alessandro explained that the streets were too narrow for it to continue and that they would have to walk the rest of the way.

Alessandro opened the carriage door, then paused, "Melody, no one will think any the less of you if you choose to remain in the carriage to wait for us. The Medina really is no place for a well-bred young Englishwoman."

Melody bristled at his words. "Where exactly is the right place for such a young woman? Perhaps nowhere more exciting than a Mayfair drawing room where she can embroider and play the piano?"

Making no more reply to her challenge than to tilt his head in acknowledgement of her words, Alessandro descended from the carriage and then handed Melody out. Rat didn't need to say anything; the waves of irritation emanating from him spoke volumes.

As soon as they entered the Medina, Melody felt transported to an entirely foreign place, and almost time, as her every sense was assaulted. The streets were extremely narrow and lined with vendors hawking everything from carpets to live chickens. One moment, the air was filled with an unpleasant smell as they passed a man using a large knife to cut up a huge fish. No sooner had they passed that stall than a far more pleasant, if unusual, scent permeated the air. It smelled exotic, and looking around for the source, Melody saw a man surrounded by brightly coloured barrels who was scooping what must be spices into pouches for customers.

As they moved past the spices, they encountered a man selling pastries and another sitting next to him selling brightly coloured shoes. The vendors were all men, but there were some heavily veiled women shopping.

Seeing the direction of her gaze, Alessandro explained, "Until quite recently, women were confined to their father's home and then their husband's. Most Moroccan women might only leave their homes two or three times in their lives. However, over the last few years, particularly since the French gained more influence here, it has become more common to see women out on the streets, though almost always accompanied by a brother, father, uncle or husband."

Now that Melody knew this, she noticed that it was indeed the case that every woman had a man close by her side. She felt even more self-conscious and pulled her scarf more closely around her head. While there were glances directed her way, Melody didn't feel that there was another meaning in the curious stares. Nevertheless, she had a little more understanding of why Alessandro had suggested she remain in the carriage.

Melody also realised why he had suggested that she join them for a visit to the Medina. He was confident that she would feel so uncomfortable that she would be deterred from any future interference in their mission. Knowing this steeled Melody's spine. Channelling Granny as best she could, Melody threw back her shoulders and determined that she would not allow Alessandro to guess any of her nervousness.

Finally, just as Melody was wondering if Alessandro had managed to get them lost, he stopped in front of a large wooden door. He knocked, and a few moments later, it was opened by an old man who seemed to recognise Alessandro immediately. Again, it occurred to Melody that Alessandro must be more familiar with Morocco, or at least Casablanca, than she had realised. Under other circumstances, she would have liked to talk with him and learn about his previous visits and experiences. However, their detente was still too fresh and fragile for that kind of conversation.

"As-salamu alaykum, Sidi Alessandro," the old man said in a very gravelly voice.

"Wa alaykum as-salum," Alessandro replied with a slight bow of his head.

"Sidi Omar?" the old man said, and Alessandro answered with a nod. The old man moved aside and welcomed them into the abode.

Melody was intensely curious about the inside of a traditional Moroccan home. From the outside, all she had seen were windowless walls. Because of this, she had expected the house to be very dark and gloomy. However, as they were led through a vestibule, she saw an open-air courtyard that the house was built around and which had plenty of windows looking out on it. Inside the courtyard were plush couches and tables to which they were led. The old man indicated that they should be seated and then he disappeared, reappearing a few minutes later with a tray laden with refreshments.

After putting the tray down, the old man removed a plate of dates, another of little cakes, and a very ornate silver teapot, from which he poured tea into glass cups with silver bases. The man then said something else in Arabic to Alessandro before disappearing.

"Omar will join us in a moment. Meanwhile, we should partake of the refreshments."

Melody couldn't contain her curiosity any further. "You speak Arabic fluently?"

Alessandro laughed. "Hardly fluently. However, I know enough to manage when I have to. Omar has taught me some phrases over the years."

So, he had previously spent time in Morocco. She did remember him mentioning Omar from 1905, but his familiarity implied more than one previous visit. Again, unable to stop herself, Melody asked, "Have you been to Morocco many times, then?"

His face immediately closing up, Alessandro merely nodded his head and said tersely, "Yes."

Oh well, thought Melody. She knew that she should have kept her questions to herself.

"My friend! As-salamu alaykum," a loud, cheerful voice boomed from the side of the courtyard.

Alessandro replied as he had to the old man. The owner of the booming voice was a man, perhaps in his mid to late fifties. He had a protruding stomach, a round, open face with a broad smile, and a large, bushy moustache. He was dressed in the traditional robes that all Moroccan men wore, but his head was bare. He approached Alessandro and enveloped him in a warm bear hug.

"It is good to see you, my friend. It has been too long."

"It has been," Alessandro agreed.

Omar, because this was who Melody assumed it was, turned towards Melody and Rat and greeted them. Rat introduced them both.

"You are welcome to Casablanca, Mr Sandworth and Miss Chesterton," Omar said warmly.

"Please, call me Matthew," Rat said.

"Then you must call me Omar," the man replied.

Melody wasn't sure what the etiquette was for an Arab man to address a woman he was not related to, so she did not offer her given name. She looked around at the windows surrounding the courtyard and noticed eyes looking down at them. Was this Omar's wife? Or did he have multiple wives? She knew that polygamy was allowed in Islam. What must these women think of her sitting there with the men? Did they think she was brazen or lucky?

"Lalla Fatima sent word that you needed my services, but I know nothing more," Omar said. "I assume you are here in an official capacity?"

Well, that was interesting, Melody thought. Did Omar know about Alessandro's role in the Secret Service Bureau? Did Fatima? Could these people really be trusted? A glance at Rat's face suggested that he shared a similar worry.

As if intuiting their concerns, Omar turned to them and said, "Long live the Queen! The British have long supported Moroccan sovereignty. In 1906, your government advocated against French dominance over my country."

Well, that at least made some sense. Melody wasn't sure that it assuaged all her fears, and exchanging a brief look with her brother, she guessed that he was similarly unsure. However, they were entirely in Alessandro's hands in Morocco. Indeed, Melody didn't even know what they were supposed to be doing there. She hoped that Rat at least had more of an idea.

"Despite signing the Entente Cordiale, the British Government is supportive of Moroccan independence from full European colonisation," Alessandro assured Omar.

Melody didn't say anything, but she wondered at how a country that happily colonised India and other countries could nevertheless stand in judgment of its European neighbour's similar ambitions in North Africa.

This question was answered at least somewhat a few moments later when Alessandro said, "Yes, while France is currently our friend, for the most part, Britain must ensure that they do not control the Straits of Gibraltar and, therefore, some of our major trade routes. It continues to be in both of our countries' interests to maintain the balance of power in the region between France, Germany, and Spain."

"Ah, yes, Spain," Omar said. "I am not sure if you have heard, but a few days ago, in response to the French troops' involvement in Fes, the Spanish government took over Omarrache and Ksar-el-Kebir. My contacts are watching the situation, and I will share more information as I get it."

It was evident by Alessandro's shocked expression that this was news to him. "The situation is even more alarming than I feared. If the Spanish reaction to this French overreach was so extreme, I am worried what the German response will be. It seems it is even more imperative that we do what we can behind the scenes to counter further French aggression, even if it is under the guise of support for the Sultan."

Melody could barely follow the tangled political web that seemed to be the situation in Morocco. When they had been investigating in Venice there seemed little doubt who the enemy was: Austria-Hungary and its partner in the Triple Alliance, Germany. She had thought that France was Britain's ally. Was that not the case? Because it now seemed as if Britain was more concerned about the ambitions of its so-called friend than its putative enemy. Well, perhaps enemy was currently too strong a word to describe Germany, but definitely not a friend. Perhaps an acquaintance of which one was highly suspicious and kept at arm's length whenever possible.

Of course, Melody had learned enough European history to know that Britain had an even more tortured history with France than it did with Germany over the centuries. Nevertheless, she had believed that in the current state of European affairs, France and Britain had one goal: to stand together against Austria-Hungary and Germany. But now it seemed that the situation was far more complicated than she believed. Perhaps if she had listened more closely on the trip from Tangier, she would understand more. Determined to make up for that lapse in attention, Melody decided to ask Rat for his insights at their next opportunity for a private conversation.

Even as she thought this, it occurred to Melody that Rat might not be inclined to educate her enough that she could then be a fly in the ointment of his nascent partnership with Alessandro. However, she knew her brother's warm and generous spirit well enough to believe that he would help her understand, whatever his feelings about her involvement.

Listening to Alessandro and Omar's conversation, it became apparent that he was far more than a mere translator. It seemed as if the man had a network of informants throughout Morocco who all shared his enthusiasm for, one might even say, allegiance to, Britain. It did occur to Melody to wonder what their Sultan might think about some of his subjects aiding a foreign power.

In reply to Omar's news about the Spanish escalation, Alessandro asked, "When was the last you heard from our friend in Fes?"

Omar shook his head and looked anxious at this question, "It has been too long. I believe it is the main reason you were summoned to Morocco. It is possible that he has been compromised. I have tried to gather what information I can through the network, but so far there has been no news. He was last seen almost a month ago."

Alessandro seemed unsure how much to say in front of Melody but finally asked, "If I need to go to Fes, can I count on your company?"

"Of course, my friend," Omar replied, his warm, wide smile replaced by a look of concern. Melody wanted to ask who their friend in Fes was and what might have happened to him. However, she suspected that even if Alessandro was inclined to reveal anything, this was not the time or place.

They didn't stay for much longer, and just before they left, Omar gave Alessandro a package of what looked like two or three books wrapped in paper.

Seeing her look at the package, Alessandro explained, "Omar is a purveyor of rare Arabic texts. Ostensibly, our relationship is based on his ability to procure items for my library. In order to maintain this charade, it is important that I am seen to leave with books."

"Do you think we are being watched?" Rat asked.

"I always assume I am being watched," Alessandro explained. "It is a good habit to form," he advised. Rat looked ashamed of his naivety, and yet again, Melody's heart went out to her sensitive older brother.

CHAPTER 6

They left Omar's home with Alessandro holding the books under one arm. Omar had promised to be in touch within a day with a plan about their "friend in Fes." Melody had no idea how far Fes was from Casablanca, but if the trip from Tangier was any indication, travel within Morocco was hard and long. Even the well-travelled route between Tangier and Casablanca had been on little more than a dirt track. The thought of getting back in another carriage to spend even more days travelling was almost more than Melody could stand.

Of course, she knew that she always had the option of staying behind in Casablanca if Rat and Alessandro had to travel within Morocco. She could imagine nothing that would please Alessandro more, probably Rat as well. As much as she loathed the idea of taking to the road again so quickly, the thought of staying behind alone with Fatima was even less appealing. So, Melody resigned herself to the possibility of another long, arduous trip.

While they retraced their route back to the carriage, Alessandro and Rat chatted about nothing in particular and Melody observed the chaotic commerce taking place all around her.

Just as they were passing the live chicken vendor, Alessandro yelled out, "Waqd!"

Melody turned her head to see him holding the hand of a young boy who was squirming in his grip.

"What happened?" Rat asked.

"This little street rat tried to pick my pocket," Alessandro explained. Looking more closely at the protesting child, he said, "And to make it worse, I believe it is the same vagabond who I saved from a thrashing, or worse, yesterday."

"Which child? The one who was accused of stealing the bread?" Melody asked.

"The very same. But this time I will not be as kind."

"Monsieur, I do not steal from you," the boy said in surprisingly good English. "I was trying to get your attention."

Alessandro adopted a look of extreme scepticism. "Trying to get my attention? Why, so you could thank me for saving your skin the other day?"

The boy lowered his voice, "Non, Monsieur. A man was following you and I saw him take out a knife. I remembered your good deed to me and did not want him to hurt you."

Seemingly unmoved by this explanation, Alessandro retained his grip on the child and asked, "And where might this man be now?"

The boy pointed up ahead. "When you yelled at me and turned, he changed his mind and moved ahead. I swear, Monsieur."

Rat looked at the young boy. "How old are you?"

The boy shrugged. "I do not know, Monsieur. Maybe eight."

There was something about the young boy that was heartbreakingly familiar to Rat. He noted how scrawny the child was and recognised the hungry look that suffused his skinny face. Without even having to ask, Rat knew the boy's story. He had lived the boy's story. Rat remembered when he had first met Wolf in Whitechapel on the day he tried to pick the then thief-taker's pocket. He remembered the grace he was shown when Wolf gave the orphaned boy work instead of turning him into the nearest constable. That work helped him to buy food for himself and his sister, Melody.

Guessing that Alessandro did not seem to be inclined to be so generous, Rat said, "Let us take the boy with us into the carriage and deal with him there. If he is telling the truth, we need to get more information from him about the man he claims was about to attack you. And if he is lying..." he paused. "If he is lying, then he is an orphaned child who is starving and cannot be blamed for doing what he has to in order to feed himself."

Immediately, Melody understood the root of Rat's compassion. She smiled at him. Alessandro did not know enough of Rat and Melody's origins to understand. However, he had no desire to hash this out further in the middle of the Medina and, instead, keeping a tight hold on the boy's arm he began walking towards where they had left the carriage. It was a short walk, and soon enough, they had bundled the boy in and were on their way back to Anfa.

"Let us start with the basics," Alessandro said sternly. "What is your name?"

"Mustafa, Monsieur.

Wary of projecting too much of his childhood onto Mustafa but also cognisant that he had at least some shared experiences with the boy that the wealthy, aristocratic Alessandro couldn't possibly understand, Rat asked far more gently than the other man, "Are your parents living, Mustafa?"

Suddenly, the boy looked very sad and shook his head. "Baba died when I was a baby. Mama died just before Ramadan. She had been sick for some time."

From what Rat knew about Islamic culture, Ramadan had been more than two months ago, so the boy had been fending for himself for several weeks.

Reflecting again on his own experience, Rat asked with concern, "Mustafa, do you have any brothers or sisters back in the Medina?"

The boy shook his head in the negative.

Alessandro was impatient. "Now that we know the boy's life history, I would like to return to the matter at hand. If you want me to believe your story, Mustafa, you might start by describing the man you claim you saw about to attack me."

The boy thought for a few moments, then said, "He was a tall, thin man, with what do you call the thing a man grows above his nose?"

"A moustache?" Melody suggested.

"Yes, that is it."

"Alright then. A tall thin man with a moustache. That is not very helpful. Was he young or old? Moroccan?" Alessandro demanded.

"He was not a Moroccan," Mustafa said with certainty. "Although he was wearing a djellaba, his fair hair made him seem European. I do not think he was too old—perhaps a little older than you, Monsieur." This was directed at Alessandro.

"And why exactly were you so sure he was going to attack me?"

"I saw him follow you to the riad and wait for you to leave. He stayed just close enough behind you for some time; then suddenly, he moved closer. It was when the Mademoiselle and the other Monsieur," at this, he looked at Rat, "they moved just a little ahead of you because the street was narrow. Then, he moved closer all of a sudden, and I saw him pull his hand out of his sleeve, and he had a knife in it."

Something in Mustafa's story suddenly puzzled Melody. "If you saw all this, you must have been following us as well. Why?"

Mustafa didn't answer for a moment. Then, in a quiet little voice, he admitted, "When I saw you come into the Medina, Monsieur, I remembered your kindness to me. I wanted to ask you if I could be your servant."

"My servant?" Alessandro asked in amusement. "And what exactly did you think that a skinny little boy like you could do for me?"

"I thought that I could take messages for you. Whatever you wanted. I know the Medina well. I speak English, Arabic, and some French," the boy said with pride.

"You do speak English very well," Melody said. "How is that?"

"My mother spoke English, and she taught me. She told me that one day if I could speak it well, I could take a boat to England and work for the King."

"For the King?" Alessandro said in a gently mocking tone. "Well, your English is good enough, I will give you that." Then, in a kind but firm voice, he said, "I am not the King, but perhaps you could be of some assistance."

Back at Fatima's home, Alessandro sent Mustafa off with Ahmed to get bathed and fed. Meanwhile, Alessandro, Melody, and Rat retired to the salon.

"Do you believe the boy?" Melody asked Alessandro.

"About the man with the knife? I think I do. His description was too specific. Unless the child is an expert liar, it had the ring of truth about it."

"I agree," Rat said. "But then that raises a much larger question: who was trying to attack you and why?"

Alessandro didn't answer immediately. Instead, he rang the bell, and a servant arrived almost immediately with a tray of more refreshments. As the morning had progressed, the day had got much hotter, and it had been particularly stifling in the Medina. Given the heat, Melody was glad to see that tall glasses of orange juice had replaced the mint tea that seemed to accompany every Moroccan meal. She happily drank more than half her glass before placing it on the table in front of her.

After taking some large sips from his glass, Alessandro said, "It seems that my presence here may have stirred up a hornet's nest."

"Surely your role with the Secret Service Bureau has not been compromised," Rat said anxiously.

"When you have worked in the shadows of European intrigue for as long as I have, you find that others in the same field might have their suspicions." Seeing the increasing concern on Rat's face, he continued, "I am not saying that they know exactly what I do for the British Government, but those who also trade in secrets often recognise similar interests in others."

This was an odd and vague answer, Melody thought. Wasn't the whole point of conducting covert espionage that no one knew your true function? To hear Alessandro explain it, one might almost think that he belonged to an elite club whose members had a secret signal they flashed to identify themselves to their brethren.

Melody decided to put aside her scepticism at his story, at least for now. If a European man had followed them into the Medina and had intended to stab Alessandro, it seemed likely that something about their reason for being in Morocco sat behind it. This did not seem like a random attack or even a robbery attempt. If the man had followed them to Omar's home and then waited for them, there was little doubt that his target had been quite intentional and specific. But why?

"If the man was not Moroccan, then what was he? French? German?" she asked.

Alessandro rubbed his chin, contemplating the question. "I do not know. There is no doubt that I have made enemies over the years. One does not succeed in business without ruffling some feathers. However, it seems unlikely that a business rival would bother to try to kill me in Morocco when Venice or London would be so much less trouble. Given this, I must assume the attempted attack was related to my more covert activities. The European community in Morocco, let alone Casablanca, is not a large one. Certainly, word gets around about new arrivals."

Melody considered the earlier conversation. "Omar mentioned a missing friend. Would I be correct in assuming that this man is a fellow operative?" She asked this in a low voice, still far from comfortable that Fatima's house was safe.

Alessandro didn't look happy to be having this conversation but nodded his head. "As you heard, part of the reason that Matthew and I were sent here was that he is missing. He had been living in Fes as an antiquities scholar but closely monitoring the situation with the French, particularly since April. Whitehall fears the worst."

Melody had so many questions that she wanted to ask. If she could, she would prefer to have that conversation somewhere more private than Fatima's salon.

"Do you think we will learn anything at the party tonight?" Rat asked.

Party? What party? Melody thought. How had she missed this?

Rat must have noticed her confused look and said, "Weren't you listening last night when Fatima told us about it?"

In truth, Melody had been exhausted at dinner and had tuned out most of Fatima's overly flirtatious conversation with both Alessandro and Rat.

Her brother continued with a sigh, "The British Envoy to Morocco, Sir Reginal Lister, is visiting Casablanca from Tangier. In his honour, the Vice-Consul, Archibald Madden and his wife are throwing a soirée."

"And we are invited?"

Alessandro explained, "The European community in Casablanca is not large and is quite tight-knit, even amongst people who might be at odds under normal circumstances. Given this, the French, German, and Spanish diplomats in Casablanca will likely be in attendance. It will be an excellent opportunity to gather some intelligence. It is even possible that my supposed attacker from earlier might be in attendance, if such a person exists."

"Then we should bring Mustafa with us," Melody pointed out. "He saw the man and could identify him."

Shaking his head at the absurdity of her statement, Alessandro asked, "How do you suggest we explain that we have a Moroccan street urchin with us?"

Melody was saved from having to formulate a response by Rat. "I assume that if we bring him along with us and explain the circumstances, or at least some of them, to Vice-Consul Madden, he could be persuaded to let Mustafa mingle with his servants as they serve food and drinks. That way, he can circulate through the room and see if he recognises anyone."

"Well, we're going to need to give him more than a bath if this idea is to work," Alessandro said, clearly giving the plan far more credence coming from Rat than he did when Melody first suggested it. She tried not to show her irritation. Alessandro stood and left the room, saying nothing. When he returned a few minutes later, he explained, "Ahmed will ensure that Mustafa has appropriate attire. He will also send the boy to us now so we can explain what we need from him."

Now that issue was dealt with, Melody considered the evening ahead. She assumed that Fatima would be accompanying them. So far that day, their hostess hadn't presented herself. Melody did not look forward to the idea of watching the woman preen her feathers in public.

No sooner had Melody had this thought than the woman herself appeared, looking as beautiful and sophisticated as ever.

"Ah, you are all back," Fatima said, sweeping into the room. "And how is dear Omar?"

Given that Omar clearly acted as far more than a translator, Melody wondered again just where Fatima's allegiances lay. After all, the conclusion of the murder investigations in Venice had revealed just how complicated but intensely felt patriotism could be. Who could have guessed that the seemingly quintessentially British Xander Ashby would have more loyalty towards his mother's homeland of Austria?

At least from what she knew so far about Fatima, it was hard to imagine why she would be willing to help Britain beyond the possibility that she felt it was somehow in either Morocco's or France's interests. Was there something more that Melody was missing?

CHAPTER 7

After a luncheon that felt far too long as Fatima held court, Melody retired to her bedroom, ostensibly to talk to Mary about an appropriate outfit for that evening. Fatima's words to her retreating back still rang in her ears, "Do not worry, Melody. No one will expect a young English woman to be dressed in the height of fashion. You are not a Parisian, after all. I am sure that you have something in your extensive luggage that will suffice."

Melody still had steam coming out of her ears as she opened the door and found Mary tidying up. Mary had known Melody most of her life and could always perfectly read her emotions. "What did she say now?" she asked, not needing to express who the "she" was. It had been clear enough the previous evening how much their hostess had managed to rile Melody up. If Mary had been asked her opinion, she might well have pursed her lips and said that Lalla Fatima was no better than she ought to be. Mary had no reason for making this judgement except that the woman had upset Melody, and that was crime enough for the always loyal servant.

As soon as she heard about the party that evening, Mary started rooting through the wardrobes where she had unpacked all the culturally and weather-appropriate outfits Melody had brought with her. There was no need for her to be told that Melody had to look her absolute best that evening.

As Mary busied herself selecting a range of dresses for them to choose among, Melody sat at the dressing table and looked at her reflection in the mirror. Her emotions were so confused that she could hardly think straight. Was she confused about what exactly she wanted Alessandro and Rat to allow her to help with, or her feelings towards the handsome, infuriating Conte Foscari, or was she just irritated at Fatima? Melody couldn't have really articulated what had her so discombobulated; she just knew that she was.

Perhaps what annoyed her the most about Fatima was that the woman seemed so self-assured. Whatever Fatima's relationship with Alessandro is or was, she seemed unaffected by his presence. It was hard to believe that Fatima had any genuine interest in Rat, and yet she flirted with both men almost indiscriminately. If she was honest with herself, Melody wished that she could pull off the nonchalant gaiety that Fatima exuded. Melody was too straightforward, too plain-talking. The idea of trifling with men's affections merely for her own amusement and vanity was repugnant to her. Yet, as much as she despised these female arts, she also wished she was able to emulate them, at least a little.

Melody knew that such feminine wiles were polished and practised in all the best drawing rooms in London. Wasn't that how one was supposed to catch a husband after all? By lowering one's eyes seemingly demurely but then glancing up from under fluttering eyelashes while saying something coy?

However, these were not the lessons that Granny had chosen to engrain in Melody. Instead, the dowager was far more interested in teaching the adored little girl the art of warfare, or at least warfare within society as the dowager countess viewed it. She had no time for simpering misses and certainly had no desire for Melody to become one. Whatever the dowager had felt was appropriate for her daughters and granddaughters to learn before their first season, she had very different ideas for the little girl she loved more than any child of her blood, perhaps more than any other person.

Up until the moment she met Fatima, Melody had been extremely grateful for the dowager's version of social etiquette lessons. Now, she wasn't quite so sure. Had she missed out on something? Was she lacking the necessary feminine skills to charm a man? After all, having thought that she had two suitors wooing her in Venice, it had turned out that both men were merely using her for their own purposes.

"Miss Melody, stop your wool-gathering and see what you think of these two options."

Melody turned to view the choices Mary had pulled out of the wardrobe. One of the options was the lovely, green silk Worth gown that Melody had worn for the first time at the party Lady Bainbridge had thrown them on their first night in Venice. As much as she loved this dress, Alessandro had already seen her in it. She certainly didn't want him to think that she only had one formal gown.

The other dress was another Worth gown, but this one was a beautiful pale blue silk. It was quite simple but beautiful cut and extremely chic. Even Fatima wouldn't be able to look down her nose at Melody in this gown. As she had for Luisa's masquerade party in Venice, Melody decided she would wear her pearl necklace. A small but perfect diamond pendant hung from the necklace. It had been a gift from Granny and paired beautifully with a pair of elegant diamond teardrop earrings that Tabby Cat had given her for her sixteenth birthday.

Melody told Mary her choice of dress and jewellery and was gratified to note the other woman's approval. "You will be the most beautiful woman at the party," Mary assured her.

"Well, you would say that, Mary. However, I do believe that I will have no reason to be ashamed."

"Ashamed! You never have reason to be ashamed; you always look elegant and beautiful. However, tonight, you will look sublime." Mary threw her a sly glance. "I am sure that Conte Foscari will appreciate your outfit."

"Mary! I do not care what Conte Foscari thinks of me or my outfits."

The look on Mary's face expressed her scepticism, but she made no further comment.

Melody decided to take a nap to be as refreshed as possible for their evening out. She lay down and closed her eyes, only intending to rest for perhaps an hour. More than two hours later, Mary finally decided that she would have to wake up. Melody awoke groggy and momentarily confused as to where she was. The ever-efficient Mary had brought up a tea tray with her and gave Melody the choice of mint tea or coffee.

Melody thought that she would need coffee if she were to clear her head. Mary had also brought up a plate with dates and some biscuits on it. Sitting up in bed with the plate on her lap and the cup of coffee in her hand, Melody tried to get herself together. Unlike many of London's society events, this party was starting quite early. She could already hear Mary running her a bath and thought that a soak would be just what she needed in order to compose herself for the evening ahead.

Finishing up her coffee and eating one more date, Melody went into the bathroom that adjoined her room. There was a heady scent of rose lingering in the warm, steamy air.

"There is some wonderful bath oil in a jar here that I added. There is also another jar with some cream that also smells of roses. When you get out, we can use some of that to moisturise your skin."

Melody removed her clothes and got into the large, clawfoot bathtub. She sunk into the warm, perfumed water with a moan of ecstasy. It was tempting to fall back to sleep again, but Mary was determined to wash her hair, so Melody sat up and submitted to Mary's ministrations.

An hour later, after being coaxed out of the bath, dried, and dressed, Melody was sitting at the dressing table while Mary brushed and dried her hair. There was a knock at the door. Mary put the brush down and went to open it. Looking over, Melody was surprised to see Rat standing there.

"May I come in?"

"Of course, silly. As long as you don't mind Mary continuing to do my hair."

Rat sat on the edge of the bed while Mary closed the door behind him and then resumed her work. Looking at her brother in the mirror, Melody noticed that he seemed nervous. Usually, Rat was the calm and collected one.

"Is there something in particular you wish to discuss?" Melody asked.

Again, there was an uncertainty that flashed across Rat's face before he answered, "Well, mostly, I wanted to check on you and make sure you're alright."

"Me? Why would you think that I am not?"

"You just seemed very out of sorts during lunch. Actually, since we arrived." Rat hesitated before continuing, "I get the sense that you do not like Fatima."

So, there it was, Melody thought. Well, she had wanted to talk to Rat about this very topic, so it was probably fortunate that he was the one to seek her out and raise the subject.

"I do not know her well enough to like or dislike Fatima," Melody lied. She did not doubt that further exposure to the woman would only deepen her immediate dislike. However, her qualms about their hostess would sound more reasonable if they were not coloured by personal animosity. Melody was sure that her concerns were valid and had nothing to do with her feelings about Fatima as a person.

Melody paused and thought about how best to phrase what she wanted to say. "Do you not find it unusual that a woman who is of Moroccan and French descent and was raised in Paris should be so seemingly willing to help Britain?"

It was a fair question, and if he were honest, Rat had thought something quite similar. As mesmerised as he was by the woman's beauty and charm, he had been surprised that Alessandro had chosen her home in which to base their mission in Casablanca. Of course, far be it for a newly minted Secret Service Bureau operative like Rat to question someone who had been working in the field for many years. Nevertheless, the decision had caught him by surprise.

Despite his reservations, Rat felt compelled by loyalty to Alessandro and infatuation with Fatima to reply in a determined voice, "Fatima also spent some years in Britain. Remember that she met Alessandro while she was there."

Melody cocked an eyebrow at her brother. "Really, Rat? Are you seriously suggesting that a year or two in a country is sufficient to push aside all loyalty to the country of your birth and that of your mother?"

Was that what he was suggesting? Of course, he wasn't. Yet, Rat couldn't find the words to express his faith in Alessandro. It was not lost on Rat that barely a couple of weeks before, he had been the one sure that the conte couldn't be trusted and berating Melody for falling under the man's sway. Yet, here he was, seemingly doing the same thing. But it was different.

Rat's self-confidence, as fragile as it already was, had been sorely strained by the resolution of the investigation in Venice. It was the undeniable truth that the murders would not have been solved without Melody's assistance. Furthermore, it was mortifying that the Venetian police had been able to follow the siblings for almost two days without him noticing. Worse even, that he had been so oblivious to his surroundings and so lacking in experience and common sense that he had talked openly, and apparently quite loudly, in public about the case such that the police knew his next steps was mortifying.

Then, as if that were all not bad enough, he had been unable to extricate himself and his little sister from Xander Ashby's clutches and had needed to be rescued by Alessandro and the police. This was really the final nail in the coffin of Rat's confidence in his abilities. No, perhaps the final nail had been the revelation that the powers that be back in London had also been so unsure of Rat's abilities that Alessandro had been tasked with following and observing him. The only redeeming part of this revelation had been that Lord Langley had not been behind this bureaucratic doubt. In fact, it seemed that Alessandro's orders had been given without Lord Langley's knowledge. Rat wasn't sure he could have borne the humiliation of knowing that his mentor questioned his readiness for the mission.

Despite all this, Alessandro had shown nothing but kindness and compassion towards the younger man. Rat would not have blamed Alessandro if he had sent Rat back to London with his tail between his legs, but he hadn't. Instead, he had taken the novice operative under his wing and had insisted that Rat accompany him to Morocco. Such graciousness had totally won Rat over.

If he had learned anything on the harsh streets of Whitechapel as a boy, it had been the importance of loyalty. Sometimes, it had been the only currency the most desperate inhabitants of the East End had to give. Ever since Wolf had caught Rat trying to pick his pocket and had employed him rather than turning him into the police, Rat had felt an unwavering loyalty to the man. That steadfast faith had been extended to Tabitha, the dowager, and then Lord Langley. And now, the Conte Foscari was part of this circle of allegiance. If Rat knew anything, it was that such loyalty could not fluctuate or be situational. If you stood by someone, you did so even when it might be hard.

Rat didn't know precisely what had taken place between Alessandro and his sister such that she had done such a complete turnabout on the man. He had a vague sense that his sister had formed a romantic attachment to the man, and he assumed that the much older Alessandro had rebuffed her. Under normal circumstances, Rat might have felt compelled to be his sister's unfailing defender and protector. However, Rat knew that there were far more important things at stake than Melody's girlish infatuation. And if Alessandro had not returned her feelings, wasn't that the right thing to do? After all, there were more than ten years between the two of them, and Rat was sure that Alessandro was worldly in ways that could only end up causing his sister pain.

So, he came back to Melody's question. He realised that he had been lost in thought and that she had turned around so that she was now facing him with that cynical, questioning look still on her face.

"I do not know," Rat confessed. "However, I do believe in Alessandro, and if he feels that Fatima can be trusted, then I must have faith in his far more seasoned judgement."

Because, in the final analysis, this was the truth: while he had his doubts, Rat felt he must subjugate them to the other man's far more experienced decision-making.

Melody had watched all of this play out on her brother's face. She knew him so well and understood the deep well of self-doubt that had only grown deeper in Venice. Despite her enthusiasm for her newly discovered investigative skills, she was profoundly sorry that this knowledge seemed to have come at the expense of her brother's confidence.

She had felt compelled to alert her brother to her fears, and she had done so. Melody had hardly expected that he would immediately embrace her concerns. She wasn't even sure what he could have done if he had. Realising that she had done all she could for the time being, Melody turned back to the mirror and said, "You should go and get yourself ready, Rat. We will be leaving soon for the vice-consul's home."

CHAPTER 8

F inally, Mary was finished with her hair, and Melody studied her reflection. She had asked Mary to try a more mature, sophisticated hairstyle, and now, as she observed the artfully placed curls, she was very satisfied.

Correctly interpreting Melody's expression, Mary assured her, "You look beautiful, Miss Melody. And no one will be able to suggest otherwise."

Mary emphasised the words "no one", which left no doubt as to who she was talking about. It made Melody feel a little self-conscious that she was so concerned about Fatima's opinion of her. Or was it Fatima's opinion she cared about? There was no doubt that Melody was very aware of how she might look in contrast to their beautiful hostess in Alessandro's eyes. But why did she care?

Determined that she would no longer worry about Conte Foscari, Melody stood and took one last look at herself in the mirror. Granny had taught her so many things, but of dowager's most enduring lessons was the importance of being clad in appropriate armour when entering a theatre of war. Whether that armour was the certainty of being dressed in the height of fashion, wearing the most coveted jewels, or being in possession of the most dangerous secrets, a woman should never step foot on the battlefield without the certainty of some strategic advantage. Smoothing down the skirt of her beautiful Worth gown, Melody was confident that Granny would approve.

Descending the stairs, Melody heard voices in the salon. Entering the room, she saw that Alessandro and Rat were dressed in evening clothes and sipping pre-party Cognacs. Fatima had not yet arrived. As Melody entered, Rat and Alessandro glanced up, and she was satisfied to see Alessandro's undeniable look of appreciation.

Both men had stood up, and now Alessandro came towards her, bowed over her hand, and said, "You look beautiful, Miss Chesterton." Melody acknowledged his compliment with a mere nod of her head. Granny had taught her well.

Whether or not Alessandro had noticed Melody's more sophisticated hairstyle, Rat had noticed it. Yet again, he was reminded that his little sister was a grown woman now and not a child anymore.

As much as he had been irritated by her insistence on joining him in Morocco, Rat was secretly a little glad that she had accompanied him. Already, Morocco felt so alien; the people, the language, the culture, it was all so far from London, even from his experience travelling through the continent so far. As much as Rat was in awe of Alessandro and taken with Fatima's beauty and grace, there was a part of him that missed home and the familiarity of London. In Britain, he felt sure of himself and his skills. At home, he knew who he was and his place in society. Even though there was a certain ambiguity to his role as Lord Langley's ward and mentee, Rat had grown comfortable with how to play that role.

In Morocco, he found himself on his back foot and was sure that the vice-consul's party would only exacerbate his discomposure. To Rat, Melody was home. She was the person who tethered him back to their family and friends in London and even further back to their roots. As much as she had assimilated into Mayfair society far more than Rat ever would, still, their relationship had a solidarity and solidity that he was suddenly very happy for in this strange, distant land.

Alessandro poured Melody a sherry, and she sat on the beautiful silk couch and sipped it, wondering how long they would have to wait for

Fatima. Not long, it seemed. It was almost as if the other woman had wanted to ensure that her entrance into the room was the grand finale. No sooner had Melody had her second sip than Fatima swept into the room.

Swept really was the right word for the woman's entrance. She was dressed in a gown of deep burgundy silk that was cut far lower than Melody would have dared in the Muslim country. Sparkling rubies dangled from Fatima's neck, ears and wrist. Granny had drilled into Melody that one could wear an eye-catching gemstone as either a necklace, a bracelet or earrings, but never all three. Except at a ball of course, and only once one was a married woman. Then, it was acceptable to be dripping in diamonds. However, for the more intimate kind of party that they were attending that evening, the dowager would have given one of her signature sniffs of disapproval, looked Fatima up and down, and made it very clear that she agreed with Mary's assessment that the woman was no better than she ought to be.

Even though this was Melody's first thought on Fatima's entrance, her second was a more generous acknowledgement that if anyone could carry off an excess of jewels, it was Fatima. Despite her petite frame, the woman exuded a larger-than-life presence. In fact, the woman's ability to transcend the physical limitations of her stature was not unlike the dowager countess' own. Melody realised that Granny would have likely felt an unwilling appreciation of Fatima's ability to command attention. Certainly, both Rat and Alessandro's eyes were immediately drawn to her, and Melody felt as if she was suddenly invisible.

"How do I look?" Fatima trilled, twirling to allow for a fuller appreciation of her charms.

"Quite beautiful, as you well know," Alessandro replied with a wry smile. Just for a moment, Melody wondered if Conte Foscari wasn't just a little exasperated with Fatima's constant need to be the centre of attention.

"And Matthew? What do you think?" Fatima asked in her most flirtatious voice.

"Fatima-a-a," Rat stammered. "I cannot imagine a more glorious vision."

Very nice, Melody thought indignantly. What about his sister sitting there in her new Worth gown?

Fatima approached Rat and gave him one of her hands. "And how debonair you look in your evening dress." Rat blushed to the roots of his hair. Melody had to control the urge to roll her eyes.

Vice-Consul Madden's official residence was not far from Fatima's home and was even larger and grander. The front door was opened by a butler who, in dress, manner, and inscrutability, could have been opening the door to any Mayfair aristocratic home. In fact, once they stepped over the threshold, Melody could have easily believed that they were on Grosvenor Square. There was not a local servant in sight. How had the government persuaded so many maids and footmen to relocate to Morocco? On closer inspection, Melody realised that the butler aside, all the servants were locals, or at least appeared to be. Rather than wearing their local costumes, they had all been styled in dress and hair to look as British as possible. To Melody's eye, it even looked as if the Vice-Consul had gone out of his way only to hire the most fair-skinned, British-looking servants.

Vice-Consul Madden was a genial, welcoming host. A mousy woman stood by his side, barely speaking above a whisper and seemingly very uncomfortable in her role as hostess. The vice-consul welcomed Alessandro warmly, pulling him in slightly as the men shook hands and said something in a low voice.

Melody noticed this interaction and wondered how much the vice-consul knew about Alessandro and Rat's roles with the Secret Service Bureau. Indeed, it would make sense if Britain's representatives in Morocco knew such things.

Alessandro introduced Rat and Melody in the same manner he had throughout their trip: Melody was the ward of the Earl of Pembroke and was travelling in Europe and now North Africa, accompanied by her brother. If the vice-consul knew that this was a cover story, it was impossible to tell from the warm, if slightly distracted, greeting he gave them. His wife's handshake was limp, and she barely made eye contact as she welcomed her guests.

They moved into the salon, which so mirrored what one might expect to walk into in London that it far more deserved the designation drawing room. The room was already quite full as people sipped on flutes of champagne and nibbled on the canapes that were being passed around by another of the highly anglicised footmen.

As soon as they entered the room, Fatima was hailed by a group of people and drifted away to greet them. Alessandro led the way across the room towards a tall, thin man sporting an impressive moustache. He was holding forth in what looked like a heated conversation with a distin-guished-looking middle-aged man with another noteworthy moustache.

At Alessandro's approach, the two men stopped talking but the tension between them was still evident as the tall man put out his hand and said, "Ah, Foscari. Good to see you." The man then introduced himself to Rat and Melody as Sir Reginald Lister, the British Envoy Extraordinary and Minister Plenipotentiary in Morocco and the guest of honour.

Sir Reginald then turned to the man he had been arguing with and asked Alessandro, "Do you know Monsieur Henri Gaillard, the French consul?"

Melody couldn't be sure, but it almost felt as if the introduction was a warning. If it was, Alessandro was far too experienced an operative to acknowledge it. Instead, he took the other man's outstretched hand and greeted him in perfect French. Of course, he also spoke fluent French, Melody thought irritably.

"Conte Foscari, your reputation precedes you," the Frenchman said, switching to English. "Your newspapers have not always been as supportive of my country as one might imagine they would be."

"I am the owner of many newspapers and the editor of none," Alessandro said dismissively and with a lightness of tone that seemed to suggest a disinterest in what his newspapers published.

"And so, you do not dictate the tone that you wish your editors to adopt?"

"Monsieur, this is a party. Surely not the appropriate place for such a conversation."

Sir Reginald chimed in, "Indeed, Monsieur Gaillard, let us not get into a discussion about our country's newspapers. Surely, that will not reflect well on your country, after all."

At this, Monsieur Gaillard's eyes shot daggers at Sir Reginald, but instead of replying, he made a short bow and excused himself. What on earth was that all about, Melody wondered. She glanced over at Rat, but he seemed as mystified as she was.

They watched the Frenchman disappear into the crowd before Sir Reginald turned back to their group and remarked, "Damn French. How dare that man make such a comment to you. Talk about the pot calling the kettle black. Did you see what Le Matin printed just yesterday? Here we are trying to talk the Germans off the ledge and dissuade them from taking retaliatory action against the French, and they print some leaked papers before there's even a chance to present them to the Huns. The Prime Minister was furious, let me tell you."

Lowering his voice, Sir Reginald continued, "Of course, the Grey faction is probably rubbing its hands with glee."

Of course, Melody knew that the current British Prime Minister was H.H. Asquith, the leader of the ruling Liberal Party. However, her knowledge of the rest of the government was much shakier. Who was Grey?

Just as Melody had racked her brain and come up short, Rat chimed in, "Why is the Foreign Secretary adopting such a provocative stance towards Germany, do you think, sir?"

Stroking his moustache in what seemed to be an unconscious gesture, Sir Reginald shook his head. He answered, "Well, of course, while this is hardly the place to discuss such things in detail, I must say that it is unfortunate that we have such an insular, xenophobic man who has barely travelled as not just Britain's Foreign Secretary, but its most powerful one in many years.

"Grey's faction's anti-German position is particularly unfortunate given that the British public seems to have drifted towards a far more conciliatory, pro-German mood of recent. Yet, here is Grey doing all he can to stir up anti-German sentiment within the government and beyond. Mark my words, if we end up at war with the Kaiser, Grey will be a significant part of the reason why."

War? Melody thought with alarm. She was well aware of much of the warmongering that the European powers had been engaged in recently. Nevertheless, it felt as if suspicion of the Germans, in particular, had been a constant hum in the background for most of her life. However, she had always assumed that it would never ignite into more than the occasional flicker of a spying incident here or a stand-off there.

"I would like to speak to you about this in more detail, Sir Reginald," Alessandro said. "Perhaps, Mr Sandworth and I can call on you and the vice-consul tomorrow?"

"Indeed, I would like to discuss our missing friend. Let us say eleven o'clock tomorrow morning." With that, the group broke up.

CHAPTER 9

A hmed had assured them that he would get Mustafa to the vice-consul's house and integrate him into the staff. Now that she had seen that all the servants were dressed indistinguishably from those back in London, Melody wondered how well Mustafa would be able to blend in. However, these concerns were assuaged somewhat when she noticed another young boy dressed in more appropriate local garb busy moving around the room silently and almost invisibly, picking up used glasses and plates.

Having made plans to return to speak to Sir Reginald the next day, the group had dispersed, with the consul excusing himself to go and greet other expatriates and local dignitaries. Alessandro had also disappeared to talk to a rather stern-looking older man, leaving Rat and Melody alone, sipping on champagne and feeling rather awkward.

As Melody glanced about them, wondering if they might just latch onto some other grouping of guests, she noticed Mustafa out of the corner of her eye. The child was dressed much as the other servant boy had been and was also discreetly sweeping up discarded glasses and serviettes. She caught his eye, and he nodded very slightly.

Seeing Mustafa reminded Melody of one of their goals for that evening: to see if they could identify Alessandro's would-be attacker. As she glanced around the room, Melody looked for a man who matched the description that Mustafa had given them of the man with the knife in the Medina. The description of a tall, thin, fair man with a moustache was not very specific. There were quite a few men in the room who might fit that description.

Melody was curious about the seeming international gathering at the party. She had assumed that the guests would all be British, with perhaps some high-born Moroccans scattered amongst them. However, based on the melange of languages she heard spoken around her, it seemed that Monsieur Gaillard was not the only Frenchman present. She could also hear some distinctly Germanic accents. That was certainly unexpected. But then, why? The countries may be warmongering and flexing their muscles, but they were not actual enemies, at least not yet. There was one obviously Moroccan man dressed in a very ornate robe. Pointing him out to Rat, her brother replied that he believed the man was the local Pasha, the highest local official representative of the Sultan, who acted as a governor of sorts.

Rat then whispered in her ear, "The man he is talking with is the French consul. One might say that he is the real governor of the region."

Casablanca was clearly a fascinating mix of European residents and visitors. Perhaps it was not surprising that they tended to socialise, even when their governments had more antagonistic relationships. After all, in London, European diplomats attended aristocratic soirees even when their countries were at odds.

After what felt like an eternity of lingering on the edge of groups, making small talk, dinner was called. Rat offered Melody his arm and led her into the large, ornate dining room. There was an empty seat to her right, and looking around the room, Melody realised that Alessandro was missing.

What she did notice was Fatima further down the table. The woman was holding court, capturing every man's attention. This included Rat, who had been placed near her. Fatima flirted, laughed coyly, batted her eyelashes, and generally sought to dominate the conversation and all male attention. From what she could tell, Melody wasn't the only female guest who was irritated by the charming Lalla Fatima. Melody caught one stout, middle-aged matron's eye and the woman made a face that perfectly captured how Melody felt.

Deciding to ignore Fatima, Melody turned to the man to her left, who turned out to be a rather dull German. It was unclear what the man's reason for being in Casablanca was because all he wanted to talk about were the various birds that he had seen since his arrival in Morocco and how different they were from those in his hometown.

Melody feigned interest in the birds of Morocco for a good five minutes before realising that the man didn't require any more interaction from her than the occasional nod of her head and vague-sounding hum of interest. Melody had sat through enough boring society dinner parties that she was able to keep up the charade adequately while her attention wandered. She realised that Alessandro had not returned and wondered where he was. As she looked around the table, Melody locked eyes with a rather handsome man, who gave her a conspiratorial smile. It looked as if the old woman to his right was engaging him in a conversation as boring as the birds of Morocco.

Suddenly, Melody noticed that one of the footmen had entered the room and was whispering in Vice Consul Madden's ear. He then rose and whispered to Sir Reginald, the French consul and then the Pasha. The four men then left the room. Melody performed another round of her perfunctory nodding and wondered what had happened.

Five minutes passed, and the soup course gave way to fish when Vice Consul Madden re-entered the room. This time, he crossed the room to where Rat sat and whispered something to him. Whatever had been said, Rat was evidently shocked and immediately rose to follow the vice-consul out.

It was unclear if the other guests were paying any attention to what was going on, but it seemed that Fatima was. She stopped flirting, stood, and made to follow Rat. Well, if Fatima was going, so was she, Melody thought. She laid her hand on the arm of the chatty German, made a brief apology for interrupting his narrative, and stood.

With two ladies and a gentleman making to leave the room, the guests had finally noticed that something was amiss. Vice Consul Madden said in an authoritative voice, "No need for alarm, Ladies and Gentlemen. Please resume your meal." As he said this, he looked very pointedly at

Melody, who ignored him and continued to follow Fatima out of the dining room.

The door closed behind them, and Fatima demanded, "Vice Consul Madden, what is going on?"

"There has been an incident," the vice-consul explained.

"What kind of incident?"

"There has been a death," Madden continued.

Melody's heart caught in her throat; was it Alessandro? Was that why he was not at dinner?

Rat must have seen Melody's face and rushed to explain, "Alessandro was found standing over the corpse. They are arresting him."

Fatima asked the obvious question, "Who is dead?"

The vice consul looked a little sheepish, "We do not know the man's identity. He was at the party uninvited, it seems."

The whole thing was too absurd for words, and Melody couldn't help but exclaim, "So, an unidentified man who was at the party without an invitation is found dead, and the Conte Foscari is suspected of killing him? Is this what you are telling me, Vice Consul Madden?"

The man turned, looking even more sheepish. "This is a difficult situation, Miss Chesterton. Perhaps we might go in here while I explain." The man pointed to a door that turned out to lead to a study of sorts.

Once inside, Fatima took a seat, but Melody was too anxious to sit. The vice consul made sure to close the door behind them, then said, "The situation in Morocco is very fragile at the moment. The French consul does not want to do anything to inflame tensions in the region, and so is willing to defer to the Pasha's authority. Unfortunately, the Pasha is adamant that his men take custody of Conte Foscari."

This was insanity and Melody couldn't believe what she was hearing. "Is it not possible that the conte merely stumbled across the body?" she asked in exasperation. "Why would he kill an unknown man in the middle of a party?"

"That is what the Pasha hopes to establish," the vice-consul explained as if talking with a slow, recalcitrant five-year-old.

Frustrated at the man's patronising tone, Melody turned to Rat. "Say something. You cannot believe that Alessandro is guilty? Why would he murder a man, let alone a random one at a party?"

Vice Consul Madden perked up at this statement. "Actually, apparently, the victim was not quite so random. It seems that one of the servant boys had identified the dead man as someone who he claims had intended to attack Conte Foscari this afternoon in the Medina. I believe that you and Miss Chesterton were with them at the time," the vice-consul said to Rat.

Melody's heart sank; Mustafa must have noticed the man and pointed him out to Alessandro. Of course, this didn't mean that the conte was necessarily guilty of killing him. However, it did complicate matters that Alessandro had prior knowledge of the murder victim.

"We need to speak with Conte Foscari," Melody demanded.

"I am sorry, but that is not possible. The Pasha has removed the conte to a local prison. At least for the time being."

At this, Fatima looked up, finally moved to action. "No! Not the Derb Moulay Cherif? This is ridiculous. The conte is a British citizen. Since when does that not count for something?"

Melody wondered the same thing. However, the vice-consul shook his head sadly. "Of course, under normal circumstances, the British Government would weigh in on such matters. However, these are challenging times. I have spoken to the French consul, and he has requested that Sir Reginald and I allow the Pasha to exercise his authority unimpeded."

"And when they decide that he is guilty and move to behead Alessandro, will you still respect Moroccan authority?" Fatima asked in an acid tone.

Beheading? Surely not in this day and age. Melody looked anxiously at Rat. Perhaps the vice consul did not realise Alessandro's role as a Secret Service Bureau operative. While Melody understood the importance of keeping his and Alessandro's roles secret, surely this was one of the situations that trumped such discretion? Rat looked very serious but said nothing.

Suddenly, the door opened, and Sir Reginald entered. For a moment, Melody hoped that common sense would prevail and that the consul would intervene and insist that Alessandro be released.

However, that hope was shattered when the man shook his head sadly and said, "Very unfortunate. But you made the right call, Madden. The British Government cannot be seen to undermine French authority in the region. Tensions are high enough as they are. If the Pasha wants him, then we must respect Moroccan authority."

"Even if they behead an innocent man?" Melody blurted out, infuriated at the bureaucrats.

The consul gave Melody a long, hard look and then turned to Rat. "Mr Sandworth, I am sure that you understand the delicate dance of foreign diplomacy in a way that a sheltered young woman cannot be expected to."

Melody looked at Rat; would he defend her? She couldn't remember when she had been as disappointed in someone as when she heard her brother say, "Of course I understand. As I am sure the conte does also."

This really was the final straw. Melody stormed out of the study, slamming the door behind her.

Rat watched her go, entirely sympathetic to her feelings. Did he understand the delicate dance of foreign diplomacy? He did understand that the situation in Morocco was volatile and that his government would not want to do anything to inflame passions in the region further. If that meant that one of their operatives, even one of high birth, would have to spend an uncomfortable night in a Moroccan prison before everything got smoothed over, then perhaps it was for the best. He knew that Melody would understand once she had calmed down.

Rat looked at Sir Reginald's determined expression and decided that there was no point in discussing this further until morning. He didn't believe that Alessandro would be left to rot in jail just to appease a local Moroccan official. However, he knew that such things often had to play themselves out. If the Pasha wanted to take a stand, he must be allowed to, at least for the time being.

Turning to Fatima, Rat suggested that they take their leave. As he was about to leave the study, Rat turned back to the consul and reminded him, "We have an appointment at eleven o'clock tomorrow morning that I intend to be at. I will spend the time between now and then doing what I can to clear Conte Foscari's name. I hope that his government will do similarly."

The consul didn't say anything, but he nodded in acknowledgement of Rat's words. Fatima and Rat found Melody sitting on a chair outside of the study, still fuming.

"There is nothing more we can do for him here tonight," Rat explained gently. Correctly anticipating Melody's response, he continued, "That does not mean that we can do nothing. Let us gather up Mustafa and leave. I want to understand what Alessandro was doing anywhere near the man who tried to stab him."

Melody rose, then turned to Fatima and asked, "Would Omar be able to help us at all?"

Fatima considered the question. "It is worth sending word to him. Once we return home, I will send Ahmed in the carriage to expedite the delivery of the message."

"Will Omar return with Ahmed?" Rat asked.

Fatima laughed lightly. "No. It is best if Omar is not seen coming to Anfa. It is hard to imagine what rare book emergency I might have that would require his presence at this time of night. But do not worry. He will come, just not in my carriage."

Melody could barely sit still for the carriage ride back to Fatima's home. They had gathered up Mustafa but had agreed to wait until they arrived at Fatima's home to question him. It seemed that the boy had been present when the Pasha's men had arrested Alessandro, and the child seemed to be quite traumatised.

Arriving back at the house, they made their way to the salon with Mustafa in tow. A maid brought mint tea, of course, and Ahmed assured them he would be off immediately. Melody encouraged Mustafa to have some of the sweet tea. She had been raised to believe that a cup of tea could solve most ills and saw no reason that this would not apply to Moroccan mint tea as well as a cup of Darjeeling.

Mustafa took a few sips, then turned to Melody and said in a plaintive voice that broke her heart, "It was my fault, Madam. I fetched the Monsieur to tell him that I had seen the bad man. I had gone out to the garden at the cook's command to pick more mint, and I had seen the man there. He did not see me but seemed to be in wait. For what, I do not know. I rushed inside to find Monsieur and told him that the bad man who tried to hurt him was in the garden. Monsieur led the way outside. I was stopped for a moment by a servant who asked me a question, and by the time I had returned to the garden, the bad man was lying on the ground with a knife in him. Monsieur bent over the man to see if he was still breathing, and at that moment, the Pasha's men came upon us and arrested Monsieur. It is all my fault," the boy repeated inconsolably.

"It is not your fault, Mustafa!" Melody assured him. Then she turned to Rat and Fatima. "Why would the Pasha's men be roaming the garden? That seems quite the coincidence, does it not?"

"Indeed," Fatima agreed. "I have never trusted that man. When the Sultan took the throne, after, well after you know what, he left this Pasha in place. I never thought it was a good idea."

Melody had no idea what "you know what" referred to. Looking at Rat, she raised her eyebrows in query.

"Well, perhaps if you'd paid more attention on the drive here, you'd know what Fatima is talking about," Rat complained. Nevertheless, he explained. "The current Sultan, Moulay Abdelhafid, well, he took over from his brother, Moulay Abdelaziz."

"Took over?" Melody asked. "Do you mean that he deposed his own brother?"

Rat looked to Fatima. "Yes. the previous sultan was perceived as being too open and close to the Europeans, particularly the French, by the tribal leaders." Fatima explained. "Morocco is still a very tribal country and the Berbers in particular, give their primary allegiance to their tribal leader. Abdelhafid allied himself with some of the more influential tribes, particularly the ones who were the most anti-European. This resulted in Abdelhafid taking the throne from his brother three years ago."

"Taking the throne" seemed quite the euphemism as far as Melody was concerned. Nevertheless, she put this thought aside for the time being and asked, "So, the Pasha here in Casablanca is the same one who was in power during the previous sultan's regime?"

Fatima nodded. Melody continued, "Why would he do that?"

"As I said, the tribal leaders are very powerful, and this Pasha is well-liked by many of the Berber leaders. His mother is a Berber, and there was a lot of pressure on the Sultan to leave the man in place. Still..." Fatima left the thought hanging.

"Still what?" Melody pressed.

The maid had returned with some dates and pastries, and Fatima used the opportunity to pour more tea and consider her next sentence. Finally, she replied, "Morocco is a complicated place. Allegiances can go back hundreds if not thousands of years. Even the Berbers are not a homogenous people. And then there is the fact that, even though he came to power by opposing his brother's support of the European powers, our Sultan has discovered that it is far easier to oppose the French demands for military and economic concessions from the sidelines than it is from the throne."

Melody wasn't sure what this meant, and she had no idea how it all connected to the murder than evening and Alessandro's arrest. Nevertheless, she was determined that she would grope her way through the morass of Moroccan politics and alliances and get Alessandro released from prison.

Mustafa's eyes were drooping, and so they excused him and sent the boy off to bed. Then, turning to Rat, Melody stated in a tone that brooked no dissent, "Fatima and I will be accompanying you to talk to Sir Reginald tomorrow morning."

It was unclear who was the most surprised by her statement, Rat or Melody herself. The truth was, whatever Melody's personal distaste for Fatima, the woman had a deep and broad understanding of Moroccan history and politics. Certainly, she understood far more than either Melody or Rat did. If they had any chance of securing Alessandro's release, they would need her help.

CHAPTER 10

The following morning, Melody was up bright and early, despite a restless night. Whatever her current feelings towards Alessandro, she did not doubt that he was innocent of murder. She did not stop to think about why she had such faith in a man who had deceived her about his romantic feelings towards her.

Despite some recent noteworthy examples to the contrary, Melody liked to think of herself as a good judge of character. She had learned from Tabby Cat and Wolf what a man or woman of good character was. They surrounded themselves with decent, honest people who they trusted. Neither one of them cared a toss for rank or fortune but instead had a knack for judging the people they encountered based on their true worth as a person.

Melody knew that Tabby Cat and Granny had a difficult past. Indeed, they often had a somewhat contentious relationship still. However, Tabby Cat had once confessed something to a younger Melody. One day, when Granny had been particularly difficult, even for Granny, Melody asked the question, "She is not actually related to you, is she? Yet, you continue to put up with her ways. Why?"

Tabby Cat had thought for a moment and then answered, "There is no one who sees to the heart of a person quite like Mama. Yes, she has her peculiarities, but at the end of the day, she does not suffer fools, charlatans, nor those who would borrow their feathers. There is much to be said for someone who sees so clearly." Tabby Cat had then added, "Of course, it is one thing to see other people's behaviour with clear eyes, quite another to so judge your own."

This caveat notwithstanding, Melody had often thought about these words. Now, when she considered Alessandro, she found that she considered him neither fool nor charlatan and certainly not a borrower of feathers. Even as she had this thought, she second-guessed herself. Was his behaviour towards her not that of a charlatan? But was it really? Now that she knew about the man's role with the Secret Service Bureau, she realised that there were things that such operatives were required to do, regardless of how distasteful they might personally find them. She put aside for the moment the question of whether Alessandro had found his inauthentic pursuit of her distasteful.

It had crossed Melody's mind over the last couple of weeks that, at some point, even Rat might have to engage in activities that he would prefer not to do. Might he even be called upon to take another's life? It was certainly possible. Yet, Melody was sure that her brother's motives in working for the Bureau were absolutely pure; his only thoughts were patriotism and loyalty to king and country. If she could make this excuse for Rat, surely, she should be able to view Alessandro's actions a little more kindly.

Omar had turned up just after breakfast. Ahmed hadn't announced him, so it seemed unlikely that he had just knocked on the front door. Instead, Rat, Fatima and Melody had entered the salon after breakfast to find the man there pouring himself a glass of mint tea.

If Fatima was surprised to see him in her salon, she didn't show it. Instead, she said, "I expected you last night."

The man stirred some sugar into his tea, even though Melody was sure it was already far too sweet. Then, after taking a sip, he replied, "It was not safe to do so. This morning, I had some book deliveries to make, including one in Anfa. It seemed best to combine this visit with that one."

Fatima acknowledged the wisdom of his decision, then asked, "Have you found anything out about our dead man?"

Omar shook his head. No one is claiming him. The French and Germans are both disavowing any knowledge of the man."

"Is it possible he is British?" Melody asked.

"It is very unlikely," Omar answered. "And why would he be following the conte if he were?"

It was a valid question. Melody considered what she wanted to ask, then said, "Omar, who do you think the man is?"

"If the Qur'an allowed me to gamble, I would put my money on the man being French," he answered.

"French?" Rat asked. "Really? Why?"

Omar laughed. "In Morocco, we are used to many different factions vying for power. The different tribes have been battling each other for many centuries. But you Europeans seem to see things as far more black and white. There are the French, and there are the Germans."

"Isn't that the case?" Rat asked, genuinely curious to hear the other man's explanation.

In answer, Omar questioned, "In Great Britain, does everyone think the same? Is everyone in power moving towards the same one goal?"

"Well, of course not," Rat answered. "We have a Liberal government at the moment, but the Tories will come back to power at some point and will pursue very different policies."

"Indeed," Omar agreed. "And do you think that everyone who works in the government agrees with everything your Liberal Prime Minister does?"

Rat thought about the question. He knew that there was a vast civil service in and around Whitehall whose job was to enact the laws that Parliament voted on. He supposed that those civil servants were tasked with implementing government policy whether or not they personally agreed with it. He hadn't really thought about it in this way before.

"Are you saying that there are factions within the French and German governments that might be working against official policy?" he asked.

"I cannot speak to your German neighbours, but I can guarantee you that is the case within France." Omar paused as if collecting his thoughts. "Have you heard of the Quai d'Orsay?"

Rat nodded that he had, but Melody shook her head in the negative.

"It is the name by which the French Ministry of Foreign Affairs is often known," Rat explained to her.

"Indeed," Omar said. "And, how can I put this politely?"

Fatima saved him the trouble, "It is staffed by overly self-confident, foolhardy men who think far too highly of their own cleverness."

Omar acknowledged the truth of her words.

"And these men are able to have that much sway over French foreign policy?" Melody asked. While she was no expert on how the British Government worked, she assumed that its elected officials were not powerless.

Again, Fatima answered, "Unfortunately, there has been a string of weak, ineffective ministers and this has led to the men of the Quai d'Orsay having undue influence. One might even say that it has gone beyond influence. I have heard rumours that some of the most nationalist, inflammatory news articles in Le Figaro and La Croix were leaked from within the Quai d'Orsay."

Melody considered all they were saying. "So, are you suggesting that the dead man is connected to this faction in the French Government? And if so, why did he target Alessandro?"

"Your government cannot be happy about the extreme nationalistic fervour coming from its so-called ally," Fatima observed.

Melody pointed out what she thought was the obvious flaw in this argument, "How would the French know about Alessandro's covert work?" She was nervous about stating too blatantly the job that Alessandro and Rat were in Morocco for. It was evident that Fatima knew something of their work, but it was unclear if she knew the full extent. If she didn't, then Melody certainly wouldn't be the one to illuminate her. Because, as she had thought previously, how did they know that they could trust Fatima? After all, one obvious answer to how the French Government might know why Alessandro was in Morocco was that the half-French Fatima had informed them.

No one had a good answer to her question, and the conversation went on for at least twenty minutes. Just as Melody looked at the grandfather clock in the corner and decided it was time to change her clothes for their visit to Sir Reginald, Ahmed entered the room with a message for Fatima.

It was clear from Fatima's expression that this wasn't good news. She folded the paper after reading it, pursed her lips, and sat silently, reflecting on what she had read. Melody wanted to scream. What was in the note? Had something happened to Alessandro?

Finally, Fatima spoke. "Sandro has been taken to Fes."

"Fes!" Rat exclaimed. "They can't do that, can they? It is bad enough that he wasn't handed over to Sir Reginald. British citizens here are protected under a special agreement. But to take him to Fes is unprecedented, is it not?" This was directed at Omar, who made a face.

"What? What are you not saying?" Melody demanded.

"You might as well say it, Omar," Fatima said in a resigned voice. "At least we now have some sense of the magnitude of what we are dealing with."

This all sounded so dire that Melody found that her palms were sweating with anxiety.

"The only reason for taking the conte to Fes would be if this somehow requires direct input by the Sultan," Omar explained.

Melody shook her head in confusion and frustration. "How did they even have time between last night and this morning to arrange this with Fes?"

"Miss Chesterton, while Morocco might not be as technologically advanced as Europe, our major cities are connected by telegram," Omar said somewhat tersely. "I am sure that the Pasha has the ability to communicate with the Sultan and his court when necessary."

"I did not mean to imply that Morocco is backwards," Melody said apologetically. "I am merely upset and concerned."

"As are we all," Omar said in a kinder tone. He then stood and said, "I must follow them to Fes. It seems as if the local British officials are unwilling to step in and assert the conte's extraterritorial rights. Someone must be there to try to intervene on his behalf."

"I totally agree, Omar," Fatima said. "And so, I will be joining you."

Omar shook his head vehemently, "Lalla Fatima, I must insist that you stay in Casablanca. The trip is far too treacherous."

In a tone that made clear that she would have her way, Fatima replied, "Omar, I realise that as a Berber you know the area better than I do. Nevertheless, I have contacts in Fes that you do not. I assume that you have not forgotten that the Sultan's favourite wife is my cousin."

Cousin? That was news to Melody and apparently to Rat as well, if his surprised look was anything to go by.

"And, of course, I will accompany you," Rat said in a determined voice. Before anyone could object, he continued, "In my official capacity."

Well, she certainly wasn't going to be the only one left behind in Casablanca, Melody decided. This resolution must have shown on her face or Rat just knew her very well. He turned and said, "Melody, you will wait for me here, if that is acceptable to Fatima, of course."

"I am not waiting anywhere," Melody said with a determination that more than rivalled Rat's.

Before Rat could even argue with her, Omar said, "Lalla Melody, the route to Fes is long, arduous and dangerous. There are bandits in the region, to say nothing of the general tribal unrest of late. It is not an appropriate trip for a young woman."

"And yet Lalla Fatima will be joining you," Melody said in rejoinder.

Omar knew that he had lost but made one final attempt at a plea to Rat. "Sidi Matthew, it is not safe."

Rat sighed; he knew a lost fight when he saw one. Turning to Melody, he said sternly, "You cannot slow us down."

"How will sitting in a carriage along with me slow you down?" Melody sneered.

"We will ride on horseback to Fes," Fatima explained, surprising both siblings. Thanks to multiple visits each year to the Pembroke Estate, both could ride a horse, but neither of them would be considered anything more than proficient. And it was one thing to go for an afternoon canter through the Welsh countryside and quite another to navigate the Moroccan terrain, particularly the foothills of the Middle Atlas Mountains that they would have to trek through before arriving in Fes.

Despite her determination to be included in the journey, Melody was taken aback to learn that it would all be on horseback.

"Have you ever ridden astride?" Fatima asked. "This is a far too long and difficult journey to make side-saddle." As it happened, Melody had ridden astride when she was young and nodded her head. Of course, she didn't have any outfit appropriate for riding, side-saddle or otherwise.

It seemed that Fatima had the same thought and said, "I have some split skirts that I will wear for the ride. You may borrow one or two. We will pack as lightly as possible. Do not bring any clothes that you cannot put on yourself."

Melody hadn't had time to consider whether Mary would be joining them, but as soon as Fatima said this, she realised that it was unfair to ask Mary, who did not ride, to make the journey.

"My men will accompany us," Fatima said to Omar. "Just in case." She didn't specify what the "just-in-case" was, but Melody assumed that it was anything that fell into the bandits and tribal unrest bucket.

"We will bring the boy with us," Fatima continued. This surprised Melody. Why was it necessary to bring Mustafa? "He is the only witness to what happened," Fatima explained. "He summoned Sandro and is the one who saw the victim in the Medina. If we are able to get an audience with the Sultan, it may be necessary to have Mustafa describe what he knows."

It seemed there wasn't much more to say. Omar returned home to prepare for their journey and said he would be back and ready to leave by early afternoon. Fatima went to gather her servants and ensure they had sufficient horses. This left Rat and Melody to pack. Fatima had said that she would send the split skirts and some riding boots to Melody's room, so there wasn't even much that had to be gathered in the way of clothes. The siblings sat in the salon and looked at each other. It seemed they were going to Fes.

CHAPTER 11

M ary hadn't been happy at the thought of Melody travelling without her. However, it was very clear that she also had no desire to travel on horseback through the wilds of Morocco. She started folding clothes until Melody intervened to explain that she was to take as little as possible.

"What does that even mean?" Mary complained.

"It means that I need to be able to carry my possessions on the horse I am riding. We will be taking some mules, but they will carry provisions, not my clothes."

Mary gave a sniff that was worthy of the dowager. "That sounds like a very inappropriate way for a well-brought up young woman to travel. I cannot imagine what Lady Pembroke would say."

Melody didn't bother to ask which Lady Pembroke Mary was referring to. As indebted as she was to Tabitha for making her Melody's nursemaid so many years before, it was the older Lady Pembroke, the dowager countess, who Mary revered. Perhaps it was because she and the old woman recognised in each other someone who adored Melody above all others.

Before they could bicker any further about the trip, there was a gentle knock at the door. Mary went to answer it and found a young servant girl holding a pile of folded clothes topped with a wide-brimmed hat and a sturdy pair of riding boots.

"Lalla Fatima has sent these for you," the girl explained. Mary took them from her, and the girl scuttled off.

"I don't know what things have come to when you are wearing hand-me-down clothes."

"I am not wearing hand-me-downs, Mary. Well, I am, but for a good reason. It will be very hot on the trail, and I do not have any appropriate clothes with me. To say nothing of needing split skirts to ride astride."

"Astride!" Mary exclaimed in horror.

"Yes, astride. This is a long journey, and there is no place for British upper-class niceties. Now, fetch the large carpetbag and let us see if we can fit everything in."

Two hours later, they had eaten a hearty lunch and were ready to set off. Omar had returned with a small travelling bag, and an excited but nervous Mustafa was waiting anxiously by the door.

Rat had struggled to find appropriate clothes in his luggage and had finally landed on two light linen suits and the most sensible shoes he had with him. He suspected that he was going to look absurd on the trail next to Omar and Fatima's men in their djellabas and with scarves wrapped around their heads. He also thought that the djellabas looked comfortable and cool compared to his suit.

"Omar, would it be seen as disrespectful if I were to wear a robe like yours?" Rat asked.

"Not at all, Sidi Matthew. A djellaba and tagelmust on your head are very practical for a trip such as ours. I am sure that we can find you something if you would prefer to travel in it." Rat indicated that he would, and twenty minutes later, the only thing that distinguished him from the Berbers he was travelling with was his fair skin and reddish-brown hair.

Rat was concerned about the sight of them all clearly setting off on such a trip. Would it look suspicious? However, there wasn't time to finesse the plan. The people holding Alessandro already had a head start.

By the time they were ready to leave, the call to prayer was beginning to echo from the city's many minarets. Fatima explained that once they were on their journey, it was permissible for the men to miss the one o'clock prayer and instead combine it with the four o'clock one. However, until they were on the road, it was best that they postpone leaving so the men could pray.

Ever since they had arrived in Morocco, Melody had found the call to prayer, particularly the early morning one, to be quite haunting. There was something so melodic in the muezzin's chanting. The sound would carry across the streets of the city, commanding all Muslims to perform their prayers.

Finally, almost thirty minutes later, they were ready to leave. Omar had explained that they usually would not ride in the middle of the after-noon, but there was no time to be lost, and they would have to do as much as they could before sunset.

Melody had no idea what to expect. Where would they sleep? What would they eat? She was worried that any questions might come across as anxious or even sound like she was whining. Instead, she kept her thoughts to herself; she would find out soon enough. It appeared that Omar was very familiar with the route they were to take, as was at least one of the servants. Between them, they took the lead with everyone else following in pairs. Two more servants brought up the rear of the caravan. It was not lost on Rat or Melody that all the servants carried rifles.

The ride out of Casablanca was pleasant. Even though the sun was high in the sky, there was a gentle breeze. The olive groves and palm trees provided some much-appreciated shade along the trail. There was a delightful scent in the air, which Fatima, who rode beside Melody, identi-fied as jasmine.

Melody looked around her with interest. It was a very different view from atop a horse than it had been through a carriage window. They passed men tending the fields and women washing clothes and shopping in the local markets. Melody noticed that people would raise their heads in momentary interest but then immediately go back to whatever they were doing. Children would chase their horses for a while, but then they lost interest and went back to playing in the fields.

By the time they stopped for the night four hours later, Melody had remembered how long it had been since she'd ridden regularly. Appar-ently, for at least that first night, they'd be camping. Melody was deter-mined not to complain or in any way show any discomfort she might feel. It seemed that there was a tent that she would be sharing with Fatima but that the men would all be sleeping wrapped in blankets. Not that it was cold. Nevertheless, she did feel for Rat, who, despite their early days of living on the streets of Whitechapel, had spent the last fourteen years in the comfort of Mayfair and had likely hoped that he would never be sleeping rough again.

Omar and the male servants quickly got a fire going and put a conical-shaped pot on it.

"It is called a tagine," Fatima explained. "All sorts of meat and vegetables can be cooked in it. We brought some supplies with us. Cook sent us off with some dough that the men will cook on the coals."

Melody saw something brown being scooped out of a jar and put into the tagine pot. "What is that?" she asked.

"We call it khlii," Fatima explained. "It is a kind of preserved meat. Usually, beef, though sometimes lamb. It is dried, spiced and then stored in fat in the jars you see." Melody must have scrunched her nose because Fatima laughed and said, "It is tastier than it sounds. And it is what we will be eating a lot of, so hopefully, you will get used to it."

Melody was embarrassed. She didn't want to come across as a spoiled young English miss and yet was worried that was how she seemed. The truth was that ever since Alessandro had been arrested, Fatima had been far nicer. Perhaps nicer wasn't the right word. She seemed genuinely concerned for Alessandro's safety and had stopped all the flirtation with Rat and the cattiness towards Melody. And if she were being honest with herself, Melody was grateful for female company on this trip. Fatima hadn't had to lend her the clothes and could have instead used Melody's likely discomfort in her own clothes as an opportunity to mock her. Moreover, it seemed very likely that Fatima's connection to the Sultan's family would prove useful, or at least Melody hoped it would.

As the sun began to set, Melody saw Rat standing at the edge of the camp, looking out at the mountains in the distance. "Penny for your thoughts," she said teasingly.

Her brother turned but didn't smile. Instead, he looked as if he had the weight of the world on his shoulders.

"What's wrong, Rat?" Melody asked, putting out her hand to touch his forearm.

Rat gave her a half-smile, "Am I that obvious?" he asked.

"Only to me," she assured him. Realising that there could be only one thing that was on his mind, Melody said, "We will find him and get this mess sorted out. I know we will."

"And what if we do not? What if I am not up to this? As it is, without Omar and Fatima, I wouldn't even know where to start."

In her gentlest voice, Melody tried to set his mind at rest or at least buoy his self-confidence. "How would you know where to start? This is a very different part of the world to Britain, or even Europe."

"Yet, Alessandro knows how to operate here. He has contacts and can even speak some of the language."

"Rat, be sensible. Alessandro is probably almost ten years older than you and, I would assume, has been an operative for some years. You have only just started. I doubt that he knew how to operate somewhere like Morocco when he started out. He probably had someone to guide him then, much as you do now."

Later, in the tent she shared with Fatima, Melody took out her diary. It seemed like forever had passed since she had last had the chance or the motivation to write in it.

Dear Diary, where do I even begin? Less than twenty-four hours ago, I was dressed in a new Worth gown and jewels and being introduced to the Envoy to Morocco, and now I am in a tent, in the middle of who-knows-where with a very sore rear end after less than a day on horseback. Though, I must admit, there is something quite exotic and romantic about sitting around the fire, eating the food the men have cooked on the coals, and watching the last of the sun dip beneath the horizon. Oh, and we passed some camels earlier. They are strange-looking creatures.

All in all, if I wanted an adventure, I have one now. I just wish that this adventure wasn't at the expense of Alessandro's freedom and perhaps even his life. What is going on? I thought that the politics of our investigation in Venice were murky, but Morocco makes that situation seem like child's play. And here is the thing I do not understand: why do any of these European countries believe that they have a right to rule here?

As Melody wrote this, she thought about something Xander Ashby had said when she had thrown in his face that the Italian people had deserved their independence from the Hapsburg Empire. His comeback had been to compare the situation to Britain's Irish situation, or even their king's dominion over Wales and Scotland. At the time, she had claimed that these were entirely different circumstances. But were they? And what about Britain's colonisation of India and beyond? She could hardly damn the French and Germans for tussling over Morocco like it was a shiny toy on Christmas morning yet have no problem with her own country's imperialism.

There were things that Melody had never questioned when she was in London, had never had a reason to question. That the population of the British Empire were not only better off than when they were independent but that they, for the most part, recognised and were grateful for that fact was a given. Yes, there were people who advocated for Irish Home Rule, and she had heard Wolfie talking about actions against the authorities in India over the past few years. She had sensed that Tabby Cat and Wolfie had a certain sympathy for the rebels. It was indisputable that they took a more measured view than Granny.

Melody's last thought before she fell asleep was to wonder how Alessandro was and to hope that they arrived in Fes in time.

CHAPTER 12

The trip to Fes was eleven days of hard riding. Most days, they set out early to avoid the brutal midday heat, resting for a couple of hours by a stream when they could and then continuing until nightfall. In the beginning, the terrain was mostly flat, fertile farmland, but the mountains in the distance whispered the promise of a more challenging ride to come.

By the third day, they had left the lush lowlands and started climbing through rocky outcrops and low hills. Goats, sheep, and camels roamed the landscape, though it wasn't always apparent to Melody what they were finding to eat in the parched, red earth.

The conversation had started to wane as the journey became more arduous. By the fourth night, Melody was sick of eating tagine and drinking mint tea. What she would have given for a cup of coffee. The soreness that she had felt after that first day of riding had morphed into a constant, dull ache in her legs. As uncomfortable as her makeshift bed in the tent was, she collapsed into it every night and was asleep almost immediately.

Increasingly, Rat was grateful that he had adopted the local costume. The robe was comfortable and cool during the day, and the tagelmust both shielded his head from the sun's rays and could be pulled across his nose and mouth to protect against the dust kicked up by the horses. He had never been as comfortable riding a horse as Melody and spent most of his days clinging on to the reins and hoping that nothing spooked his steed; he wasn't ready for a gallop.

Omar, Mustafa and Fatima's men seemed to take the journey in their stride. During the sporadic conversations during meals, Melody had learned that while Omar and the other men were Berbers, Mustafa's family were Arabs. The adult men would often talk together in a language that Mustafa didn't understand and which she assumed was their Berber language.

"I selected the Berbers from amongst my staff to come with us," Fatima had explained on the first night as they were preparing for bed. "The deeper we go into the country, and particularly once we are in the Atlas Mountains, the people are mostly Berber. The tribes are semi-autonomous, and the Sultan's authority is nominal. We are much better off surrounding ourselves with Berbers for this trip, even if they are from other tribes."

This explanation made total sense to Melody, and yet again, she found herself surprisingly grateful for Fatima's presence on the journey. The further they had travelled from Casablanca, the more the other woman had ceased to remind Melody of the unpleasant London socialites with their veiled barbs. Would that all change once they reached Fes? Was the difference from when they were in Casablanca that there was no Alessandro to display for?

As their journey took them through villages, Omar would ask about the caravan of men ahead of them which included Alessandro. From what he could glean, they were maintaining a good enough pace that the Pasha's men were no further ahead than they had been. That was some consolation, at least.

Melody could sense an increased tension in the group. Pulling her horse alongside Rat's, she whispered, "Is there something going on? All the men seem on edge."

"I am not entirely sure, but Omar mentioned that we are entering the tribal lands of a particularly insular Berber group who are very suspicious of outsiders," Rat explained. Seeing the concern on Melody's face, he hastened to add, "Omar says that there is nothing to be overly worried about. As long as we are just passing through, they will not interfere with us. However, we do need to be on our guard and ensure that there are no incidents that might be perceived as threatening."

Melody wasn't sure what Rat's last sentence meant. What might they do that could be so perceived? Looking more closely at Omar and Fatima's men, she realised that their rifles were no longer on display and assumed that this was part of their adoption of an unthreatening posture.

At some point, Melody noticed that the terrain had become rockier and more uneven. She was grateful that her horse seemed to know how to pick its way carefully as the path became narrower and more treacherous. Omar explained that they were entering the foothills of the Middle Atlas Mountains. The air felt cooler, which was a pleasant change from the usually brutal afternoon sun, but did portend a chilly night if they had planned to camp out. As they climbed through the Middle Atlas Mountains, the vista became increasingly dramatic and quite awe-inspiring, with the highest mountains in the distance still snow-capped.

On day seven, as they broke for their midday meal and rest, Omar said that they should plan to ride to a settlement in the lowlands past the Middle Atlas Mountains, Sefrou. While it would require them to ride for a little longer than they usually did in a day, there was a riad where they could get shelter for the night, and the town's souq would give them the opportunity to stock up on supplies. The idea of spending even one more hour than usual on horseback was enough to make Melody groan in anticipation of even more sore than usual muscles. Counterbalanced to her stiffness was the possibility of a real bed for the night and a meal that was something other than khlii tagine and bread. Shivering against the crisp mountain air, Melody was glad that they would have shelter in Sefrou for the night.

As the afternoon wore on, Melody was unsure how much longer she could stay upright on her horse. Because of the coolness in the mountains, they had not had to stop for their customary afternoon rest, and so she had been in the saddle for five hours without a break. Just as she was determined to ask Omar and the men to stop, if only for a few minutes, they came over a ridge and saw a village nestled in the verdant valley below. A clear river snaked through the village, its water sparkling from the late afternoon sunlight. There were fields of crops surrounding the village as well as clusters of trees, which Omar explained were primarily olive and palm trees. Even from this distance, they could see the minaret of the mosque.

The horses had come to a standstill as the group surveyed the village. Omar pulled his horse up next to Melody and Rat and explained, "Every village must have four things: a mosque, a community bread oven, a well, and finally a market, or souq as we call it."

"Are you sure we will be welcomed here?" Rat asked nervously.

"Indeed. We will make our way to the riad of my mother's cousin, Aksel, a wealthy trader."

The horses began to pick their way down the rocky path down to the village. From what Melody could see, Sefrou was a modest settlement, its flat-roofed, clay-brick houses blending into the earthy tones of the surrounding hills. It was hard to imagine that more than a few hundred souls lived in the village. And if that was the case, then every single one of them was out on the streets that afternoon. The streets were bustling with people, donkeys and the occasional goat.

Their caravan was an interesting enough sight to cause some glances, but most people were too busy going about their business to care about the strangers. Melody had noticed that the women they had passed on their travels, much like the ones now in Sefrou, were dressed quite differently from those in Casablanca. In the city, there hadn't been many women out on the streets, but when they had been, they had been dressed all in black. Here, the robes were embroidered with colourful threads. Many of them had veils over the lower part of their faces.

As they rode through the village's streets, Melody and Rat marvelled at the souq stalls. One had colourful rugs, another copper pots, and next to that, a stall selling olives from large vats. Delicious smells of freshly baked bread, roasted almonds, and rosewater hung in the air. Smelling the bread reminded Melody how hungry she was. She hoped that they would be at the riad soon.

The caravan stopped at a rather ramshackle wooden building. This couldn't be the riad where they were hoping to stay, could it? It didn't look much better than staying in a tent for the night.

Perhaps anticipating Melody's concern, Fatima explained, "This is called a caravanserai. It is where we will leave the horses and my men for the night before we proceed on foot to the riad. The boy will stay here with the horses."

The idea of getting off the horse and stretching her legs, even for a few minutes, was very appealing. Five minutes later, Omar, Fatima, Melody and Rat proceeded on foot through the village. It wasn't long before they arrived at quite a plain-looking building that had a rather magnificent wooden door with a huge brass knocker. The building had no windows. Remembering Omar's home in Casablanca, Melody realised that it was likely that the spartan exterior masked a far more comfortable, lavish interior.

When Omar knocked on the door, a small, wiry-looking man opened it. His eyes lit up when he saw Omar and a huge grin suffused his face. The man burst out into a joyful stream of a language that Melody couldn't recognise, but that didn't sound like Arabic; she assumed it was a local Berber dialect. The man gathered Omar into a bear hug.

A few more words were spoken and then Omar turned to them and said, "This is Mansour. He has been with my family since he was a child. He now runs my cousin's household."

They followed Mansour down a short corridor, which led to an open-air courtyard bigger and even more lavish than Omar's. The walls were decorated with elaborate, colourful mosaics, which also served as the decorative background for a large fountain built into the building's rear wall.

As Melody looked around, she marvelled at the intricate carvings framing each doorway and the top edge of the walls and arches.

"It is made of egg white and marble dust carved in place," Omar explained. Melody couldn't get over the beauty and craftsmanship of the engravings.

Large, colourful silk pillows were scattered around the courtyard, and Mansour gestured that they should settle themselves. Before they could take a seat, Omar suggested that they wash their hands and faces in the fountain. After the dust of the mountains, the cool, fresh water splashed onto her face felt delightful to Melody. After washing, they sat on the cushions.

"Mansour will bring us tea and tell my cousin that we are here."

Melody hoped that there would be something to eat to accompany the tea. She breathed a sigh of relief when Mansour returned with a silver tray with the customary teapot and glasses on it but also a plate laden with a variety of biscuits. Mansour placed the tray on a low table and raised the teapot high over the glasses before pouring tea into each one.

They had seen tea poured like this before, but now Rat wondered aloud, "Why does he hold the teapot so high when he pours?"

Omar laughed. "If someone does not do that, then they are showing you how unenthusiastic they are for your visit and making clear that it should be of short duration. By pouring the tea from a height, and causing all those bubbles in the glass, Mansour is indicating that we are welcomed guests and that he hopes our stay will be long."

The tea was a welcome balm to their parched throats, and the biscuits were delicious. It was a curiosity of Moroccan cuisine that Melody had noted that while savoury dishes could be quite sweet, particularly the tagines, filled with prunes and apricots, traditionally sweet items, such as biscuits, often had far less sugar than they did in other cultures. However, the mint tea here was served as tooth-achingly sweet as elsewhere in Morocco.

They had been sipping their tea and nibbling on the biscuits for a few minutes when a large man burst into the courtyard. His resemblance to Omar was obvious, but this man's stomach was even rounder and his moustache even more extravagant. It was clear from the rich fabrics of his clothing that this was their host. His djellaba was made of fine cotton with richly detailed embroidery around every edge. On his head, he wore a bright orange silk turban.

On his entrance, everyone stood, and Omar went towards the men. They hugged warmly.

"As-salamu alaykum," Aksel said.

"Wa alaykum as-salum," Omar replied.

Omar then turned to Melody, Rat and Fatima and introduced them. Melody had wondered if Aksel would speak any English, but his greetings made clear that he spoke it well enough.

"You are blessed guests. Anyone my dear cousin brings into my home is welcome."

CHAPTER 13

As they sat and sipped tea, they chatted. Initially, the conversation was Casablanca gossip. It seemed that as a merchant, Aksel regularly moved around the country and seemed quite familiar with the local politics and intrigue.

When his need to catch up on Casablanca society was satiated, Aksel asked, "So, why are you making this trek, my cousin? And with such company?"

The question almost sounded rude to Melody's ears, but she hoped that it was nothing more than Aksel's command of the English language. Certainly, in every other way, he had been a very gracious host.

As Omar began to speak, Melody wondered just how much he would reveal. He seemed aware of Alessandro and Rat's roles working for the Secret Service Bureau, but she was sure her brother would prefer that not be revealed widely.

"A man, a friend, who is British, has been arrested and is being taken to Fes for trial."

Aksel raised his eyebrows. "Taken to Fes rather than handed over to the British authorities. Is that not unusual?"

"Indeed," his cousin answered. "The consul feels that passions are running high enough at the moment, and they don't wish to interfere and make matters worse. The French asked him to allow the Pasha to handle the situation, and it seems that his response was to send my friend to Fes."

"To the Sultan, may God bless him?" Aksel asked.

"That is what we believe, yes."

Aksel stroked his magnificent moustache as he considered Omar's words. Then he asked, "I am sure you have been travelling for many days. Did you hear about Spain's actions?"

Spain? Melody thought that only France and Germany were vying for power in Morocco. What did Spain have to do with it? Then she remembered the conversation at Omar's riad days ago.

Aksel continued, "It was a few days ago, but word only just reached me today."

Omar replied, "Yes, we heard that our Spanish friends were so alarmed by Morocco's French protectors' rush to aid the Sultan that they have sent their army to occupy Larache and Ksar-el-Kebir, claiming it is to maintain order in the wake of the rebellion in Fes."

"This will be viewed badly by Germany, I fear," Omar continued, shaking his head.

"I do not understand," Melody said. "Why will Germany care what Spain has done? Are they not competing with France rather than Spain for dominance here?"

Smiling in a rather annoying manner that suggested she was amused at Melody's ignorance and naivety, Fatima explained, "It is very likely that Germany will view this as an alliance by France and Spain against it to assert de facto control over Morocco."

"Is it?"

Fatima shrugged her delicate shoulders. "Does it matter? All that matters is that it is highly likely that this inflames tensions in Morocco even further. And that will not be good for Sandro."

This time, Rat asked, "Why will this affect how Alessandro is treated? Doesn't the Sultan have bigger issues to contend with?"

"That these foreign powers have solidified their positions in Morocco cannot reflect well on the Sultan, may God bless him. Our Berber brethren have made clear their displeasure with him and what they saw as his betrayal of his people as he increasingly relies on foreign advisors. That these foreign powers are now even more entrenched than they were before must make the Sultan's position even more precarious," Omar explained.

After their tea, Melody and Fatima were led to a lavish guest room, where they could bathe in rose-petal-scented water. Melody was so relieved to be able to wash off the grime and dust of their travels that she was tempted to linger in the water. However, the delicious smells coming from outside their room were even more alluring. Their clothes had been taken away to be laundered, and traditional robes were left for them to wear for the evening.

As Melody dressed, she asked Fatima, "Do you really believe that this latest move by the Spanish will make things go even more badly for Alessandro?"

The other woman was already dressed and was brushing her long, dark hair. She stopped her strokes of the brush and considered the question. "I believe that Alessandro has somehow become entangled in a web of intrigue between the various countries that seek to dominate Morocco, the Sultan, and the various Berber tribes who would loosen the foreigners' hold over this country. This latest move by Spain will surely escalate the tensions and make it even harder for the Sultan to justify excusing behaviour in a foreigner that would surely be fully prosecuted with a Moroccan suspect."

Seeing that Melody was about to interrupt, Fatima put up her hand and said gently, "It is not fair, but it is how the situation is. I believe that nothing short of unequivocal proof that Sandro is not guilty of the murder will be sufficient to ensure his release."

Melody shook her head in frustration. "We do not even know who the dead man is. How can we hope to prove Alessandro's innocence without that basic knowledge? Perhaps we should have stayed in Casablanca. We are so far from the scene of the murder that it is hard to believe we will have any luck finding evidence in Alessandro's favour in Fes."

Fatime assured her that their travels to Fes was the right move. Her ability to get them an audience with the Sultan was a significant step towards getting Alessandro released. "As soon as the Pasha's men took Sandro to Fes, we had no choice."

Their conversation at an end, the two women descended to the courtyard. The table was already piled high with delicious-looking food and included three large tagine pots. Melody's heart sank.

Melody had thought that she was sick of tagines, but as she tasted the delicious chicken version they were being served, flavoured with preserved lemons, olives, and spices, she realised that she was just ready for something other than khlii. This tagine was as far removed from the basic meal she had been eating for days as possible. It was served with the traditional flatbread, cooked over coals, but again, the one served at Aksel's table was far superior to the rather dry, tough bread that Fatima's men had cooked for every meal.

As she looked at the table set before them, laden with olives, roasted vegetables, couscous and various bowls filled with enticing-looking items, Melody found herself wishing, just for a moment, that their stay might be more than one night. She immediately berated herself for such selfishness. Alessandro might already be in Fes, rotting away in a dank prison, being fed who knows what maggot-infested food. How dare she wish to extend their trip by even an hour.

They all ate until they could not find room for even one more olive. Then, the mint tea was brought out, and Mansour performed his pouring ceremony again. As she sipped on the tea, Melody found that she could make room for a couple of dates after all. Having finished his tea-pouring duties, Mansour pulled a small pipe out of his robe and began playing for them. The tune was beautiful and soothing. So soothing that Melody found her eyelids becoming heavy as she struggled to stay awake. It didn't help that the conversation had become rather boring as Aksel, Omar, and Fatima explained the rivalries and political tensions between the various Berber tribes in the region surrounding Fes. She knew that she should be paying attention. After all, it seemed that these tensions were at least tangentially relevant to why Alessandro was being held. Yet, Melody was too weary and the information too dry to hold her attention.

Eating at the low table while sitting on the cushions was surprisingly comfortable once one got used to it. Melody could only imagine what Granny would make of such a dining scenario. Unfortunately, the very comfortable cushions only added to Melody's sleepiness. In an effort to stay awake, Melody looked around the courtyard. The riad was two storeys high. There were three doors surrounding the courtyard, with a corridor leading off from the fourth side. There were also shuttered windows that looked out onto the courtyard. Except one of these shutters was not entirely closed.

As Melody noticed this ajar shutter, she realised that someone was behind it, peering out at the courtyard. Now that she was paying attention, she realised that she could hear giggles coming from that direction. While various servants, male and female, had brought out the various dishes during their meal, as with Omar's riad, none of Aksel's female relatives, wives, daughters, or even a mother had joined them. One fresh-faced young man of perhaps sixteen, introduced as one of Aksel's sons, had been part of the dinner, but he had sat quietly next to his father, not participating in the conversation. Were the women of Aksel's family sitting in the room adjacent to the courtyard observing the dinner?

When Melody finally fell onto her feather mattress later that evening, she was asleep almost immediately. The following day, she woke after one of the longest, deepest nights of sleep she had experienced since they left Venice. As much as she stood by her decision to force herself on Rat and Alessandro for their trip to Morocco, the deprivation of the comforts Melody was used to during their trip to Casablanca was in stark relief compared to the opulence of their time in Venice. She had thought the trip from Tangier to Casablanca difficult as they spent their night in a variety of guesthouses and inns that, while they were considered luxury accommodations by Moroccan standards, were quite basic in their facilities. However, these past nights camping had made those hard beds and lack of plumbing seem sumptuous by comparison. The riad's comfortable bed and other luxuries had been a welcome reprieve.

Melody found her freshly laundered clothes at the end of her bed and gratefully put on a split skirt and shirtwaist that didn't feel grimy.

After a quick breakfast, the group thanked their host heartily and left the riad. They then made their way back to the caravanserai, where Fatima's men and Mustafa were waiting for them. The horses were refreshed and ready for the final leg of their journey.

As she was moving towards her horse, Mustafa came up alongside Melody and tugged on her sleeve.

"Lalla Melody," the boy said in a whisper.

Melody looked around at the other men, but they were all too busy preparing the horses and packing their minimal possessions. She bent down to the boy's height.

"Sidi Alessandro was brought through here the night before we arrived. The Pasha's men stayed in this caravanserai with him," the boy said in the same low voice.

Melody considered this information. Why hadn't Fatima's men mentioned anything? Come to that, why hadn't Aksel? The village was small enough that it seemed unlikely that the Pasha's men had come through and hadn't been noticed. Fatima had said that she had chosen to bring men who were Berbers to help them navigate the complex tribal allegiances they would likely encounter along the way, but did those men have questionable fealties of their own?

Again, Melody came back to the question of where Fatima's loyalties lay. While the two women had certainly moved past overt hostility to something perhaps even more than civility, could Fatima be trusted?

What was clear was that she couldn't put her faith in anyone except Rat. As much as Alessandro had vouched for Omar, he was also Berber. She now realised that Morocco's Berbers had complicated loyalties, and she shouldn't make any assumptions about which side they were on. And what did "side" even mean? As Omar had pointed out, they couldn't even be sure precisely what Britain was aiming for in Morocco. She had to find time to talk to Rat about her concerns, but he had hardly been open to her thoughts on Fatima's trustworthiness previously.

One good thing about this trip was that Rat's infatuation was, if not muted, at least far less on display during it. Of course, the hardships of horseback riding through the Atlas Mountains hardly lent itself to flirtations. The more she thought about it, the more Melody realised that the big difference was that Fatima had stopped preening for and flirting with Rat. Again, she wondered if the difference was that Alessandro was not present as an audience.

None of these thoughts were of any use now. Eyeing up her horse, Melody could hardly bear the thought of getting back on it. Omar had estimated that they had another two days of travel ahead of them and said it was unlikely they would spend that night in another village. Melody thought about her comfortable sleep the night before and steeled herself for at least one more night wrapped in a blanket in a tent after a long day in the saddle.

CHAPTER 14

Within the hour, they had left Sefrou and were riding through lush, fertile plains on their way to Fes. As they rode past farms and small villages, the path became smoother and the riding easier. It was warmer than it had been in the mountains, and the scent of tilled earth and blooming orange trees filled the air. For a while, Melody was able to forget her sore muscles and the challenge ahead of them and try to enjoy the verdant scenery.

Omar and Fatima were riding together, and the other Berber men were clustered in front and behind them, clearly still anticipating possible trouble from nearby tribes. Melody had been riding alone when Rat pulled up beside her.

They trotted together in companionable silence for a while before Rat looked around to ensure that everyone else was preoccupied in conversation and far enough away, then said in a low voice, "Melody, what do you think is going on?"

Melody looked at her brother in surprise. He was seeking her opinion. He really must be feeling out of his depth.

She considered the question and the thoughts that had been buzzing around in her brain for the last few days. She answered carefully, "It has been interesting to learn that Berber tribes are so against French involvement in Moroccan affairs and were behind the Fes rebellion in April."

Rat looked at Melody. Where was she going with this?

Melody continued, "That first day when we went with Alessandro to meet Omar, it seems that we were being watched when we entered the Medina, but how did that person know to find us there? The man's subsequent appearance at the vice-consul's home and death makes clear enough that his appearance in the Medina that day was no coincidence."

"Is this about Fatima again?" Rat hissed in an even lower voice.

"Not just her. Presumably anyone in her household could have overheard our plans. And then, there is Omar himself."

"Melody, really! Think what you're suggesting," Rat protested. "Omar has been nothing but gracious and helpful since the moment that Alessandro was arrested. Well, even before that, really. Why would either he or Fatima put themselves through this horrendous trek unnecessarily?"

While it was a question that had flitted through Melody's brain on occasion, she now gave the answer she had landed on, "They would have no choice, would they? Anything other than a full-throated defence of Alessandro backed up by this kind of action would immediately cause suspicion to fall upon them."

Rat conceded the point but pointed out, "You originally thought that we shouldn't trust Fatima because she is half French, yet you are now saying that we can't trust Omar because he is Berber, and they are against the French. Which is it?"

Melody shook her head. She didn't know. All she did know was that they were surrounded by people who might all have their own reasons for stirring up a hornet's nest in Morocco during those turbulent times.

"I do not know," she admitted. "However, I think we need to assume that it could be anyone travelling with us or in Fatima's household." She then voiced something she had been chewing on for a few days, "It is possible that our murder victim was alerted to Alessandro's attendance at the party and went there for the express purpose of attempting a second attack."

"So, what do you believe happened? That Alessandro actually did kill him but in self-defence?"

"That is certainly one option," Melody stated, trying to remember

Mustafa's exact words on the night of the murder. "From what Mustafa said, he went to fetch Alessandro and they both were returning to the gardens when another servant stopped the boy to ask him something. Alessandro continued to the gardens and when Mustafa joined him, Alessandro was bending over a body. We need to talk to the boy again and determine how long that delay was. There is a big difference between a few seconds and a few minutes."

Rat still couldn't get his head around what his sister was suggesting. "So, you think Alessandro is guilty of murder?"

"All I am saying is that it might be self-defence, which I assume is as valid in a Moroccan court as it is in a British one." As she said this, Melody wondered whether it was true. She had a hazy enough understanding of British law, let alone Moroccan. Nevertheless, she was sure that if Alessandro had killed the mysterious man, it had been in self-defence and that had to count for something. Particularly given that the man had made a prior attempt on Alessandro's life.

One thing that Melody was certain of was that she would assume that anyone in their caravan might be involved, directly or indirectly, with whatever Alessandro was caught up in. Well, anyone except Mustafa.

Though, should she be casting aside the boy as a suspect so quickly? It was awfully convenient that a young boy, who just happened to speak fluent English, had crossed Alessandro's path multiple times, had saved him from an attack, and had been the person to call him into the vice-consul's gardens. Was she being naive in crossing the boy off her list of suspects? As much as it pained Melody to consider that a young child might not be as innocent as he seemed, she realised that no one could be above suspicion, at least for now.

Omar had promised that if they kept up a good pace that day, rested for the minimum time needed, and left as soon as the sun rose the next day, they could reach Fes by the following evening. The thought of only spending one more night in a tent was motivation enough for everyone, and they passed the rest of that day moving at a good clip, helped by the flatter terrain.

Whatever novelty the trip had initially held for Melody had long faded. Now, even this new terrain had lost its appeal, and she barely moved her head to look at the changing landscape, increasingly frequent villages, and groups of children who would occasionally run alongside the caravan. Melody was used to the shepherds with their flocks, the nomadic tribes with their herds of camels, and the women gathered by streams washing clothes and gossiping. Any charm in it all had been lost days before.

Melody found the last night in the tent more bearable now that the end was in sight. Or, hopefully, was in sight. She had spent the ride that day thinking about how she might approach Fatima with her concerns. If Fatima's loyalties were all Alessandro claimed, then wouldn't she want to know if she had a treacherous servant in her household? And if Omar was the culprit, again, wouldn't Fatima want to know?

Speaking with the woman did risk alerting Fatima to Melody's suspicions, which wouldn't be good if, in fact, she was the guilty party. Even so, there seemed no better alternative.

Because the day was Friday, their meal that evening had been couscous. Omar had explained that couscous was the traditional dish on the holy day of the week. Always happy to have a break from khlii, Melody enjoyed the meal more than usual. Given that they were planning to leave at sunrise, everyone bedded down for the night as soon as the meal was over rather than lingering around the fire as they sometimes did.

Melody and Fatima retired to their tent. As they removed their dusty clothes and prepared to wrap themselves in their blankets against the chill of the evening, Melody said as casually as she could, "Do you have any idea why Alessandro might have been targeted, Fatima?"

The two women's conversation during the trek had been pleasant enough but relatively superficial for the most part. Now, Fatima looked over at Melody and asked, "What are you asking me?"

There it was, a direct question that demanded either an equally direct answer or a full retreat. Stealing herself for a difficult conversation, Melody said, "I assume that you are aware of Alessandro's work for the British Government."

For a moment, she worried that Fatima was not fully aware and that she had just given away Alessandro's secret. However, to her relief, the other woman nodded and replied, "Yes, I am."

Fatima didn't explain why or how, and Melody decided that now wasn't the time to press her for more of an explanation. Instead, Melody pointed out, "Then is it possible that someone in your household has overheard something, and that is why Alessandro was attacked."

Melody wasn't sure what she had expected Fatima's response to be. Anger? Denial? Irritation? Instead, the woman seemed to be taking the question seriously. "You doubt the loyalty of my staff?" She asked in a concerned rather than defensive tone.

"Someone knew where to find us in the Medina when we went to see Omar. And then that same person turned up at the vice-consul's party. Don't you find that strange? Why would anyone want to harm Alessandro unless they realised the work he does as an operative?"

Fatima laughed, "Sandro is hardly an angel. The man owns many businesses and newspapers. It is possible that he has become a target for far less nefarious reasons than international intrigue." While that was obviously true, something sat behind Fatima's words that made Melody wonder just how much the woman herself believed them.

As her eyelids started to feel heavy, Melody's last thoughts were that she needed to talk to Rat about what he knew of the mission that he and Alessandro had intended to complete in Morocco. The trek to Fes had not been the time or place for such a discussion, but as soon as they had some privacy, she would press her brother to reveal all that he knew. If someone was aware of Alessandro's work for the Secret Service Bureau and that was why he was targeted, then it made sense that the attempted attack on him was aimed at preventing him from completing his mission.

Melody's eyes were closed, and she was starting to drift off into sleep as she had this thought. But no sooner had it flickered in her consciousness than her eyes were wide open, and she sat up. If Alessandro's mission had been compromised in some way, then so had Rat's! Was her brother in danger? Now, she was even more determined to talk to Rat and discover what he and Alessandro had been tasked with achieving in Morocco.

After her epiphany, Melody took some time to fall back to sleep. She was in the middle of a lovely dream when Fatima abruptly woke her up with aggressive shaking.

"Heavens, Melody. I've been calling to you and trying to wake you more gently for some time," Fatima complained. "The men are getting the horses ready. We need to be ready to go as soon as possible." The woman held out one of the round breads that the men cooked on the coals for every meal and a glass of mint tea. "Eat and drink as quickly as you can. I am packed and ready to go. I'll wait for you outside."

Melody took a bite of the still-warm bread and a sip of the tea. Then another. She didn't have much to pack and dressed quickly before finishing what remained of her breakfast. By the time she left her tent, it was evident that she was holding everyone up. Two of the men quickly took down the tent and packed it up as Melody apologised and made her way to her horse.

They broke for a brief, hurried midday meal, and then, instead of resting under palm trees as they usually did, everyone remounted their horses for a gruelling ride in the afternoon sun. Now that they were no longer in the mountains, there was no respite from the heat. Melody felt sorry for the horses, who were clearly as miserable as their riders.

Finally, just as Melody thought that the day's ride might never end, one of the men at the front of the caravan called out something.

Omar was riding in front of Melody and Rat and turned to tell them, "The men can see Fes up ahead. It should not be much more than another hour."

As relieved as Melody was to hear that, it felt like the longest hour of her life. The sun was starting to set when suddenly she caught sight of the city in the distance. Melody could see Fes's minarets and rooftops rising out of the farmlands to great the waning sun.

Over the previous hour or so, the road had become busier, with traders riding or leading donkeys and mules laden with goods, villagers carrying sacks of grain, and camel caravans adding to the congestion. As their caravan mixed in with the other traffic, the air buzzed with the hum of voices in Arabic, Berber, and even Spanish and French. The voices mixed with the call to prayer.

As they heard the prayer call end, their caravan came to a halt. The men dismounted, pulled out their prayer rugs, and bowed towards Mecca in the east. Melody had watched this ritual many times. At that time of evening, the men were usually done in a little over five minutes, and this was no exception. In no time, they had remounted, and the group was again on their way.

Even in the dusk, Fes was clearly visible, lit by lanterns all along its fortified walls. Suddenly, Melody was fully alert and fascinated by the city appearing before them. The massive, ochre-coloured walls encircling Fes were dotted with watchtowers. A massive gate, made of heavy wood reinforced with iron and framed by intricate geometric patterns and Arabic inscriptions, was open and seemed to be serving as a bustling checkpoint. Merchants and travellers were coming and going, sometimes being stopped for inspection and questioning.

Omar turned again, "This is Bab Ftouh, one of Fes's most prominent gates. We should expect to be questioned. Lalla Fatima will speak for our group."

Considering Omar's words, Melody assumed that this was because of Fatima's status and connection to the Sultan. As they pulled up to the gate, the crowds parted for the obviously illustrious visitors, and Fatima moved to the front of the group. A stern-looking guard approached her horse, and they spoke for no more than a minute before he waved them on.

CHAPTER 15

They were barely through the gate before the sights, sounds and smells of Fes overwhelmed their senses. After coming through the gate, the group found themselves in an open marketplace. Omar and his men dismounted from their horses. Fatima, Rat and Melody followed suit.

"The alleyways are far too narrow to ride through," Omar said. My men will take the horses. I think the boy should come with us." Omar didn't explain, but it made sense that they keep Mustafa close, given that he was their only witness to the near attack on Alessandro.

Everyone took their luggage, such as it was, and the men led the horses off while Omar directed everyone to follow him into the Medina proper.

Now that they were really in the Fes Medina, the alleyways were narrow with tall walls that felt rather claustrophobic. Most of the alleyways also had partially covered tops that just added to this feeling. The alleyways were made even more challenging to navigate because of the stalls set up on either side. It seemed that commerce didn't stop after sunset, and shoppers and vendors haggled over everything under the sun. Melody had thought that the Medina in Casablanca had been a crazy, eclectic mix of offerings, but it was nothing compared to Fes. The smells rivalled the sights and sounds; a mix of exotic spices, freshly baked bread, leather from nearby tanneries, and wood smoke filled the air as well as less pleasant smells of donkey dung and freshly slaughtered meat.

Omar seemed to know where he was going, but Melody was nervous about getting separated from him in the press of people thronging the alleyways. She grabbed Rat's hand and ensured that they were never more than a step behind Omar.

They had only been walking for a few minutes when Omar stopped beside a large wooden door covered in an intricate pattern of metal studs. Melody noticed something she had seen at Omar and Aksel's riads: there seemed to be a door within the door.

Melody asked Omar what the second, smaller door was for. He laughed and said, "Ah, so you noticed that. We call the smaller door a khokha. It is primarily for everyday use. Only on special occasions or for the most esteemed guests is the larger, much heavier door opened." As Omar said this, he rapped the large brass knocker on the khokha. As they waited, Omar explained, "I telegrammed ahead from Casablanca. This is the riad belonging to my friend of many years, Lahcen. He is a good man and is well-connected in Fes. The Pasha is his father's cousin, in fact."

As Omar said these words, the smaller door opened, and an aged, wizened servant greeted them. Omar spoke in what sounded like a Berber language, and after just a few words, the servant welcomed them into the riad.

Melody had thought the two riads she had been in so far had been opulent, but this one took her breath away. As with Aksel's riad, the courtyard was decorated with mosaics and engraved carvings, but these were even more ornate than those had been. There were two additional stories rising above the courtyard, and the balustrade was a highly decorative ironwork. Intricate brass lamps hung from the ceilings of the area surrounding the courtyard, and smaller versions were on its walls.

As they entered the courtyard, Melody saw that the left side, under the overhang of the above storey, was filled with burgundy silk-covered couches set around a low table topped with beautiful mosaics. The entire setting was one of sumptuousness but also comfort. The servant led them over to a couch and then left, Melody assumed to get the requisite mint tea.

Their host, Lahcen, was a slim man with a long, expressive face that was quick to light up in a smile. It seemed that Omar had not seen his friend for many years, which was hardly surprising given the difficulty of the trip from Casablanca to Fes. Lahcen also spoke English fluently and was very welcoming to his guests. He was particularly deferential towards Fatima, which Melody assumed was because of her familial link to the Sultan.

Melody was pleasantly surprised to find that dinner that evening was not a tagine but, instead, something that Omar called a pastilla. Each person was served a round pastry. Melody was intrigued to see that it was topped with what looked like confectioners' sugar and cinnamon applied in a pretty decoration. Was this dessert? Melody was too shy to ask the question and risk offending their host, so she was surprised when she cut into the pastilla to find that it had a chicken filling. The meat was shredded and mixed with slivered almonds and raisins. It also seemed to be sweetened with sugar and cinnamon. The pastilla was a curious but delicious dish.

As they had in Aksel's home, Melody and Fatima had bathed, and their clothes had been taken to be laundered and replaced with beautiful silk robes. Melody appreciated that the loose costume was far more comfortable for sitting on low couches and cushions.

They finished their meal with dates, fruit, and mint tea. For most of the meal, Omar and Lahcen had been catching up on each other's news. Melody wondered what Omar had told his friend about why they were in Fes. She caught Rat's eye, and he shrugged his shoulders and cocked his head; it seemed he was also curious.

It seemed that they would not learn that evening if and how Lahcen might be able to help them in their mission. Melody and Fatima each had a lavish room, and Melody's sleep was as deep and refreshing as it had been in the previous riad. She luxuriated in the silk sheets, and it would have been tempting to spend the following morning napping if she hadn't been so cognisant that Alessandro was likely already in Fes and in prison. They had no time to waste.

The breakfast feast was lavish. It included fruit and dates, various types of bread, and an intriguing item that resembled a pancake.

"That is a msemen," Fatima explained, helping herself to one. Melody thought the msemen must be quite special to tempt Fatima to eat breakfast, given that she didn't usually eat before noon. Melody also took one and followed Fatima's lead in slathering it with butter and honey. She took her first bite of the msemen. It was delicious. While it resembled a pancake, it was more like a light, flaky flatbread.

Lahcen had not joined them for breakfast, but as they were finishing up and taking their last bites of the food and sips of mint tea, he entered the courtyard and came and sat on the couch.

"I have had word from the Pasha," Lahcen said. "It seems that your friend is being held at the palace of the Sultan, may God bless him."

"The palace?" Rat asked in a surprised tone. "Is that usual?"

Melody wondered the same thing, but she also noted that Lahcen had had time to send and receive such a message that morning. That indicated that Omar had found time to discuss Alessandro with his friend, even if he hadn't done it over dinner. She wondered again how he had described the situation.

"It is not usual," Lahcen agreed. "However, given your friend's status, it is not unprecedented."

Did this mean that Alessandro was in some dank dungeon under the palace or that his accommodation was more civilised? Melody wondered.

"Are we able to see him?" she asked.

"When I informed the Pasha that Lalla Fatima is one of your party and wishes to speak with the Sultan, may God bless him, he promised to send word from the palace as soon as possible. If you are able to speak with Conte Foscari, it will be at the whim of Al-Sultan, Amir al-Mu'minin."

Yet again, Melody gave thanks that Fatima had accompanied them. Whatever the truth of the woman's loyalties, they would not have had even a chance to plead Alessandro's case to the Sultan without her as part of their group.

Now that they knew that they had to wait for word from the Pasha, there was no reason not to linger over breakfast. More mint tea was drunk, and the conversation meandered through local politics and gossip. Finally, when Melody was unsure how much longer she could wait for an answer, a servant came in and whispered in Lahcen's ear.

"It seems that you are in luck," he announced. "The Sultan will see you this afternoon. In deference to Lalla Fatima, you will receive a private audience."

At his words, Fatima clapped her hands and stood. "In that case, we do not have long to shop."

"What are we shopping for?" Melody asked.

"Appropriate attire for an audience with the Sultan," Fatima explained with a shake of her head and a roll of her eyes. "Even if we had anything other than our travel clothes with us, we need to show our respect and deference to His Majesty by our costumes." Turning to Lahcen, she asked, "Do you have someone who can guide us through the Medina?"

"I do. Her name is Hakima, and she will take you to the best stalls in the souq to buy what you need." Turning back to the servant, he said something, including the name Hakima. The man nodded and left.

"I have sent word asking her to meet us here within the hour. Hakima acts as the Wakil for my wives. She knows all the best weavers, jewellers, and tanneries."

"What is a Wakil?" Rat asked.

"A Wakil is an intermediary who procures the finest cloth and other fineries on behalf of women such as my wives. She will also be a superb guide through the souq."

As promised, within twenty minutes, Hakima the Wakil was at the riad. She was a short, pleasantly plump woman with intelligent eyes and a kind smile. She had a no-nonsense way about her, and Melody did not doubt that they were in good hands. Rat did not have any appropriate clothes with him, and there was little chance of finding him a three-piece suit at such short notice. Hakima was unfazed by this and, with Fatima translating, assured them that they would return with an appropriate djellaba for Sidi Matthew.

Her worries about their meeting with the Sultan aside, Melody was excited about their shopping expedition. Just her brief glimpse at the edge of the Medina the day before had whetted her appetite to explore further. Melody, Fatima, and Hakima set off, accompanied by one of Lahcen's male servants for protection. Melody had little doubt that Hakima was more than capable of handling whatever situation they encountered. However, it seemed that it was unheard of for young women, even European ones, to traverse the Medina without a male escort.

As they exited the riad, Hakima looked down the street thoughtfully as if plotting their route. She spoke no English, so Fatima translated from Arabic: "She says that we'll need shoes, robes, headscarves, and jewellery."

"Jewellery?" Melody questioned. "Is that really necessary?"

"It is vital that we represent our rank and status as highly as possible," Fatima explained. "At the very least, we will need multiple bangles, rings, a bold necklace, and earrings." If that was the least, Melody hated to imagine what the most was.

After an exhausting but productive three hours, the women had chosen caftans, wide, ornate belts, the largest, most extravagant necklace and earrings Melody had ever worn, and beautiful silk headdresses with jewellery attached.

Hakima had proven to be a methodical navigator of the Medina and a savvy negotiator. Melody had no idea what the woman had said to all the merchants she haggled with, but there seemed to be a lot of handwringing and pleading, followed by acceptance of the woman's offer.

Melody was particularly enamoured of the buttery, soft leather slip-on shoes she had chosen. Backless with a distinctive pointed toe, they were dyed a vibrant shade of magenta and embroidered with gold thread onto which little pearls were woven. Even the slippers she had worn to her last ball were not as beautiful or comfortable as these shoes.

The caftan was made from beautiful gold silk and had delicate embroidered flowers on the skirt and sleeves. It was as lavish, if not more so, than the most exquisite Worth gown. The jewellery was all much bolder and more ornate than anything Melody had ever worn. She could only imagine what Granny would have to say about a young, unmarried woman flaunting herself in such showy pieces. Of course, she could only imagine what Granny would have to say about the entire outfit!

By the time Hakima led them back through the labyrinth of the Medina with the servant carrying all the packages, they had barely an hour before it was time to leave for the palace. This was just enough time to eat a light snack, wash off the dirt of the Medina, and put on their new clothes.

CHAPTER 16

As part of their shopping expedition, Fatima and Melody had bought Rat an ornate white djellaba with red embroidery on the edges of the hem and sleeves. To accompany this, they had bought one of the distinctive red velvet hats with a black tassel that was the usual formal headwear for men of the upper classes in Fes.

Looking at the outfit laid out on his bed, Rat worried that he would look absurd. He wished there had been time to get a more European suit of clothes ordered. It had been one thing to wear a djellaba to travel in; that had been practical. However, donning this outfit to visit the Sultan, of all people, felt inappropriate. He had brought one western suit of clothes with him to Fes, but it was hardly smart enough to visit a palace. It seemed that he had no choice at this point, so Rat dropped the djellaba over his head, slipped his feet into the soft-leather shoes that had been purchased for him, and put the hat on his head. Glancing at himself in the mirror, Rat thought he looked ridiculous, but there was no looking back now.

Walking down the stairs into the riad's courtyard, he found Fatima and Melody already dressed and waiting for him. He might look ridiculous in local garb, but Melody looked beautiful. She carried herself in the caftan, headscarf and jewellery as if she was born to wear such an attire. As for Fatima, well she had never looked more elegant and unobtainable. There was something about seeing her in her native Moroccan attire for the first time that underscored just how foreign she really was and how absurd any hopes that he might harbour were.

Rat noticed that Omar had not changed. "Are you not coming with us?"

"No. I am not worthy of the presence of the Sultan, may God bless him," the other man intoned very seriously.

"How will we find our way to the palace?"

"Three of Lahcen's servants will lead the mules."

Mules! Melody thought. She had hoped that her days in a saddle were over for a while. It seemed that was not the case.

Soon enough, the three of them were seated on asses and being led to the palace. The servants led them back the way they had come the previous evening to the market past Bab Ftouh. As their group moved past the market, Melody noticed the architecture changed. Now, the narrow alleyways were lined with whitewashed houses and had a distinctly different feel about them. She asked Fatima about the neighbourhood, who then, in turn, asked one of the servants.

"This is the Andalusian Quarter," she repeated.

Looking to her left and right, Melody could now see the distinctly Spanish influence in the architecture. The houses had intricately carved wooden balconies and colourful awnings hung over the alleyways.

After some minutes of travelling through that quarter, they noticed the neighbourhood change again. Melody thought that the souq they were passing through looked familiar from their shopping expedition that morning. It was bustling with people and donkeys, the neighbouring tanneries emitting sharp, pungent smells that vied with the far more pleasant aromas of spices and perfume wafting off the surrounding shops and stalls.

As their guides expertly wound their way through the Lalla, the clattering of their mules' hooves added to the clangourous cacophony of metalworkers beating brass pots, vegetable sellers hawking their wares, sharp-elbowed shoppers haggling for the best deal, and donkeys whose braying rang above it all.

The Medina's streets were such a labyrinth, and Melody wondered how the men leading their mules were able to pick their way through the maze of narrow alleyways with such certainty. She was sure that she would be lost very quickly if left on her own.

Sitting on the mule with no idea where she was going, Melody allowed her mind to wander from contemplation of the raucous commerce going on all around her to consideration of the audience ahead of them. She tried to remember the conversations between Alessandro and Rat during the interminable ride from Tangier to Casablanca but couldn't recall much. What she did know from the conversations in Casablanca was that the current ruler had taken the Sultanate by force from his brother a few years before. What kind of man did that? Then she thought about her own country's long history of royal interfamilial tussles and realised that perhaps this was not so different after all.

As she tried hard to dredge some useful information from her memories of those half-listened to discussions, she remembered Alessandro mentioning that the struggle between the brothers was at least in part over the then Sultan's perceived concessions to the various foreign powers jostling for influence in Morocco. Actually, she did remember the conversation. Her brother and Alessandro had talked about how the now Sultan Abdelhafid had managed to amass support behind him by capitalising on widespread discontent with the undue influence of the foreign powers in Morocco. Yet, if she had understood the various conversations that had swirled around her during their trek to Fes, it seemed that the current Sultan was now seen as cooperating with those same powers, particularly the French, that he had come to power denouncing.

Given this history, Melody wondered about the man they were about to plead Alessandro's case to. Would they find brutal ruthlessness? Was he willing to do whatever he had to to seize and keep power, including overthrow his brother? Or was he a pragmatist caught between the idealism that had brought him to power and the realities of the colonial powers' entrenchment in his country?

Melody was jolted out of her wool-gathering by the sudden change in her surroundings. It seemed they had left the dense, overcrowded Medina behind and emerged onto a street notable for its calm. Ahead of them, a vast, ornate gate was flanked by high, imposing walls. It seemed they had arrived at the palace.

The gate was guarded by intimidating-looking men in red, green, and white djellabas with matching turbans. The men carried rifles and looked ready to use them if necessary. They eyed the approaching group with wariness. Suddenly, it occurred to Melody that they might not be admitted into the palace despite the assurance of a private audience with the Sultan.

It seemed this concern was unnecessary. Melody sighed with relief as one of the servants accompanying them pulled out a letter, and after a quick perusal by one of the guards, the gate was opened for them to enter the Royal Palace of Dar al-Makhzen.

Just before leaving for Venice in May, Melody had taken part in one last event for the Season: a Royal Garden Party at Buckingham Palace. She had been impressed with the sheer scale of the palace and its grounds, but they were nothing to the vista that opened up before her. The Sultan's palace could more accurately be termed a small village. The grounds stretched far before her with clusters of buildings dotted about. The King's gardens had, of course, been perfectly manicured with nary a rose petal out of place. Yet, for all their pristine formality, they lacked the charm of the grounds they were moving through now. Heavenly scents of orange blossom and jasmine hung in the air, and everywhere Melody looked, there were roses. So many roses.

One of the guards had accompanied them as they made their way to their audience with the Sultan. He steered the three mules, their riders and the servants guiding them to a large building whose entrance was highly decorated with intricate patterns of mosaic. Enormous bronze doors were guarded by yet more men in the red, green and white robes. The guard who was accompanying them spoke to his comrades and one of the bronze doors was open.

The guard then said something in Arabic, which Fatima translated as a request that they dismount from their mules and follow him. As they walked down a long marble-floored corridor, Melody looked up at the ceiling, which was resplendent in its intricate, brightly coloured decoration.

The corridor ended at a large courtyard garden, which looked to have multiple fountains and even more orange and jasmine, as well as palm trees. In the middle of the courtyard was a seating area with a low couch covered in red silk and an equally low table with a mosaic top. Seated on a slightly higher chair facing the couch was a man in his mid-thirties dressed in a simple but very elegant silk djellaba with a matching turban. Melody assumed that this was Sultan Abdelhafid. While there were servants busy around the courtyard, it was surprising to find the Sultan sitting alone.

Hearing their approach, the Sultan looked up from the book he had been reading. He asked the guard something and nodded at the reply.

First, he acknowledged Fatima and said something briefly in Arabic before switching to English. "Cousin of my honoured wife, we are charmed to have you grace our court."

"Moulaya Abdelhafid, I am humbled by your generosity in receiving me," Fatima replied. "Might I introduce those I travel with?"

With a slight incline of the head, the Sultan indicated that she might continue.

"This is Miss Melody Chesterton. She is the ward of the Earl and Countess of Pembroke. She is accompanied by her brother, Matthew Sandworth, the ward of the Earl of Langley."

If the Sultan wondered, as so many people often did, why the siblings were wards of different aristocrats, there was no indication in his expression. Instead, he said, "You are welcome. Please take a seat."

They settled themselves on the low couch and, as if by magic, servants appeared carrying trays of refreshments. Of course, there was mint tea. Jugs of orange juice, whose colour was so vibrant that it almost seemed unnatural, were also placed before them, as were huge platters of fresh fruit, dates, and nuts.

The Sultan helped himself to a date and asked, "How do you find my country, Miss Chesterton?"

He was an attractive man with dark, soulful eyes that gleamed with intelligence but also mischief. There was something in the tone of his question that caused Melody to wonder if the man was mocking her. Nevertheless, she answered in as polite and formal tone as possible, "Morocco is a wonder, Your Majesty. I find my senses quite overwhelmed by its beauty and rich culture."

The man nodded as if she had given the correct answer to what was perhaps a trick question. What on earth had he expected her to say?

Turning his attention to Rat, the Sultan asked, "And so you are to accompany your sister through her travels, Mr Sandworth? Are you not needed for more important tasks in London?"

If she had been in any doubt as to the hidden meanings behind the Sultan's seemingly innocent words to her, Melody did not doubt that something else sat behind his questioning of Rat. What important tasks was he alluding to? How on earth would Rat answer such a question?

"Your Majesty, I believe that it is also customary in your country for male relatives to accompany women outside of their households. Certainly, in Britain, a young woman travelling alone is uncommon in the upper echelon of society." Melody was very proud of how Rat answered the challenge with great politeness but also with a quiet strength behind his words.

"Indeed," the Sultan answered. He then spoke some sentences in Arabic to Fatima, even though it was evident that he was fluent in English. Melody wondered if he spoke of family matters or if it was pertinent to Alessandro's imprisonment.

Once a servant had poured tea for everyone and offered orange juice, the Sultan began to speak again. "I have heard that your English country-side is very green. Very unlike Morocco," he observed.

"While that is true for the most part, during our journey, we passed through valleys and farmland that was not unlike the British landscape," Rat replied.

Pivoting immediately, the Sultan said, "I hear that you have a new king. Perhaps that is for the best, given the stories I heard of the last one."

Neither Melody nor Rat allowed themselves to be provoked by this seeming challenge. Instead, Rat decided to plunge straight into the reason for their meeting. "You Majesty, my sister and I, accompanied by Lalla Fatima, have made the long journey to Fes in order to plead the case for our friend who was arrested and brought here."

The Sultan steepled his hands and lightly tapped the tips of his index fingers together as if pondering Rat's words. Finally, he spoke. "Do you believe that a European who stands accused of a crime should be treated differently than anyone else, Mr Sandworth?"

Without considering the wisdom of her words, Melody pre-empted whatever Rat was about to say. "Is it usual for someone arrested in Casablanca to be brought to Fes and imprisoned within the walls of your palace, Your Majesty?" Almost as soon as the words had flown out of her mouth, Melody wished she could unsay them. Her challenge had been impertinent under any circumstances, but spoken to royalty by a young, foreign woman might cause them to be turned out of the palace before they could say any more. Or worse.

"I apologise for my words, Your Majesty," Melody said quickly. "Yet, I do not apologise for my concern for my friend."

The Sultan did not answer immediately, and from the inscrutable look on his face, it was unclear if he was about to erupt in a temper and order them arrested. Finally, just as the tension was almost unbearable, the man did erupt, but into laughter.

"You are; what is the word in English?" he turned to Fatima to help him, saying something in Arabic, to which she replied. He then continued, "You are plucky. Not unlike Lalla Fatima, in fact. You are correct; it is not usual to bring a prisoner to Fes. Even one who is accused of murder." They all looked at the Sultan expectantly. "However, there is reason to believe that your friend's crimes go beyond murder."

Again, everyone waited for him to continue, but it seemed the man had said all he intended to for the time being.

Frustrated by the vagueness of the accusation against Alessandro, Melody looked over at Fatima and quirked her eyebrows. Whether or not the other woman understood the facial expression or merely had the same thought as Melody, Fatima said in a tone of voice that was almost flirtatious, "You Majesty, may Allah continue to grant you wisdom and strength in your rule. We do not wish to question that rule. We are merely concerned for our friend. Would it be possible for you, in your munificence, to allow us to see our friend and assure ourselves of his wellbeing?"

"Do you believe that he would not be treated well?" came the challenge. However, the words had no teeth and were followed by the concession, "You may visit your friend. However, you will be watched by one of my guards at all times."

Once the Sultan had permitted them to visit Alessandro, Melody and Rat were both impatient for their royal visit to be over. They exchanged glances multiple times as they wondered how long the sovereign would prolong the meeting. As Rat endured more inane observations about his country, he wondered if their irritation was the point. The Sultan must have realised how agonising the situation was for them and was enjoying watching them have to grit their teeth and mask their frustration.

Finally, when yet another question about Britain's incessant rain had been answered tersely, the Sultan seemed to decide that he'd had his fun and stood abruptly. "This has been an interesting conversation, Miss Chesterton and Mr Sandworth." He then called a servant over and said something in rapid Arabic.

Had it been? Rat wanted to ask. As far as he was concerned, most of the conversation had been ridiculous.

The Sultan began to turn to leave, then reconsidered, looked directly at Rat and said, "Perhaps Britain should keep its colonial dominance for India and elsewhere and stay out of Moroccan affairs entirely." Having uttered this enigmatic statement, he retired into an adjoining room.

Rat and Melody were unsure what to do next, but Fatima explained, "His Majesty instructed the servant to fetch a guard to take us to Alessandro." As she said these words, the guard who had led them into the courtyard returned and indicated that they should follow him.

Melody wasn't sure what she had expected a palace jail cell to look like, but it seemed that Alessandro was merely locked in a room in a small building adjacent to the main palace. The room was well-guarded but once they were inside, it wasn't uncomfortable. There were three small windows high enough up to be useless for escape, but which gave the room some natural light. Glancing around as they entered, Melody saw a narrow bed with a small table next to it. Another larger table had books piled upon it and the remains of a meal. While the room was hardly opulent, she was relieved to see that it wasn't the dank dungeon she had been imagining.

Alessandro had been lying on the bed reading when they entered. When he saw who his visitors he leapt up, relief writ large on his face. It was evident he hoped they were a formal rescue party.

This hope was immediately shattered when the guard said, in good enough English, "I will stay here for the visit, which will be no more than ten minutes. There will be no physical contact with the prisoner."

Alessandro's disappointment was evident, yet so was his gratitude for their presence. "How did this happen?" he wondered. "Casablanca is a long way from Fes, amore mio."

In the sultry tones of a lover, Fatima replied, "There is no distance too great, cara."

Was Alessandro making love to Fatima, there in front of her? Melody wondered in shock.

The woman then continued to say something in Italian in the same loving voice.

The guard noticed that they weren't speaking English, but Fatima's romantic tones were unmistakable, so he just raised his eyebrows at these foreigners and their ways and went back to staring at the wall.

Melody's happiness at seeing Alessandro unharmed was immediately beaten back by her pique at the obvious romantic relationship between Alessandro and Fatima. If there had been any doubt in her mind that what was between the two of them was more than flirtation, it was gone now. She was tempted to storm out of the room and leave the lovers to their cooing.

She might have done just that if it were not for the following words Fatima said in Italian. In the same tone as her endearment, she said, "Now, tell me quickly what happened."

Melody's Italian was not good enough for her to follow their few hurried exchanges, which were all said in voices that would persuade any non-Italian speaker that they were amorous. However, she caught the word "recognised" and something about a telegram. Finally, she gave up trying to follow along; surely Fatima would tell them everything later.

It was apparent that the guard was beginning to take more notice of their continued conversation in Italian, and so they immediately switched back to English. "Do not worry, my love. We will do all we can to ensure your release," Fatima cooed.

Alessandro turned to Rat and scolded, "You should never have let Melody come. It is far too arduous a trip."

Before her brother could answer, Melody snapped, "I thought that it was now clear that no one, not even my brother, is able to force my actions. I go where I choose."

Whatever Alessandro had been about to reply was forestalled as the guard said, "Your time is up."

Melody doubted it had been ten minutes yet and was about to argue, but Rat quickly shook his head, so she said nothing.

CHAPTER 17

Before they knew it, the group had mounted their mules and were being led out of the palace and then back through the Medina. Rat's Italian was worse than Melody's, but he had also sensed that Fatima and Alessandro were playing out a charade to allow them to speak privately. He was on tenterhooks to hear what Alessandro had relayed to Fatima. However, finding a place where they could speak without being overheard might be a challenge.

Rat had spent some time considering Melody's theory that there was a traitor within Fatima or Omar's household and realised that he couldn't entirely discount it. He was unwilling even to countenance the possibility that Fatima herself was the turncoat, and he was almost as unwilling to believe that Omar's friendship towards Alessandro was not all it seemed. Still, there was a very real possibility that one of the Berber men who had accompanied them was not all he appeared, and they still did not know enough about Lahcen to be sure where his loyalties sat. Given this, trying to have this discussion securely in the riad seemed reckless. Yet, where else were they to go without arousing suspicion?

As they wound their way back through the chaos of the Medina, Rat considered where he, Fatima and Melody might plausibly go alone or at least with nothing more than a servant to accompany them. He was tempted to try to have the conversation then and there; they had no reason to believe that the servants leading the mules understood English. However, yelling back and forth from mules was hardly the best way to conduct a clandestine meeting.

Interspersed amongst the shops of the Medina were cafes where men sat drinking mint tea and discussing the news of the day. But "men" was the keyword. If Rat were to lead two women, even foreign women, into such a place, they would cause a stir. He didn't want word to get back to either the riad or the palace that they had been trying to speak privately.

At some point, the alleyway widened enough that Rat was able to spur his mule on to pull alongside Fatima's. He leaned over and said as quietly as he could while still being heard over the Medina's noise, "We need to speak before we return to the riad. Do you have any suggestions?"

Fatima nodded in answer and shouted something to the servant leading her mule. Rat wasn't sure what she'd said because they continued their journey for some minutes. Then, they turned down a particularly narrow alley that was barely wide enough for the mules. At the end of it, they came to a storefront with colourful fabrics and scarves hanging up outside.

"This is a Hanout An-Nassaj, or a weaving shop," Fatima explained.

They descended from their mules, and Fatima told the servants to wait outside with the animals—or at least, Melody and Rat assumed she must have said that. Inside, the shop was much larger than it had seemed from the outside. In one corner, an old woman was using a huge loom to weave a beautiful piece of multicoloured fabric that resembled the sun setting as it moved from red to orange to yellow.

Melody was immediately drawn to the loom. The fabric looked like it was silk as it shimmered in the rays of sunlight coming through the window behind the weaver.

Seeing her interest, the savvy shopkeeper approached Melody and spoke in Arabic. She shook her head, and Fatima stepped in. "He said that he has another piece in the same colours and style and will give you a good price."

"It is beautiful. I have never seen silk like it," Melody said in awe.

"It is not the kind of silk that you are used to," Fatima explained. "It is made from Saharan aloe vera cacti and is a Berber traditional fibre." Then, seizing the moment, Fatima said something to the shopkeeper and walked towards a pile of scarves gesturing to Rat and Melody to follow her. Speaking loudly in English, she said, "Come and look at some of the other colours and patterns and choose one that you like."

Sure of a sale, the shopkeeper left them to their perusal of the fabric. When they were confident they would not be overheard, Fatima said quickly in a low voice, "Sandro said that he recognised the murdered man. He was a rogue British operative who disappeared perhaps a year ago. That must have been how he was able to recognise Alessandro. Matthew, Sandro said that you should send a secure telegram to London asking for more information on the man. He said that you would know what secure meant. He said to mention there has been mischief from Skylark in the telegram and that the Bureau would know what that meant."

Rat nodded. He would send a telegram to Lord Langley as soon as possible. His mentor was the only man in the Secret Service Bureau in whom he had complete faith and trust. If the man sent to attack Alessandro had been a one-time British operative, who knew what nefarious schemes might be in play?

Now that they were in the shop, Melody decided that she would need more clothes if they were to stay in Fes for any length of time. She and Fatima spent a happy hour choosing from the beautiful fabrics and ordering clothes to be made up from them.

Finally, they left the Hanout An-Nassaj with enough packages to more than explain their detour. Remounting their mules, they continued their journey back to the riad. As they rode, Rat considered how he'd accomplish his task. Sending a coded message to Lord Langley was the least of the issues. His guardian and mentor had been the one who set the young Rat on the path to cryptography and there were numerous codes that he knew the earl would immediately recognise. The more significant issue was sending the telegram. Ideally, he would like to send it via the consul in Fes; he assumed that the man had access to telegraph equipment. Though, how was he to explain the need to send one to Omar and Lahcen?

As he chewed away on the puzzle, Rat considered whether Alessandro's revelation about the man who tried to attack him and ended up dead in Casablanca justified a reassessment of the suspicions that Melody had made him consider.

What did they know or believe they knew? The man they were referring to as Skylark had also worked for the British Government in some capacity in the Secret Service Bureau. Because of this, he knew of Alessandro's role. Did he know about Rat's work for the Bureau? If so, was he also in danger? It seemed unlikely that the threat had been neutralised just because Skylark was now dead.

Who had hired the rogue operative to attack Alessandro and why? And had the same person then killed the man? Perhaps then setting Alessandro up for the murder? As Rat considered all these questions, he wondered what Melody made of the explosive news that Fatima had shared.

Even as he had the thought, it also occurred to Rat that he wanted to talk to his sister about what they had learned. During the investigation in Venice, he had come to realise that she was not only a good sounding board but that she had a very logical way of dissecting an investigation. As much as he had railed against her accompanying him to Morocco and then to Fes, Rat realised that he was glad that she was there. He would have to find a way to be alone with her to talk through what they had learned.

Sitting on the mule behind Rat, Melody's thoughts were diverted in quite another direction. As intrigued as she was about what Alessandro had told Fatima, she couldn't get her mind off how he had told her. While it had been immediately apparent to Melody, even with her limited Italian, that the words of love were merely a smokescreen so that he might speak Italian without the guard becoming suspicious, even so, there had been something about the conversation that had pierced her heart.

Alessandro and Fatima had been very convincing as lovers. Too convincing. Melody couldn't shake the thought that it had not been an act. Even as she thought this, Melody berated herself; what did it matter to her? Alessandro had made a fool of her in Venice, and even if the man came to her begging on his knees, Melody would never trust him again with her heart.

By the time the group had returned to the riad, Rat had decided that his best course of action was to hew as closely to the truth as possible without being explicit as to the nature of the message he wanted to send.

While he was Italian, Alessandro was also a British citizen. A British citizen who was being held in a foreign jail. Rat had met and talked with him. It would only be natural to want to relay that information to the highest local British official. This was the story that he gave to Lahcen, who promised to send a servant to the consul in the morning with a request for a meeting.

Rat was eager to send the telegram as soon as possible. However, they had arrived back at the riad just before evening prayers. The sun was setting, and Rat realised that he would have to be patient and wait until the following day. While Omar, Lahcen and the other men prayed, Rat took the opportunity to make a stealth trip to Melody's room, where she had retired to wash her hands and face before dinner.

Rat knocked lightly at her door. It was opened by a pleasantly surprised Melody, who hurried him into the room. "I am so glad you have come, Rat. I want to talk to you about what Alessandro told Fatima." She paused, "Why did you come?"

"I want to talk to you about the same thing," he confessed, taking a seat on the end of her bed.

There was much Melody wanted to say about this admission, but she decided that it was not the best use of their time before dinner. Instead, she asked, "What do you think is going on here? Why would a British operative, even a rogue one, try to murder Alessandro?"

"It certainly isn't unheard of for people to be accused of working against their own governments. You were too young to remember the Dreyfus Affair and its repercussions in France, but internal betrayal is always a worry. Take Xander, for example. People become disillusioned by their governments and countries for all sorts of reasons."

Melody then asked the next obvious question, "So, who do you think this rogue operator was working for? And more to the point, who killed him?"

Rat shook his head; he had no idea. "What I do know, or at least I believe, is that the initial attack on Alessandro must have been planned. Someone knew that we were coming to Morocco and had been watching us and waiting for an opportunity. I assume that the plan was that in the chaos of Casablanca's Medina, the attacker would be able to come up on Alessandro, slip a knife between his ribs, and then slip away.

Indeed, he might have managed this if it weren't for Mustafa's sharp eyes."

The mention of Mustafa reminded Melody of the lingering doubt that had taken root and that she couldn't shake, much as she wanted to. "It was quite a lucky coincidence that he happened to be there just as this so-called attacker was approaching Alessandro, was it not?"

Rat narrowed his eyes as he realised the full import of what Melody was saying. "Are you suggesting that Mustafa, a young child, is somehow caught up in this scheme?"

"I hate even to consider it, Rat, but you have to admit that it was awfully lucky that the young boy Alessandro saved the day before just happened to be there at the right time the following day."

"So, what do you imagine might have happened? What would be the point of having the rogue operative try to kill Alessandro merely to be thwarted by someone who was in league with him? That all seems terribly convoluted."

Melody sighed; sometimes Rat could be surprisingly dull-witted for such a usually intelligent man. "No. What I am suggesting is that perhaps there never was an attacker that day in the Medina and that Mustafa's warning against the supposed attack was nothing more than a way to ingratiate himself with Alessandro and gain admission to our group. After all, look what happened: he travelled with us from Casablanca and is privy to everything we do and who knows what conversations we do not realise that he overhears."

As her brother continued to look sceptical, Melody pointed out, "Mustafa is around the same age as you were when you first met Wolfie in Whitechapel. You were desperate for money and would have done, probably did do, whatever he asked of you without question. You were a young child; did you stop to question the morality or legality of the work he gave you? I am not suggesting that Mustafa might be anything other than what he claimed: an orphaned child who desperately needs to make money. However, that truth suggests that it is at least possible that someone else hired him to spy on us."

Rat thought back to those desperate days on the streets of Whitechapel after their parents had died. He was trying not just to provide food and shelter for himself but also the four-year-old Melody.

Would he have turned down any work offered? The truth was that he had not been in a position to be picky about how he made coin. It was just a lucky quirk of fate that brought him into contact with a decent man like Wolf rather than one of the many criminal gangs of the East End. His story might have unfolded very differently, and more to the point, Melody's story might have, too.

Finally, acknowledging the logic behind Melody's words, Rat asked, "So what would you have us do? Confront the boy?"

"Not at all. All I am doing is pointing out that this is one possible scenario. If it is, then perhaps our murder victim, this rogue operative, was never in the Medina that day. Perhaps Mustafa's role was to lure Alessandro that night at the vice-consul's party so that he might be found in an incriminating position by the Pasha's men. I have no idea why, but it's possible. However, it is also possible that this is not the case and that everything about Mustafa is as it seems. I believe we should be careful what we say and do around the boy, at least until we have incontrovertible evidence either way."

Rat agreed. Now that Melody had brought this possibility to his attention, he started mentally to review every interaction with the child. He thought about the boy's words to Melody at the caravanserai that the Pasha's men had passed through and how it had caused Melody to voice suspicions about Fatima's men, Omar and Aksel. Was it possible that the child was capable of such machinations? Would he have been at that age? Perhaps he would have been if an adult had been guiding his actions behind the scenes. Rat had identified so strongly with Mustafa that day in the Medina. Was it possible that he hadn't thought deeply enough about the other similarities with Rat's desperation all those years ago?

Shaking his head as if to dispel such thoughts, Rat said, "Yes, let us keep a closer eye on the boy, but also not discount other possibilities. This does make it even more important that I communicate with Lord Langley." Saying this caused Rat to realise that he should hurry to dress for dinner so that he might take his time composing a telegram that would be short enough while also relaying the key information and then encrypting it.

After Rat had left her room, Melody considered their conversation. She understood her brother's reluctance to see Mustafa as anything other than the innocent but desperate child he had presented himself as. Putting aside her concerns about the boy for a moment, Melody reconsidered her suspicions about Fatima. If her loyalties were anything other than Alessandro claimed, would she have been truthful about what he had said to her in Italian? Of course, she might have worried that either Melody or Rat knew enough Italian to catch her in a lie. Though if Melody were honest with herself, it was probably clear from their blank looks during most of the exchange in Italian that they were clueless.

As much as it satisfied her petty jealousy to imagine that the beautiful, charming Lalla Fatima might not be all that Alessandro thought she was, Melody had to acknowledge that the woman was almost certainly not their shadowy enemy.

CHAPTER 18

The following morning, Lahcen sent his servant to the consul's residence. The man returned while everyone was breakfasting with a note inviting Mr Sandworth to wait on Consul James MacLeod at his convenience. Rat had composed his telegram, encrypted it, and then destroyed the original message. He was eager to send it to Lord Langley and asked if the servant could take him immediately.

Rat wiped his mouth, rose from the low couch, and, on the spur of the moment, asked Melody, "Would you like to accompany me?" It occurred to him that the vice-consul might be a valuable source of information on the political machinations playing out in Fes. One of the many skills he had come to appreciate his sister possessed was the ability to put people at ease such that an interview felt more like a casual conversation.

Melody was pleasantly surprised by the invitation and immediately agreed to accompany Rat. Her travelling clothes had been laundered and, while a little worse for wear after their trek across Morocco, were sufficient for such a meeting. More to the point, while it had been appropriate to wear her caftan to visit the Sultan, it seemed far less so to visit the British vice-consul. Without the need to change her outfit, Melody was ready to go immediately. She acknowledged her pleasure in the offer with a slight tilt of her chin before rising to join Rat and the servant.

Fatima looked at them quizzically, but she kept any questions she had, particularly about her exclusion from their party, to herself. As it happened, Rat had considered inviting her. However, his next thought was that she was a French citizen, and despite his faith in her loyalty to Alessandro, the vice-consul might be less inclined to a candid conversation with her present.

Lahcen had assured Rat that the walk to the vice-consul's residence in the Batha district would take no more than thirty minutes on foot. Given that neither he nor Melody were eager to get back on the mules any sooner than they had to, they indicated their willingness to walk.

They followed the servant as he wound his way through the Medina. Looking at the stalls that lined the narrow alleyways, Melody wondered whether they had been this way previously. After walking for perhaps fifteen minutes, she noticed that the narrow alleyways began to be replaced by wider, uncovered streets. Slowly, the frenetic energy of the part of the Medina where they were staying began to wane. As they passed through a gate, the feeling of the city changed quite suddenly as a more European style of architecture emerged.

Even the jasmine-scented air felt cooler as they entered the Batha district. There were fewer people, donkeys, and street vendors, and the neighbourhood felt much less chaotic. Within a few minutes, Melody guessed that they were not far from the vice-consul's residence, as the now whitewashed buildings began to look far more ornate and expensive. Perhaps most noticeable were the windows in these buildings, suggesting that the inhabitants were foreigners who were not keen to hide their womenfolk away.

At the end of the street, the servant halted outside a building whose architectural theme seemed to be understated elegance. It sat behind a beautiful, peaceful courtyard with two fountains surrounded by lush orange trees laden with plump fruit. A highly polished brass plate on the wall announced that they had arrived at their destination.

Melody was pleasantly surprised to find that Consul MacLeod's staff were wearing their native Moroccan costumes rather than mirroring the attempt by the vice-consul in Casablanca to anglicise his servants as much as he could. Rat introduced them both, and it seemed that they were expected. They were shown into a light, airy drawing room that, while it would not be mistaken for a room in a riad, nevertheless had enough Moroccan pieces to seem exotic in an expensive, polished way. There was a large Berber rug on the floor, leather ottomans scattered about the room and a low table with a mosaic top that was not unlike the ones they had encountered in the riads they had stayed in.

The servant who had answered the door accompanied them into the drawing room and then left, returning five minutes later with a tea tray. As he poured the tea into porcelain teacups, Melody was relieved to see that it was Darjeeling and not more mint tea. Melody had never thought that any people could drink tea more frequently than the British, but it seemed that Moroccans could. While she quite enjoyed the beverage, it was nice to have something else for a change.

Melody and Rat sipped their tea and nibbled on jam tarts that were as British as could be. They had only been waiting a few minutes more when the door opened, and a tall, distinguished-looking man who was probably in his mid-forties entered the room. He had a neatly clipped moustache above a mouth that curled into a welcoming smile.

"Mr Sandworth, welcome," the consul said in a mild Scottish accent. He crossed the room with an extended hand.

"Thank you for seeing us on such short notice, Consul MacLeod," Rat replied. "I would like to introduce you to my sister, Miss Melody Chesterton."

The greetings were followed by small talk. The consul had not returned to British shores in some years and was happy to chitchat and hear whatever society gossip Rat and Melody had to share. So happy, in fact, that Rat worried there would be no occasion to talk of weightier matters.

He was starting to wonder how he could change the course of the conversation when the vice-consul asked, "Is the telegram you wish to send somehow connected with Conte Foscari's current sojourn in the Sultan's palace?"

That was an interesting way to phrase Alessandro's imprisonment, Rat thought but didn't express. Instead, he replied, "Yes. My sister and I made the acquaintance of Conte Foscari in Venice and then accompanied him to Morocco."

"Not an easy journey, let alone for a well-bred young woman," the consul observed. "What inspired you to make the trip?"

Melody watched MacLeod closely. It had been evident in Casablanca that the consul, Sir Reginald, knew something of Alessandro's covert role. Was it safe to assume that Consul MacLeod was similarly well-informed?

It seemed that Rat had been thinking along the same lines. "Consul MacLeod, how aware are you of why Conte Foscari was in Morocco?"

The consul didn't answer immediately, instead stroking his moustache and choosing his words carefully. "Sir Reginald sent me a telegram when the conte was taken into custody by the Pasha, bringing me up-to-date on all things pertaining to the arrest. Can I take it that you share the conte's line of work, Mr Sandworth?"

"Indeed," Rat replied. "May I ask what you know about our other missing colleague?"

"Very little. I was unaware of his mission in Morocco until Sir Reginald sent the telegram about the conte. It seems that I was not considered important enough to be trusted with that information." The man's tone as he said this made quite clear what he thought of such an omission. "Of course, the British community in Fes is small enough that I knew the man quite well. However, like the rest of the hoi polloi, I believed him to be nothing more than an antiquities scholar."

Melody thought about the coincidence of Alessandro being arrested for murder just as he arrived in Morocco to investigate the other operative's disappearance. "What else can you tell us about the man?"

The consul's surprise at being asked this by a young woman was obvious. He glanced briefly at Rat but then answered, "His name, or the name I know him by, is Brett Rothnie. Seemed a nice enough fellow, a little scatterbrained at times, but that's what you expect these scholarly types to be, isn't it? Always seemed to have a camera bag slung over his shoulder. I asked him about it once, and he said that he never knew when he might stumble across an item or a place he wanted to document for his work. It was a vague but plausible explanation. Of course, now I realise that he might have had other reasons for wanting to document things."

"Is he married?" Rat asked.

The consul shook his head. "Well, I don't believe so anyway. If there's a Mrs Rothnie, I never met her. It is common practice for British residents to register with my office when they arrive. It's hard for us to help them if we don't know that they're here. I can have my private secretary look through the records. We should have an address for the man as well, if that would be helpful."

Rat indicated it would be, and the consul rose and left the room for a few minutes, returning with a sheet of paper. "I confirmed there is no wife on record, but I do have an address. It isn't far from here, in fact." He passed the paper to Rat, who pulled out a pocket notebook and copied it down.

There was one more question that Rat wished to ask the consul. "Why do you believe that the Sultan had Conte Foscari brought to Fes? From what we have heard, it is unusual enough that a foreigner of his rank would be taken into custody by the local Pasha, let alone then brought here."

Consul MacLeod raised his eyebrows and rolled his eyes a little. "Abdelhafid finds himself caught between a rock and a hard place," he said, referring to the Sultan with an informality that surprised Rat. "The man overthrew his brother on the grounds that he was too cosy with the foreign powers, yet here he is allowing the French to occupy Fes. This has caused him some heartburn recently when he felt French pressure at the end of last month to remove the Grand Vizier, Madani El Glaoui, from his position. El Glaoui had been a key supporter when Abdelhafid sought to overthrow his brother."

The consul seemed to be choosing his next words carefully. "El Glaoui is a reformer, an idealistic true believer in Moroccan independence. He believed that he had supported a like-minded man in Abdelhafid only to be greatly disappointed when the Sultan seemed to reverse his position and allow the French to assert such authority here."

Rat thought about this explanation. "What was El Glaoui's position on the Berber rebellion in April then? He must have felt quite torn, given his own views about foreign influence."

"Indeed, particularly as his family are Berbers. However, in the end, he was driven by loyalty to the Sultan and a real belief that the rebels were playing into French hands by weakening the Sultan's position and providing the French justification for intervention. He personally led troops against the Berber rebellion."

Melody was having a hard time following the political machinations. Now, she remembered why she had tuned out so much of the similar conversation on the journey to Casablanca. There was only one part of this that concerned her. "As my brother asked initially, what does any of this have to do with Alessandro, Conte Foscari, being arrested and brought to Fes?"

The consul grimaced. "I think after the French occupation, Abdelhafid wanted to prove his independence to the rebellious Berber tribes. Foscari's arrest was the perfect opportunity to demonstrate this. That he wasn't French or Spanish, I am sure, made the situation even more perfect."

"Because he could be seen not kowtowing to foreigners while not actually alienating any of the countries that have real power in Morocco?" Rat guessed.

"Indeed."

Melody thought about all they had learned about the combustible situation in Morocco and asked, "If Mr Rothnie had discovered some information that might affect the balance of power here, which country do you think most likely to want to prevent that information from seeing the light of day?"

"Take your pick. It depends on what Rothnie found, assuming he found something. Even factions within our own government have conflicting views on what is in Britain's best interests here. I have been in this business for long enough that I do not discount anything."

As shocking as this statement was, it made it even more urgent that they get word to Lord Langley. Rat retrieved what he had written for the telegram from his jacket pocket.

Consul MacLeod took the letter, looked it over and observed, "There is nothing in this letter that seems urgent enough to send by telegraph. I will assume it is in code, Mr Sandworth." Rat neither confirmed nor denied the statement, and the consul rose and left the room to have his secretary send the telegram. At the door, he turned and said, "As it happens, I am having a gathering here tonight to formally welcome Colonel Henri Gouraud who arrived recently to run the region, taking over from General Paul-Charles Moinier who led the French occupation of Fes."

Seeing the surprise on his guests' faces, the consul explained, "Britain's position on France's involvement remains cautiously neutral. France is our ally, and we need to be supportive of her government officials abroad. However, this might be a good opportunity if you wish to meet some of the personalities involved in the political maelstrom that is Fes at the moment. We dine at eight o'clock." With that, the consul left the room.

"Should we wait for a reply?" Melody asked.

"There is not much point. It is only nine o'clock in the morning here and so eight o'clock in London. It will be some time before Lord Langley receives this telegram and even longer before he is able to learn what we need to know. I am sure that the consul will send us the reply immediately. He clearly knows the urgency of the request."

CHAPTER 19

They bid farewell to the consul and received his assurance that he would send a servant with Lord Langley's reply as soon as he had it in hand. In turn, Melody and Rat graciously accepted his dinner invitation for that evening.

Melody and Rat showed Brett Rothnie's address to Lahcen's servant, who nodded his head and indicated that he knew the way. As the consul had said, Mr Rothnie's home wasn't far, and they arrived there within five minutes. While it wasn't as grand as many of the houses in the Batha district, there was a charm about it that made Melody feel that anyone who lived in such a delightful house must be a good sort of man. She knew that it was an irrational thought but felt it nonetheless. Up until that morning, the missing operative had been a nameless, faceless abstraction. Now that they had a name and she was looking at his home, she imagined a somewhat absent-minded professor-type, bumbling around this cosy house, searching for spectacles that inevitably he would discover were on the top of his head and constantly misplacing items. Of course, it was hard to reconcile this image with the idea of a covert operative sneaking around in the shadows. Perhaps that was the point; it was an excellent disguise.

From what they knew, the man had been missing since sometime in mid-May, so several weeks at that point. Did Brett Rothnie have servants, and if he did, were they even still in residence at the house? Rat knocked at the door. There was no answer. Then he knocked again. They were almost about to give up and leave when the door was cracked open.

"What do you want?" a terse voice asked. It didn't sound Moroccan, but it also didn't sound British. It was impossible to see the woman attached to the voice, such was the gloom of the inside of the house.

"We would like to ask you about Mr Rothnie," Melody said gently.

"He's not here."

"We know that," Rat explained. "That is why we want to ask you a few questions. We are, well, we are friends of his, of a sort."

The door cracked open a little more and the owner of the voice was revealed to be a middle-aged woman with dark hair and olive skin that suggested she might be Spanish or from somewhere else in southern Europe. She had a kind face and gentle eyes, even if they darted back and forth nervously at that moment.

"Might we come in?" Melody asked in the same soft voice.

For a moment, she thought the woman would refuse and shut the door in their faces, but after a moment, it was opened, and the woman stepped back to allow them to enter. She led them down the gloomy hallway and into a sitting room that had the comfortable charm that Melody would have expected based on its exterior. Walking into the room was like being transported to Britain, perhaps to a slightly cluttered yet welcoming parlour in a country vicarage. There was nothing in the room that indicated that it was many miles from Great Britain. Instead, from the quaint landscape paintings on the wall to the embroidered cushions on the couch, the room spoke to English rural homeliness.

"I am Melody Chesterton, and this is my brother, Matthew Sand-worth," Melody explained, holding out her hand.

"I am Olympia Rothnie, Brett's wife," the woman explained. At least now they understood why a wife wasn't registered with the vice-consul's office; she neither looked nor sounded British. "Won't you take a seat? Can I get you some tea?" Olympia asked.

Rat and Melody indicated that they needed no refreshments and took a seat. Olympia Rothnie perched anxiously on the edge of a battered but comfortable-looking armchair. "How do you know Brett?" she asked.

Melody exchanged a look with Rat; they hadn't discussed how to explain their interest in Brett Rothnie. Deciding to stick as close to the truth as possible, she explained, "Well, we do not know him. However, our friend, Conte Alessandro Foscari, is acquainted with your husband. The conte has been wrongly accused of murder and is imprisoned. We spoke with him yesterday, and he told us that he had intended to contact your husband but had been informed that he went missing some weeks ago."

At this, Mrs Rothnie's eyes filled with tears. Melody rose and rushed to her side. Kneeling next to the distraught woman, she said, "I am so sorry that we have upset you. We merely want to help. Do you have any idea what happened to your husband?"

"I will be alright in a moment. Let me just collect myself. Please, sit. I will be fine in a moment," Mrs Rothnie promised them.

"Please, do not feel concerned on our behalf," Rat assured her.

Olympia Rothnie took a couple of deep breaths and began her story. "My husband is a scholar of antiquities," she explained. Rat wondered if she knew that was merely a cover story but made no comment. Olympia continued, "He had been quite distracted of late. Typically, Brett is such a placid, even-tempered man. I tried to get him to tell me what was bothering him, but he claimed it was nothing."

Melody searched Olympia's face; she didn't seem to be dissembling. Was it possible that she had no idea about her husband's true reason for being in Fes?

Deciding to probe that question further, Melody asked, "How long has your husband been in Morocco?"

Olympia considered the question. "I believe that he first came around 1906." She then added, "I did not know him at the time. We have only been married three years."

"You mentioned that Mr Rothnie is an antiquities scholar. What era does he study?" Rat asked.

"His area of interest is the early Islamic period in Morocco in the late seventh and early eighth centuries. This includes the Islamic conquest of Iberia. He travelled quite frequently between Morocco and Southern Europe for his work."

Rat considered her words. This was undoubtedly a well-thought-out cover. "You mentioned that you have not been married long. You do not seem Moroccan, Mrs Rothnie. How did you meet?"

The woman smiled for the first time since they had arrived. "I am Greek. Brett was travelling to Constantinople to study the Ottoman-era archives. His travels there from Tangier took him through my country which is where we met. We married and travelled on together."

This account did not seem in any way disingenuous. Rat considered the predicament they were in. They needed to learn what, if anything, Brett Rothnie discovered, but he couldn't imagine how to raise the topic of rifling through the man's papers without some kind of explanation of his covert work. He glanced over at Melody, but then realised that it was his decision alone to make. Choosing to reveal a covert operative's identity was not something to be taken lightly. Yet, it was also quite possible that Brett Rothnie was no longer alive and perhaps his wife deserved to know the actual reason why that might be.

Finally, making a decision, Rat probed tentatively, "Mrs Rothnie, did it ever occur to you that your husband might be in Morocco for another, more secretive reason?"

Olympia stiffened at his words. Melody, who was still kneeling next to the woman, gently touched her arm. "Mrs. Rothnie, we are only trying to help uncover what has happened to your husband. Anything that you might know or even suspect could be useful information."

Taking a deep breath, Olympia said, "I do not know precisely what Brett was up to, but I have suspected for some time that there was something going on. At first, I worried that he had taken a mistress, but that is not who my husband is. He would leave the house at odd hours, sometimes staying out all night. He seemed increasingly agitated just before he disappeared and was very secretive about his activities. Do you know what he might have been so worried about?"

"Mrs Rothnie, your husband worked for the British Government in a covert capacity," Rat explained tentatively.

Whatever Olympia had expected them to say, this clearly wasn't it. "No. He was an antiquities scholar," she protested.

"This was nothing more than a story to explain his presence in Fes and perhaps certain activities he engaged in. Like taking lots of photos, for example, when I suspect he was instead gathering evidence."

"Evidence of what?" she asked, perplexed.

"We are not entirely sure. However, our government is very concerned about the activities of our European neighbours in the region. It seems that there are worries that the French occupation of Fes could become a much larger issue, perhaps even a direct conflict between France and Germany which Britain might then get dragged into. I would imagine that if your husband had evidence that would in any way undermine France's position, there are various factions who might want to suppress this information."

"I do not understand what you are saying, Mr Sandworth."

Rat apologised. Just saying the words out loud highlighted how confusing the situation was. However, he did know one thing, "May we enter your husband's study and search through his papers?"

"I would let you, but he had the key with him when he disappeared."

Melody knew that her brother always carried his small set of lockpicks with him. She replied, "I believe we will be able to open the door—with your permission, of course." Olympia nodded her consent.

Melody and Rat stood to move to the study. Just then, Melody remembered one detail they hadn't asked about. "Mrs Rothnie, when was the last time that you saw your husband?"

Olympia Rothnie considered the question, finally answering, "It was a Tuesday. I remember that because it is the day I always go to the souq to shop. Brett was here when I left. He told me that he was going out. I told him not to be home late because I was making his favourite meal. That was the last thing I ever said to him." The woman began crying again.

An hour later, Rat and Melody left Brett Rothnie's home. Rat had picked the lock to the study, and they had methodically gone through all his papers and photographs. To their frustration, they could find nothing obviously noteworthy. Whatever Brett had been hiding in his study didn't seem to be there anymore or else was very well hidden. Olympia had watched them search in hopeful anticipation of some explanation of what had happened to her husband. Melody felt awful about having raised the woman's hopes only to dash them.

They left the Rothnie home with the servant leading them back to Lahcen's riad. Neither sibling said much for the walk, both lost in their thoughts. Up until now, all Melody had been concerned with was exonerating Alessandro. However, now that she had met Olympia, there was another pressing concern: discovering what had happened to Brett Rothnie and getting justice for the man, if indeed it turned out that he had been killed.

When they returned to the riad, they found an anxiously pacing Omar waiting in the courtyard. "Where have you been for so long?" he asked frantically.

"What has happened? Is it Alessandro?" Melody demanded, catching his anxiety.

"No, no, Lalla Melody. It is just that a servant has come from the palace and has been waiting for you for some time."

A servant from the palace? What on earth could that mean? Melody and Rat looked at each other. Was this a good or a bad thing? Omar called for the servant to be brought to them. A young, heavily veiled woman was brought into the courtyard. Omar said something to her, and she replied in a soft voice.

Omar then turned to Melody and said, "You have been invited to the harem by Lalla Rabia, one of the Sultan's wives. You are to return with her immediately."

Melody was intrigued by the invitation but was dusty from their walk and hardly dressed appropriately to visit the palace. She expressed this to Omar and requested that the servant wait so she could wash and change. He repeated her words in Arabic, and the servant girl replied.

"She says that there is no need. Lalla Rabia invites you to visit the hammam with her. This is a great honour, Lalla Melody. You should not keep her waiting. Take the mule and the girl will lead the way."

As uncomfortable as Melody was with the idea of visiting royalty without even washing her face, it seemed that she had no choice. Then she had a thought, "Is Lalla Fatima not joining us?"

Omar shook his head. "The servant was very clear that this invitation is only for the young British woman." Seeing how wary Melody was of the situation, Omar assured her, "This can only be of benefit to our friend. The harem yields far more power than you might think."

Melody wasn't convinced that women who lived in a gilded prison, never able to see the world or be seen, could be considered power brokers. Still, an opportunity had presented itself, and, more to the point, there was no gracious way to turn down the invitation.

CHAPTER 20

After another mule ride through the Medina, Melody found herself being led into the palace yet again. They hadn't entered through the large main gate that had been used for their previous visit but instead through a small side gate manned by just one guard. The clandestine nature of the visit became more apparent as they entered a large building that Melody assumed was the harem by a side door.

The servant girl knocked three times on the door, and a tall, burly male servant opened it. Melody remembered Omar mentioning that only eunuchs could attend to the women in the harem and wondered if this was also true for the guards. This guard seemed very threatening, not merely because of his giant size but also because of the large, very sharp-looking dagger in one hand.

The guard seemed to be expecting them and ushered them into the building. Melody followed the girl through highly decorated corridors, each step muffled by the many beautiful soft rugs lining the floors. Melody felt the air grow warmer and more fragrant, which she assumed meant they were nearing the hammam. Trying to identify the delightful scents, Melody thought she smelled rosewater and perhaps sandalwood.

Turning from the corridor to a doorway, the girl led Melody into a plain room where another servant girl awaited her. That girl indicated that

Melody should disrobe and offered her a plain, very loose-fitting white muslin robe. She then brought over a basin of warm orange blossom-scented water and mimed that Melody should wash her hands.

Then, the other servant girl led Melody through an archway draped with silk into a much warmer, mosaic-tiled room. In the middle of the room, there was a low fountain surrounded by large silk cushions. A young woman lay on the cushions, one hand lazily playing with the water in the fountain. She was dressed in a white robe similar to Melody's, except that hers was threaded with gold.

At Melody's entrance, the woman looked up. Melody thought that, as a rule, Moroccans were very attractive people and that the women with their almond-shaped eyes and dark glossy hair were quite beautiful. Unfortunately, the woman waiting for Melody, who she assumed was Lalla Rabia, was the exception to this rule. Every feature on her visage was at odds with the others. Her nose was too large for what was an overly long face. Her chin was too pointy, her forehead rather too dominant. The one saving grace of Lalla Rabia's countenance was her eyes which were dark brown with large pupils, framed by thick eyelashes of extraordinary length. The eyes were intelligent and kind but also a little guarded.

"Lalla Melody, welcome," the woman said in a melodic voice. "Please, come and join me in the harara," Rabia said, rising and leading the way through another door.

Melody followed into a very hot and steamy room. The room was quite dark, its only illumination coming from the daylight filtering through the small, star-shaped cutouts in its domed ceiling. In the middle of the room, there was a large, smooth marble slab that glistened with moisture. Her hostess went and sat on the slab and patted a spot next to her. Melody accepted the invitation and took a seat.

Attendants brought two copper bowls of hot water and placed them on the floor. Lalla Rabia reclined on her front on the slab, and Melody went to follow suit. She was surprised that before she could lie down, one of the attendants had gently opened the robe Melody was wearing and pulled it from her shoulders. Melody was used to being naked in front of Mary, but she wasn't sure she was prepared to be so in front of a stranger. Luckily, in one swift motion, the attendant replaced the robe with a light cotton sheet and encouraged Melody to lie down on her front with the sheet covering her. Glancing over, Melody saw that Lalla Rabia was similarly covered.

Over the next twenty minutes, every inch of Melody's body was scrubbed and exfoliated. Once she got over the embarrassment of having a stranger perform such an intimate act for her, she found the experience quite relaxing. After the exfoliation, the attendant used the water in the copper bowl to rinse off Melody's body. Lalla Rabia said nothing the entire time. Melody knew enough to realise that she could not initiate a conversation and must wait for the royal wife to speak.

After the exfoliation, the attendants left for a few moments. Melody wondered what would happen next. As if reading her mind, Lalla Rabia explained, "They will return with Ghassoul Clay that we use for deep cleaning and softening the skin."

Clay? Melody wasn't sure how she felt about having her body covered in clay, but there didn't seem to be a gracious way to decline. In the end, it wasn't as unpleasant as she had feared, though she was happy when, finally, it was washed off. Still, Lalla Rabia hadn't said anything of note. After the clay had been thoroughly rinsed off, Melody's hair was washed. When this step was complete, she was helped back into her loose robe and led into yet another cooler room. After the humid heat of the harara, this room felt refreshing.

Melody followed Lalla Rabia's lead in lying on a mosaic bench slightly elevated at one end. As with the warm room, the only light came from the cutouts in the ceiling. Given that Melody's robe was once again removed, she was glad for the relative darkness. She wasn't sure what was going to happen to her in this room, so she was surprised when she felt oil being rubbed into her from the tips of her feet through her hair.

"You are being treated with Argan oil," Lalla Rabia explained. "There is no more luxuriant way to moisturise one's body and hair. The oil keeps my skin youthful and my hair healthy and shining." Melody was surprised that the oil only had the lightest scent. She had expected it to feel greasy on her body, yet it didn't. When she was fully oiled, the attendant then sprayed her body with a light rose scent.

Finally, with her robe back on, Melody was led to a low cushion-covered couch with a table in front of it. Lalla Rabia followed. While the two women reclined, another servant brought long, cool glasses of orange juice and dishes of dates and nuts.

When all the food was set on the table, Lalla Rabia clapped her hands and said something in Arabic. At her words, all the servants melted away, and the two women were alone. Lalla Rabia still said nothing. She took a long sip of orange juice and savoured a date.

Finally, when Melody felt she could not bear the anticipation any further, the other woman asked, "How do you find Morocco?"

Melody thought about the question. "I find it a fascinating country. The landscape changes so dramatically and sometimes quite quickly. You have both sand dunes and snowcapped mountains."

"Indeed. Morocco is a beautiful country. How do you find its people?"

"I believe that people are people no matter where you travel to. Some of them are good and kind, and some are evil. In between are most people who want nothing more than to take care of their families and live a life of health and happiness."

Lalla Rabia sat up from her leaning position and looked very meaningfully at Melody. "So, you believe that all people are fundamentally the same and that no one group is significantly different or better than any other?"

This wasn't precisely what Melody had said. However, now that the words were said out loud, she realised that she did believe that. Melody knew that she was one of the fortunate few to live a charmed life of wealth, ease and influence. Still, it was but a random quirk of fate that had given her that life. If not for Wolfie and Tabby Cat, Melody and Rat might have lived all their lives in Whitechapel. Rat would have joined a criminal gang, most likely. As for Melody, well, the best she could have hoped for was to find a husband who didn't beat her more than most instead of a life as a prostitute prowling the streets of the East End. Both of those options assumed that she had lived past childhood, which was hardly a guarantee.

Given these far more likely possibilities, how could Melody hold any opinion other than the basic equality of mankind? While there was no doubt that she was a very different person in many ways than if she hadn't come to life in Mayfair, in the fundamentals, she was who she always would have been. Fate might have made her bitter, and certainly, she would be less carefree. However, she would have been no less intelligent, no less worthy of an education, no less deserving of a full stomach and a roof over her head.

As these thoughts flashed through her head, Melody nodded her head in agreement. "Yes, that is what I believe," she answered.

"And so why are my people deemed unable and unworthy to rule themselves without foreign interference?"

Melody realised she had been led into a trap and was unsure how to respond. As she had reflected on days before, Xander Ashby, of all people, had recently pointed out to her that many of the citizens of the British Empire might feel as Lalla Rabia did. She now realised that foreign involvement in other countries was an incredibly complex subject.

Then, without considering the wisdom of her words, Melody pointed out, "Did the Arabs who now inhabit Morocco not invade here many centuries ago and impose their rule on the native Berbers?"

There was a long, pregnant pause. Melody worried that she would be thrown out of the harem or worse. Then, Lalla Rabia threw her head back and laughed. It was a deep, pleasant gurgle of a laugh. "Either you are very wise or very foolish," she observed. "If you are wise, you will never make such a statement within the Sultan's hearing."

Then, changing tack without warning, Lalla Rabia said, "My father is one who has always passionately felt that no good comes from having foreigners impose their will on our land. He believed that my husband felt similarly. Yet now, my father is no longer Grand Vizier and French troops occupy Fes." Perhaps sensing a question Melody wished to ask, Lalla Rabia explained, "We wives and consorts may not leave the harem, and so we ensure that the news of the world comes to us."

Lalla Rabia suddenly looked quite sly. "For example, I heard the news that you came to plead with my husband for clemency towards a very handsome Italian gentleman he has arrested. Who is this gentleman to you that you cross the Atlas Mountains on his behalf?"

Melody blushed. She didn't want to but couldn't help it. Rabia saw the blush and laughed. "Ah, I see how it is. You have a tendre for this man I believe."

Unsure how best to answer, Melody said nothing. Lalla Rabia noted her embarrassment and said sagely, "Sometimes I believe that the

Moroccan way has its advantages. I never had to wonder if I loved Abdel-hafid and if he held me in high regard. There was no delicate dance. It became strategically beneficial to both my father and Abdelhafid to link our families. My now husband was not yet the Sultan, but he sought to challenge his brother's authority. My father, Madani El Glaoui, was the elder of a powerful Berber family. More to the point, my father could command the loyalty of other local Berber tribes, something the then prince would need if he were to seek to overthrow his brother."

"And so marriage to you was nothing more than a business arrangement?" Melody asked. Even as she said this, she realised that things were not so different with her own Royal Family. This was how alliances had been cemented for many centuries. Maybe Lalla Rabia was correct; perhaps it was easier this way than marriages based on romantic love.

Seeking to move the conversation away from her romantic entanglements, Melody observed, "Your father seems to have made a wise choice for you. Now, you are the wife of the most powerful man in Morocco."

Lalla Rabia laughed, but this time, it was a hollow sound. "My husband may inhabit the Dar al-Makhzen, the Royal Palace, but his authority is hollow. Every promise and dictate he makes is measured by men who will never bow to him. Do you call that power?"

Melody was surprised that the Sultan's wife was willing to say such things openly, but then she considered how unlikely it was that any of the servants understood English. Still, what of the other wives? Surely, it wasn't wise for Lalla Rabia to express such treasonous thoughts. Certainly, Melody did not wish to be overheard agreeing to such a statement.

Instead, she said archly, "Certainly, the Sultan has the power to arrest foreigners and hold them prisoner. As for the rest, it is not for me to speak to Morocco's relationship with the French."

"A very diplomatic answer, Lalla Melody. How far might that diplomacy stretch? I wonder, if you were to discover something damning, something that showed the French for what they truly are, would you act on it?"

"Does such a thing exist?" Melody wondered, unsure where this conversation was leading but curious to learn more.

"My father has reason to believe it does. He was alerted to the existence of such proof but then, before he could do anything about it, he was removed from his post. He believes that this was done at the urging of the French. This despite valiantly leading the troops against our own Berber people during the rebellion and almost losing his life."

As she said these words, Lalla Rabia rose. "It has been an interesting conversation, Lalla Melody. Be careful. The situation in Morocco these days is as venomous as a snake charmer's viper." And with that, she turned and left abruptly.

CHAPTER 21

During the ride back to the riad, Melody considered Lalla Rabia's words. There was no doubt that the woman had been trying to set Melody onto a particular investigative path, and yet she had been so vague that it was unclear what path that was. If she had wanted to say something, why not just say it? There had been enough said explicitly, seemingly without fear of being overheard and understood. Why stop where she did? Was it possible that the Sultan's wife didn't know anything beyond the shadowy allusions she had made?

What Melody was sure about was that she needed to talk with Rat as soon as possible. Just as they were approaching the riad, another possibility occurred to her: perhaps she should include Fatima in that conversation. Melody was quite sure now that Fatima was as loyal to Alessandro as Rat believed, or at least she was reasonably sure. If that was the case, why not include the other woman? Melody went back and forth with herself about the pros and cons of such a decision. Finally, Melody concluded that she and Rat had neither the language skills nor the local knowledge to make as much of Lalla Rabia's hint as they needed to. If only for practical reasons, she would share the information with Fatima as well as Rat.

Now that Melody had made that decision, she was faced with a more practical one: where to have this conference. It was one thing for Rat to slip into Melody's room quietly. However, the addition of another person ran far too high a risk of drawing attention to their conversation. While Melody had, however, grudgingly, come to trust Fatima, there was no reason to extend this faith to the woman's servants, Lahcen or Omar.

Thinking about the last time the three of them had managed to talk privately, Melody realised that another shopping trip might be the answer she needed. Melody guessed that she had been in the hammam for a couple of hours and that it was now mid-afternoon. If she was prepared to leave almost as soon as she returned to the riad, there should be enough time to make the trip back into the commercial hubbub of the Medina. Of course, that assumed that Fatima and Rat were both available and willing to make the trip. Most importantly, she had to make the request in such a way that it didn't raise any suspicions.

As it happened, Melody had been considering returning to the weavers and commissioning some more clothes. She had greatly appreciated the ease of motion that Fatima's split skirts had provided on their trip to Fes and wished to have one or two more made for her. If they were going to stay much longer in Fes, it might also be worth having more caftans made, including perhaps a slightly less formal one.

Arriving back at the riad, it seemed that Melody's guess as to the time was correct, and she had long ago missed lunch. Though she had nibbled on some dates in the hammam, they had not been a sufficient snack to alleviate the hunger of missing a meal. Her growling stomach aside, Melody concluded it would be a little odd if she were to return to the riad and almost immediately suggest another outing. Instead, she asked one of the servants if it would be possible to bring some food to her room.

Luckily, it seemed that none of the household beyond the servants were around the courtyard, and she was able to slip unnoticed up to the first floor and Rat's room. Crossing her fingers that she'd find her brother there, Melody knocked lightly on the door.

Rat had been sitting in the armchair in his room reading one of Lahcen's books. It seemed that their host had a wide-ranging and eclectic library and that at least some of his books were in English. Determined to distract his thoughts from Melody's visit to the harem, Rat had chosen one of these books and was now quite engrossed. So engrossed that he almost missed the light tap on his door.

As soon as Rat opened the door, Melody pushed her way inside without saying a word.

"What's the matter?" Rat asked in a worried tone. "Was there a problem during your visit?"

"Not a problem, though something we need to discuss. But not here. I would like to include Fatima in the conversation, and I can see no way that we can do that discreetly in the riad. I would like to revisit the weavers. What did Fatima call it? The Hanout An-Nassaj? That seemed to be a safe place to talk; anyway, I want to order more clothes."

Intrigued by his sister's plan for a covert operation, Rat could see one flaw in her plan, "How will you explain my accompanying you, Melly?"

"You will say that you wish to get another djellaba made for the trip back to Casablanca. You did find it a comfortable travel garment, did you not?"

Rat acknowledged the truth of her statement. "I believe that Fatima left some time ago to pay some social calls. She had said she would be back about now. Why do we not wait downstairs in the courtyard? We can ask for some mint tea and wait to catch her as she returns." This seemed like a sensible plan.

Luckily, they had only just started on their first glass of tea when Fatima swept into the courtyard. "How was your morning with Lalla Rabia?" she asked with a hint of resentment. It appeared she had been informed as to Melody's invitation.

"I got to experience the harem's hammam," Melody answered. Fatima raised her eyebrows in reply by which Melody inferred that she should be honoured at such treatment.

"In fact," Melody said quite loudly in case anyone was nearby, "what the visit made me realise was that I may need more clothes while we are in Fes. I was thinking of returning to the Hanout An-Nassaj." Showing Fatima the item of clothing she was holding, she explained, "I am going to bring one of your split skirts and ask them to copy it. I saw some lovely fabric there the other day that I think would work well. Matthew is going to join us. He would like another djellaba. We were wondering if you would join us."

As she said this last line, Melody tried to communicate through her facial expressions that Fatima should say yes because there was more to this trip than merely shopping. Whether or not Fatima gleaned that, she agreed. They assumed that she would want to freshen up and rest before venturing out again, but it seemed that indefatigable was yet another word that could be applied to the woman.

It was unclear where Omar and Lahcen were, so Rat left word with a servant before they headed back out and mounted the mules. The same servant who had led them the other day led them again, and it wasn't long before they were deep in the souq.

After their extensive purchases the previous day, the shopkeeper was thrilled to see them back again so soon. He spoke rapid Arabic to Fatima, who explained what they were looking for. Suspecting that Rat and Melody had an ulterior reason for suggesting the outing, Fatima suggested that the shopkeeper bring them a range of fabrics to choose from so that he would be gone for some time. While she didn't believe he spoke English, it was prudent to be careful.

Finally, the shopkeeper left, eager to pull his most expensive fabrics for the Barani. The man had no love for foreigners, hence his description of them as Barani, outsiders, to his helper in the back. Despite this sentiment, he was a savvy businessman and knew a good opportunity when he saw it.

With the man safely out of the way, Fatima demanded, "Well? I assume that you dragged me back out because you wished to discuss something. So, what is it?"

Melody tried her best to ignore the irritation in the other woman's voice and, as quickly as she could, relayed the key parts of her conversation with Lalla Rabia.

"So, she didn't say what this supposed thing that proves the French coerced the Sultan is? Is she even sure that such a thing exists?"

With a resigned shake of her head, Melody admitted that Fatima's concerns were valid. The other woman continued, "And even if it does, my only concern is freeing Sandro and it is unclear to me, very unclear, how this supposed clue from Lalla Rabia helps us with that end."

Melody had been thinking about this very question. Now keeping her voice low, just in case anyone could understand, she explained, ticking points off her fingers, "We have a few strands of this mystery which I believe are more interwoven than we have previously thought. Firstly, Lalla Rabia accused her husband of being entirely subservient to the

French. We know that Brett Rothnie had been acting quite erratically recently, and we believe that he discovered something, though we're unsure what. He then disappeared sometime in early to mid-May."

Turning to Rat, Melody asked, "When did Alessandro tell you that you had to leave for Morocco?"

Rat considered the question. "I believe that it was May 12th. Wait, no, it was May 11th. We left on the 12th, which I believe was a Friday."

"I remember that Mrs Rothnie said that her husband disappeared on a Tuesday in early May. I am assuming that it was Sir Reginald who sounded the alarm that Brett was missing, but do you know how he discovered this?"

Rat shook his head at his sister's very valid question. He should have asked Alessandro this, and now he was frustrated with himself for omitting to inquire about such a salient point of information.

Melody was as frustrated as Rat about this missing information. Nevertheless, she knew the importance of having a cohesive theory that one could adapt to new information as it presented itself. For now, she was going to hypothesise that Brett Rothnie disappeared on May 10th. She was also going to assume that Sir Reginald had been expecting some kind of communique from Brett Rothnie and had become worried when it never arrived.

As she thought through this timeline, Melody remembered one thing. "Consul MacLeod told us that he hadn't known that Mr Rothnie was in the employ of the British Government. So, we know Sir Reginald didn't receive news of the disappearance through him."

"Yes, you're right, Melly," Rat confirmed. "I'm not sure what that tells us, but it is a piece of evidence at least."

Returning to counting off her fingers, Melody continued, "Brett Rothnie had been acting quite erratically, according to his wife, and had become very secretive before he disappeared. Do we think he had some warning that he might be in danger?"

Again, Rat thought it was a valid question but one to which he had no answer.

"Who is Brett Rothnie?" Fatima asked, reminding Rat and Melody that they hadn't brought her up-to-date on their morning excursions. They quickly filled her in on their trip to Consul MacLeod's home and his revelation of the missing operative's name and address. They then told her about their conversation with Olympia Rothnie.

"So, you think he discovered something, but you didn't find it in his study?" Fatima asked, scepticism writ large on her face. "What is your hypothesis for this? That he had it on him when he disappeared?"

Irritated but determined to ignore Fatima's sarcastic tone, Melody replied, "Perhaps. Or perhaps it was in the study, and we didn't find it. What we do know is that Lalla Rabia implied that there is something, perhaps a document, that would reflect badly on the French. Is it possible that this is what Brett found? She certainly believes that this evidence is somehow tied up with her father, the then Grand Vizier, being removed from his post. Something that she believes happened at the behest of the French Government."

"And I ask you again: what does this have to do with securing Alessandro's release?" Fatima asked impatiently. So impatiently that Melody second-guessed her decision to bring the woman into their confidence. However, she also didn't have a good answer. Every instinct she had told Melody that this was one investigation and that the reason Alessandro had been followed and an attempt had been made on his life was that he had come to Morocco to investigate Brett's disappearance. Was his arrest yet another attempt to interfere with Alessandro's mission?"

Deciding to articulate this theory out loud, Melody said in a hesitant voice, "What if this is all about whatever Brett found? Perhaps the French Government killed Brett, and then, when Alessandro was sent to investigate, they used this rogue operative to identify and then attack him. While the attack failed, Alessandro had now been identified by the French as a British Intelligence operative, and so this rogue operative was then unnecessary and was himself killed."

Rat considered Melody's words. "It isn't a terrible idea," he admitted. "Perhaps a decision was made that it might be more useful to have Alessandro in custody than to make another attempt on his life. And so, the rogue operative's last unknowing job for his employer was to be killed in a public enough place that Alessandro could be immediately discovered leaning over the body."

"Ha!" Fatima's face said all they needed to know about the credence she gave their theory. "This convoluted story is why you dragged me out this afternoon? And even if you are correct in places, what would you have us do?"

The dismissiveness of Fatima's tone was annoying, but she had a point: what did Melody think they should do next? Suddenly, she snapped her fingers. "We have that dinner invitation for this evening. We may be able to learn more there."

Fatima raised her eyebrows, "What dinner invitation?" Melody explained that Consul MacLeod and invited her and Rat to meet the new French official in charge of Fes. "Then I will join you," Fatima declared. Melody's very British horror at making a social faux pas by bringing along an unexpected guest must have shown on her face, for Fatima added, "I am a French citizen. And anyway, I have never met a man who was not charmed to have me grace his table."

Well, that seemed to be that, then. Melody had to admit that it might be helpful to have the French-speaking Fatima with them.

Rat glanced at his pocket watch. "If we are going to return to the riad, bathe, dress and return to the consul's home, we ought to leave soon."

Her brother's words brought a new difficulty to light: what were they to wear? None of them had any Western clothes that were appropriate for a formal evening gathering. As speedy as the dressmaker had been with their Moroccan garb, it was doubtful that they could get evening wear made up within the new few hours. Melody voiced this concern.

"We will wear caftans, and Matthew will wear his djellaba," Fatima said dismissively as if the answer should have been obvious.

"Is that appropriate?" Rat asked in horror. It was one thing to wear native garb to visit the Sultan, but he couldn't imagine wearing it amongst fellow Europeans.

"Pfff," Fatima exclaimed. "Why wouldn't it be? And anyway, do we have a choice?" Melody and Rat had to acknowledge that they really didn't. Twenty minutes later, laden down with more packages and even more outfits ordered, including the split skirts, they left for their return trip through the souq.

CHAPTER 22

Dressed in one of her new silk caftans and resplendent in her Moroccan jewellery, Melody looked at herself in the mirror in her room. Apart from anything else, these clothes were far easier to get in and out of without Mary's help. While Melody shared Rat's concerns about attending the consul's dinner dressed in local garb, she had to admit that the clothes suited her. While she did not doubt that Fatima would outshine her in every way, Melody felt that she wouldn't be ashamed to meet the local dignitaries dressed as she was.

Thirty minutes later, Melody, Rat, and Fatima were shown into the consul's drawing room. There was a small group gathered there already, all of them men. If Consul James MacLeod was married, it didn't seem as if his wife was with him in Fes. The man himself caught sight of them and crossed the room.

"Ah, Miss Chesterton and Mr Sandworth, I'm so glad you could make it." Turning to Fatima, his glance full of admiration, he said, "And I see you have brought a beautiful friend with you. How delightful."

Fatima held out her hand, batted her eyelashes, and said in a sultry voice, "I am Fatima Amrani. My late father was the Moroccan Ambassador to Paris. Consul MacLeod, I hope you will forgive me for attending your dinner without an invitation. I have been hoping to meet you since I arrived in Fes and insisted that Miss Chesterton and Mr Sandworth bring me along."

Melody had to work hard not to roll her eyes at this blatant flattery and flirtation. However, she had to admit that it worked. The consul kissed the outstretched hand and replied in an equally flirtatious tone, "What could there possibly be to forgive? I can only regret the time you have been in Fes so far when we were not acquainted."

Turning to Melody, Fatima declared coquettishly, "Why, Melody, you did not tell me how handsome and charming the consul is. I hope that you did not mean to keep him to yourself."

Unsure how much more of this she could stomach, Melody remarked, "Consul MacLeod, I did not realise that we would be the only women here tonight."

"Indeed. These are military men whose wives and families are back in Europe, and I am unmarried." He glanced back over at Fatima, "For now."

"Is everyone here French, sir?" Rat inquired.

"Not at all. Of course, we have General Paul-Charles Moinier and Colonel Henri Gouraud here tonight over there." He pointed at two men standing together, both wearing the kepis and high-collared tunics adorned with medals and epaulettes that indicated they belonged to the French military.

Then, pointing beyond them to a younger, very handsome man with dark, close-cropped hair and soulful brown eyes who was dressed in British military uniform, the consul continued, "And over there, we have Captain William Somerset of His Majesty's armed forces. Captain Somerset is in Morocco currently as a representative of the Foreign Office."

Perhaps sensing their eyes on him, Captain Somerset turned and began walking towards them. He really was a very attractive man, Melody decided. She couldn't help but be interested in him. Of course, she thought, Fatima was sure to flirt with Captain Somerset and take all the man's attention. To her great surprise and pleasure, the man barely glanced at Fatima and instead seemed only to have eyes for her.

As he came to a standstill by their group, he asked, "Consul MacLeod, it is very unfair of you to monopolise such beautiful female companions. Particularly when they are the only ladies at this party. Can I ask that you introduce me, sir?"

While he said this, Captain Somerset never took his eyes off Melody. Pre-empting Consul MacLeod's introduction, she held out her hand and said, "I am Miss Melody Chesterton, and this is my brother, Matthew Sandworth."

Irritated at her exclusion from Melody's introduction and at the handsome captain's lack of notice, Fatima pushed herself forward. She said in the same sultry voice she used on the consul, "And I am Fatima Amrani."

Captain Somerset took the proffered hand but gave it an almost cursory shake while barely taking his eyes off Melody. Even if he hadn't been such an attractive man, it would have been flattering. As it was, his captain's uniform made the already very handsome man even more dashing. The captain had a deep voice with the clipped tones of the British elite. Was he a duke's third son or something like that? Melody wondered. Certainly, a career in the armed forces was a common path for such men to take. Perhaps a new flirtation was just what she needed to get her mind off her last romantic disappointment with Alessandro.

"And what brings you and your charming companions to Fes, Mr Sandworth?" Captain Somerset asked.

Ever since they had decided to attend this dinner, Rat had been wondering how best to answer this inevitable question. Fes was not an easy place to get to, and most visitors to Morocco were happy to go no further than Tangier or Casablanca. It wasn't credible that the three of them had chosen to make the arduous trek through the Middle Atlas Mountains merely to take in the scenery.

Finally, Rat had decided that, as was often the case, sticking as close to the truth as possible was the safest option. "My sister and I travelled to Morocco with our friend, Conte Alessandro Foscari. We were staying in Casablanca at Lalla Fatima's home when the conte was mistakenly arrested for a crime he did not commit. He was brought to Fes, and we followed him here in the hopes of facilitating his release."

Melody couldn't be sure, but she thought that she noticed an expression cross the captain's face as Rat explained this. If she'd had to put a name to it, she would have said that it was a surprise, but there seemed to be something else that she couldn't quite put her finger on.

Perhaps his surprise was explained by his next words. "You made the trek from Casablanca? That is a long and difficult trip, particularly for a well-bred young woman."

As much as Melody bristled at being thought too delicate to be capable of such travel, the truth was that it had been a long and difficult trip. She wasn't looking forward to making the return journey, whenever that might be. Could she really be angry at the handsome Captain Somerset for pointing out the truth?

Deciding to err on the side of forgiveness, Melody interrupted whatever Rat might have been about to say in reply. "It was a very long trip and certainly not easy. However, Lalla Fatima has been friends with Conte Foscari for quite some time and felt certain that my brother would have need of her local knowledge and contacts in order to secure the conte's release. I stubbornly insisted on accompanying them."

"Something that I can only be grateful for," the captain said smoothly, executing a little bow as he spoke.

This was all very charming and flattering, but it wasn't why they were at the party. Melody could sense the irritation and impatience emanating from Fatima at her side. Of course, it was unlikely the other woman would be quite so vexed if Captain Somerset was flirting with her. Nevertheless, Melody knew that they could be using their time more productively. She just wasn't sure what they might be doing.

Just as Melody was pondering this question, she sensed a new nervous energy in the room. She had her back to the door but could see Captain Somerset glance up and tense. Turning to see what or who was causing such consternation, Melody saw that an elderly, dignified-looking man with a long white beard had entered and was surveying the room. He was dressed in a white djellaba and turban and leant on an intricately carved wooden walking stick. Standing a little behind the man as if out of deference was a young, similarly dressed man. All conversation in the room had stopped, and every face was turned towards the newest guests.

Melody turned back to Captain Somerset, who had quickly schooled his face from his initial look of displeasure. "Who is that man?" she whispered to the captain.

"That is Muhammad al-Muqri, the Grand Vizier of Morocco," the captain said in a low, tense voice.

"Ah, so he is who was appointed after Madani El Glaoui was removed from the role last month."

Captain Somerset narrowed his eyes. "You are very knowledgeable about Moroccan politics for a young woman," he observed.

"It seemed wise to educate myself once we discovered that the Sultan was holding Conte Foscari," Melody answered as vaguely as she could. She certainly had no intention of letting her trip to the harem be widely known.

It wasn't immediately clear if this answer had satisfied Captain Somerset. However, after a brief moment, he replied, "You are evidently as intelligent as you are beautiful, Miss Chesterton. Nevertheless, I must excuse myself to go and pay my compliments to the Grand Vizier. I hope we can pick this conversation back up during the evening." With that, he bowed again and crossed to where the Grand Vizier was now standing, talking with their host, who had left their group to welcome his illustrious guest.

Rat had overheard the whispered conversation. "So that's al-Muqri, is it?"

"You say that like you know all about the man."

"You would, too, Melly, if you had listened to anything Alessandro had told us during our trip to Casablanca."

Choosing to ignore her brother's judgemental tone, Melody said instead, "Tell me what you learned."

Rat sighed but replied, "Prior to this most recent appointment, al-Muqri had been Grand Vizier twice before. His most recent tenure in the role was for Sultan Moulay Abdelaziz."

"The current Sultan's brother," Melody interrupted, determined to show that she wasn't entirely ignorant about the situation.

"Indeed. Al-Muqri's close association with Abdelaziz made it politically untenable for the new Sultan to leave him in the role. Such had been the widespread discontent with Abdelaziz that Sultan Moulay Abdelhafid sought to distance himself from his brother's former administration and its unpopular policies. However, al-Muqri somehow managed to keep some influence in the new regime. So much influence, in fact, that he has now regained the role."

Fatima had said nothing up to now, but now she asked, "Why do you think he is here?"

"Do you mean why was he invited or why did he accept the invitation?"

Before Fatima could answer Melody's question, Rat explained, "From what Alessandro told me, when al-Muqri was last Grand Vizier, he was known for his very pragmatic embrace of France's influence in Morocco. Indeed, while this position was not popular throughout Morocco in 1908, with many seeing it as a capitulation to foreign interests, his willingness to work with the French is likely the reason that Sultan Abdelhafid has reappointed him now. Unlike his predecessor, al-Muqri's pro-cooperation stance is now seen as an asset for managing relations with the French."

Realising that he still hadn't answered Fatima's question, Rat continued, "Given that this is a party to welcome Colonel Henri Gouraud, who will now be running the region on behalf of the French Government, it makes sense to invite the Grand Vizier, if he is so pro-French involvement."

Fatima and Melody nodded at this explanation, which made a lot of sense. Now, they watched the consul lead the Grand Vizier and his companion across the room to meet the two Frenchmen. Captain Somerset did not follow them. In fact, he seemed to have left the room.

Melody looked around at the few other groupings of men. Captain Somerset had not attached himself to any of those. She assumed the captain was availing himself of the facilities and turned her attention back to the Grand Vizier.

"I am assuming that if anyone were able to persuade the Sultan to release Alessandro, it would be al-Muqri," Melody said almost to herself. Then she turned to Fatima and urged the woman to insert herself into the conversation between the French officials and the Grand Vizier. "As we know, there isn't a man you cannot charm," she said in what she hoped was a persuasive voice.

"Except perhaps this one," Fatima replied caustically. "The Grand Vizier is a traditionalist to his core, and I am sure will be appalled by my very presence here, let alone if I, a mere woman, were to be so bold as to speak to him."

No sooner had Fatima said these words than she found the consul once more by her side. "Miss Amrani, the Grand Vizier has asked to meet you. It seems that he knew your father many years ago. Would you allow me to escort you over and introduce you?" he said, offering his arm.

"I would be honoured," Fatima said with a knowing look in Melody's direction.

As Fatima swept off with Consul MacLeod, Melody turned to Rat. "What do we do now?"

"Well, I see Captain Somerset is returning, so perhaps I should allow the two of you some privacy," Rat teased. "The man seemed quite besotted at first sight."

Melody blushed, but Rat's words gave her an idea. "Why don't you attempt to find the consul's private secretary and see if a telegram has arrived yet?"

"Surely Consul MacLeod would have mentioned something if it had."

"Perhaps. However, the room was quite full when we arrived, so he has probably been occupied greeting his guests for some time. The private secretary may not have known that we were invited tonight and would have no reason to bring the telegram in here. He might even have sent word to the riad."

That was a lot of perhaps, maybes and mights. Still, if there was even a slight possibility that Rat had received a reply from Lord Langley, it was worth going to inquire.

As Captain Somerset reclaimed his spot by Melody's side, Rat asked, "By any chance, do you know where I might find the consul's private secretary?"

Fixing Rat with an inquiring gaze, Somerset asked, "May I ask why you need him?"

"He sent a telegram for me earlier and I wished to see if there had been a reply." As soon as Rat said this, he worried that he shouldn't have done so, even to someone who worked for the Foreign Office. He hurried to explain further, "I am the ward of the Earl of Langley. I received word in Casablanca that he hasn't been well. I have been worried and sent a telegram to ask if he is feeling any better."

For a moment, Melody was gripped by worry; this was the first she had heard of Uncle Maxie being ill. Then she realised that Rat was merely attempting to account for his urgent desire to check if his telegram had been answered. It seemed as if his ruse had worked. Captain Somerset's face relaxed, and he gave Rat directions to the secretary's office.

"I walked by it a few minutes ago, and I saw that he was still there. So, you should be in luck." Rat thanked him and left.

CHAPTER 23

R at followed the captain's directions and came upon what he hoped was the secretary's office. His sharp knock at the door was answered by a hearty "Enter!"

The consul's private secretary was a cheerful-looking young man. He looked up from some papers as Rat entered and then stood. Rat approached the desk with an outstretched hand and said, "I am Matthew Sandworth. I believe that Consul MacLeod asked you to send a telegram on my behalf this morning. I am attending the dinner with my sister and thought I would pop in to see if a reply had arrived yet."

The secretary shook the outstretched hand and said, "Alister Black-adder at your service. Good to meet you, Mr Sandworth. As it happens, I heard a telegram come through a few minutes ago but I was absorbed in some paperwork and did not have a chance to check."

As he said this, Alister Blackadder pointed to a wooden table in the far corner of the room. Standing on the table was a classic telegraph machine with a polished wooden base, brass fittings and visible wiring.

Alister stood and moved toward the machine. "Have you ever seen one of these beauties in action?" he asked. Rat shook his head in the negative. "Well, we used to have to listen to incoming sounds and translate them into Morse code, but the modern ones have a paper tape recorder which inks the dots and dashes straight onto this paper strip here."

Picking up the long paper strip, Alister brought it over to show Rat. All he could see were dots and dashes printed on the long strip. "Can you decode this?" he asked, hoping that the answer was yes. He didn't want to have to wait to see what Lord Langley had replied.

"I can!" Alister said proudly. He went back and sat behind his desk, pulled a fresh sheet of paper out, took his pen and started translating the coded message. He gestured towards a chair in front of his desk and suggested that Rat take a seat. A few minutes later, Alister looked up and handed Rat the sheet of paper. "Done. Here you go."

Rat took the paper and glanced over it quickly. It was evident that Lord Langley had replied to the coded message that Rat had sent with one similarly encrypted using the Playfair cypher. Rat knew that he should probably wait until they returned to the riad to decrypt the telegram, but he was too anxious to wait. Instead, he asked Alister for a pencil and paper, explaining that the telegram was encrypted.

Ever since Lord Langley had first started teaching Rat about cryptography as a child, they had always used the fourth word, whatever it was, as the keyword in their encrypted messages. The message on the paper that Alister handed him had the word birthday as the fourth word.

Just as he was about to write the keyword down and begin to decrypt the message, he looked over at Alister Blackadder and said, as almost an afterthought, "It is awfully rude of me to ask this, but..."

"But would I give you some privacy while you deal with the telegram?" Alister said, finishing Rat's sentence. "Of course, old man. Nothing rude about that. Totally appropriate. I should have thought of that myself. Will ten minutes be enough time? I need to get a cup of tea anyway." With that, Alister stood and left the room.

Now that he was alone, Rat concentrated on his task and had fully decrypted the message in little more than five minutes. While he didn't regret the pivot he had made recently in his career, he would always find cryptography fascinating and got great satisfaction out of the puzzle-like aspect of the field. Looking at the decrypted message in front of him, he reread it to make sure he hadn't missed anything.

It seemed that the murdered rogue operative's name was Timothy

Shandling. In 1910, it had been discovered that Mr Shandling was selling classified British information to the highest bidder, sometimes the Germans, sometimes the French. By the time it was discovered, he had disappeared. The telegram had one rather cryptic comment that Rat pondered for some minutes, trying to determine what Lord Langley meant. It said, "Be careful. There is a rumour that Shandling has a highly placed friend who may have helped him escape. I will send more information when I have it."

"Highly placed friend," What on earth did that mean? And when might Lord Langley have more information? Rat sat back in his chair and considered the rest of the news. What was particularly interesting was that the rogue operative had sold British secrets to the French. Was he still working for his French paymasters, perhaps in Morocco? Rat thought back to Melody's theory that the French Government was behind Brett Rothnie's disappearance and the attempt on Alessandro's life. While he hadn't given it a lot of credence when Melody had floated the theory, this new data point made it much more likely now.

As he was thinking through the possible ramifications of Melody's theory being correct, the door opened, and Alister Blackadder came back into the room. "Is the coast clear?" he joked.

"Yes, I'm done. You can have your office back," Rat answered, folding the paper and putting it, the telegram tape, and the paper with Alister Blackadder's decryption of the Morse code in the pocket of his djellaba. Better safe than sorry. He stood, shook the other man's hand, thanked him again, and left the office. Fine man, Blackadder, Rat thought as he walked back up the corridor.

Back in the drawing room, Rat found that the rest of the guests were making their way into dinner, and he rushed to join them. He wouldn't have an opportunity to share what he'd learned with Melody and Fatima for some time. He was also curious as to how Fatima's introduction to the Grand Vizier had gone.

Dinner was long and tedious as far as Rat was concerned. Because of the lack of female guests besides Melody and Fatima, Rat found himself with a French government official on one side of him and Consul MacLeod on the other. The consul had insisted that Fatima sit next to him and spent the entire meal absorbed in his flirtation with her. The French official did not speak much English, so Rat concentrated on eating his meal and observing his fellow guests.

Captain Somerset had managed to get himself seated next to Melody, who looked as if she was very much enjoying the man's attentions. Rat was glad. He knew what a blow to her self-esteem Melody had suffered when Xander Ashby's true intentions had been exposed. And while he wasn't sure what exactly had happened between his sister and Alessandro, Rat was astute enough to recognise his sister's hurt feelings. It was lovely to witness her finding herself the object of such determined male attention. Captain William Somerset seemed like a fine, upstanding young man. Just as Melody had, Rat had caught the cultured tones of the man's accent and assumed that he came from a good family, if not an aristocratic one.

As he watched his sister giggle at some new flirtation from the infatuated captain, Rat thought about the light that the telegram might have shone on this investigation. He looked around the table at the various French officials enjoying the tasty smoked haddock appetiser. Was it possible that the man responsible for engineering Alessandro's arrest was in this room?

Colonel Henri Gouraud was sitting next to Captain Somerset, with the Grand Vizier to his left. From the snippets that wafted across the table to Rat, they seemed deep in conversation in French. Yet again, he wished he had more proficiency in foreign languages.

In deference to the Grand Vizier, Rat presumed, there was no wine served with the meal. In the absence of port with which to potentially enjoy a cigar, Consul MacLeod stood as the dessert plates were being removed, offered his arm to Fatima and said, "Shall we retire to the drawing room for some coffee or mint tea?"

Luckily, at least as far as Rat was concerned, the evening ended not long after when the Grand Vizier put down his glass of mint tea and announced his departure. Once the guest of honour had left, everyone else soon started trickling out.

Melody's company had been monopolised throughout dinner and afterwards in the drawing room by the charming captain. As she sipped her coffee and listened to more of Captain Somerset's amusing stories of growing up the youngest of a family of six boys in Hertfordshire, she caught Rat looking at her intently. He widened his eyes, raised his eyebrows, and slightly inclined his head towards the doors, indicating his wish to leave.

Reluctantly, Melody told the captain, "I believe that my brother is trying to tell me that it is time for us to make our thanks to our host and depart."

As she said this, she stood and held out her hand. The captain stood and took her hand. Looking very serious all of a sudden, he asked in a tentative voice, "May I call on you, Miss Chesterton?"

"I would love that, Captain Somerset. I do not know how much longer we might be in Fes. It all depends on how quickly we are able to secure the conte's release. However, I would be happy for your company during whatever time I have left here."

Captain Somerset smiled. "When you put it like that, there seems to be a great incentive for me to ensure that Conte Foscari's detention is of a long duration." He said this lightly and laughed at the end, but Melody must have looked shocked at his words because Captain Somerset quickly added, "Not that I have any power to do so. And, of course, nor would I even if I did."

Melody relaxed, gave Lahcen's name and the general location of the riad to the captain and said she hoped she would see him soon. She then turned and joined Rat, who now had Fatima by his side. They found Consul MacLeod, who expressed great sorrow at seeing Fatima leave so soon.

Finally, they had extricated themselves and found the servants and mules who had brought them there that night. The streets were wide enough in the Batha district that two mules could walk side-by-side. Fatima rode next to Melody with Rat bringing up the rear.

"Oh my, but that man is a bore," Fatima exclaimed when they were safely out of earshot.

"Who? Consul MacLeod?"

"Who else? I could barely stifle my yawns during dinner. At one point, I tried to turn to speak with the French gentleman on my other side, but the consul was having none of it. Honestly, one would think that there are only so many stories of salmon fishing one man had to tell, but it seems there is no limit!"

Melody was amused at the idea of Fatima's legendary charms back-firing on her. However, more pertinent was learning about her conversation with the Grand Vizier.

"Well, he was quite charming and speaks fluent French. It seems that he had known my father when they were both quite young men. In fact, during his very first tenure as Grand Vizier, he had been the one to recommend my father for the posting to Paris."

Impatient for Fatima to get to the critical part of her conversation, Melody said, "But what about Alessandro? Did you ask?"

Fatima shook her head sadly, "Al-Muqri refused to discuss Sandro. As soon as I tried, he shut down the conversation and excused himself from the group." It was evident that Fatima was as frustrated by Melody at this news.

From behind them, Rat, who had overheard the conversation, said, "I have news. However, I don't want to yell it out in the street like this. Before we go into the riad, let us talk for a few moments." Once Rat had said this, Melody was so impatient to hear what he had to say that she was tempted to spur her mule on to move faster.

Soon enough, though it felt like an eternity, they were outside the riad and had dismounted from the mules. The servants led the animals away, leaving Rat, Fatima and Melody the privacy for Rat to tell them about the telegram. The one part he left out was Lord Langley's vague warning. Until he had a better understanding of what was meant, he didn't want to alarm the women. Instead, he focused on Shandling's possible connection to the French Government.

"Do you think that I am right and that the French are behind this?" Melody asked.

"Yes," Rat agreed. "The evidence certainly points in that direction."

Given her earlier poohpoohing of Melody's hypothesis, Fatima didn't want to admit that she was wrong too quickly. Instead, she said, "What evidence is that? That the dead man once sold secrets to multiple countries, including France, hardly proves that he was working for them in Morocco."

Melody was well and truly fed up with Fatima's attitude and snapped, "Then do you have a better theory?"

Fatima was forced to admit that she didn't, but she was still disinclined to accept Melody's. Instead, she said, "And if you are right, then what? What is our next move?"

Neither Melody nor Rat had a good answer to that question.

As she undressed for the night, washed her face and then got into bed, Melody considered what Rat had told them. She'd had an immediate reaction to his news, but she wanted to reflect on it more to be sure that she wasn't just seeing things the way she wished them to be. Finally, as she lay in bed, staring up at the ornate, highly decorated ceiling, she decided that her first instinct had been the right one: Lord Langley's telegram ruled out Mustafa being anything other than the helpful, sweet child he seemed to be.

What had prevented her from immediately accepting this was the thought that Timothy Shandling could be all the telegram implied he was. Yet, even so, Mustafa might still not be the innocent he purported to be. Instead, he might have been in Shandling's employ. If that was the case, then the seemingly lucky coincidence of him being in the right place at the right time to warn Alessandro about the attempt on his life had indeed been a ruse to ingratiate himself with their group.

However, one rule that she knew that Wolfie and Tabby Cat ran all their investigations by was that the most straightforward answer was almost always correct. While it was, of course, possible that a highly convoluted solution was right, it was rarely the case. Wolfie referred to this principle as Occam's Razor. And if she applied this principle now, employing Mustafa seemed overly complicated for a seasoned operative such as Shandling. What would have been the point of inserting the child into their household? After all, it was beyond the bounds of reasonableness to assume that Shandling had planned his own murder. In which case, the point couldn't have been to have Mustafa in place to lead Alessandro to the body.

Melody's instincts told her that the young boy was all he seemed to be. She knew that she wanted that to be the case, but she also truly believed it was. She hadn't seen much of Mustafa since they had arrived in Fes. The boy had been absorbed into Lahcen's household, and she'd only caught a brief glimpse of him helping to serve breakfast the day before. Now that she had deduced that there was nothing to fear from the child, Melody was determined to call Mustafa up to her room to talk the following day.

While she was sure of his innocence, Melody still had some doubts about Omar and very much had concerns about Fatima's men. Mustafa had now spent enough time in their group, mingling with the servants, that he might have overheard something. She knew well enough from her childhood that adults tended to underestimate how much children understood and absorbed what was being said in front of them.

CHAPTER 24

After he had retired for the night, Rat had sat in his room for some time pondering the telegram from Lord Langley. More specifically, he had sat wondering what additional details might be forthcoming about this so-called "highly placed friend". What did that mean, and when might Lord Langley have the additional information that he promised?

Rat sat and considered whether there was any more information that he might provide that could in any way help Lord Langley with his inquiries. He reflected on what they had learned, both directly and through indirect, anecdotal conversation. Rat had the greatest respect and admiration for Lord Langley and would never presume to explain world affairs to his mentor. However, he was unsure how much of the sentiment on the ground was being transmitted back through official channels by the likes of Sir Reginald. Was the consul even aware of the extent to which the French might be manipulating the situation behind the scenes?

Finally, Rat had decided that there was nothing to lose by returning to the consul's home and sending another telegram laying out what they believed they knew so far. If it helped Lord Langley, all the better, and if it didn't, well, there was nothing to be lost. Rat was far too secure in his mentor's professional and personal regard to worry that the earl might think less of him for sending possibly superfluous information. Having made this decision, Rat was determined to write and encrypt a note immediately.

Sitting at the desk in his room, Rat considered what he wanted to tell Lord Langley. Then, using the Playfair cypher again, he wrote the note in code. Satisfied with what he'd written, Rat determined to return to the consul's home as soon as possible the following morning to send another telegram.

The next day, Rat rose and dressed quickly in the djellaba from the previous evening and was ready to leave as early as was acceptable for a morning call. Rat was disinclined to get back on another mule if he didn't have to. He believed he remembered the way through the Medina to the Batha district, so he felt he did not need to bother a servant to accompany him.

As he walked through the courtyard, he encountered Fatima, who was sipping mint tea and considering how she might spend her day. She looked up as Rat advanced. "Are you heading out, Matthew?" she asked.

It was astounding how Fatima managed to turn even the most mundane sentence into a flirtation when she so wished. Rat blushed and answered, "Yes. I wish to return to the consul's home to send another telegram." Then as much out of politeness as a desire to spend more time with the beguiling woman, he asked, "Would you care to join me?"

Fatima shook her head vehemently. She had no desire to run the risk of encountering the consul. Of course, as much as she found the man a roaring bore and had no interest in being courted by him, she was also irritated that he hadn't bothered to send even a note, let alone a token of his esteem that morning. If Consul MacLeod had sent such a thing, she would have loudly and publicly expressed her exasperation at the man's annoying persistence. However, now that he hadn't, she was seething quietly at the consul's neglect. The last thing in the world she intended to do was to turn up at his home and have there be even a whiff of desperate interest inferred.

As much as Rat was always happy for Fatima's company, in this instance, he was not unhappy to have her decline the invitation. To travel with her would mean getting the mules and servants and turning the entire outing into a far bigger endeavour than if he were just to stroll there alone and ask a servant to take him to Alister Blackadder's office. Blackadder was such a good chap that Rat did not doubt that the man would excuse him dropping by uninvited.

Rat's certainty that he remembered how to navigate the Medina to the Batha district might have been overly confident. In fact, it took him quite a few wrong turns before he finally stumbled, more by luck than judgement, across the consul's home. Rat walked up to the large, oak front door and rapped on the knocker.

A huge, hulking manservant opened the door. The man's size and visage reminded Rat of Wolf's bosom friend, Bear. Certainly, in Bear's case, his terrifying look belied a very sweet and gentle nature. Rat wondered whether the same could be said of this man. Certainly, he didn't seem particularly sweet as he informed Rat that the consul was not at home. Rat said that he had actually come to see Mr Blackadder in order to send a telegram back to London. The servant's dismissive look as he opened the door and invited Rat in told him all he needed to know about how the household staff viewed their European overlords.

Easily remembering his way back to Alister Blackadder's office, Rat strode down the corridor and knocked on the door. There was no answer. Rat considered what he should do. While it was possible that Alister had merely stepped out for a few minutes, it was also possible that he was out running some errand for Consul MacLeod and might be gone quite some time. Now that Rat had determined to send the telegram, he was eager to see it transmitted. How hard could it be to use the machine? He wondered. Surely, the most challenging part of sending a telegram was the knowledge of Morse code. If nothing else, Rat was too impatient to send the telegram and wondered if he could translate his message into Morse code. After all, he was trained in cryptography.

Determined to at least examine the telegram machine to see if its use was self-explanatory, Rat entered the office and made his way over to the machine and examined its buttons and wires. Wasn't it merely a case of using it almost like a typewriter? It looked simple enough.

Out of an abundance of caution, when he had left Alister Blackadder's office the evening before, Rat had taken his decrypted note, the translation from the Morse code and the original telegram. These were still in his pocket. Now, Rat wondered whether he might be able to work backwards from the telegram that had been decoded to figure out the right

Morse code symbols to use. Then, he could write his encrypted note out in Morse code and then send it himself. Of course, there was the possibility that not all the necessary letters were represented on the telegram from the day before. Still, the note had been long enough that Rat was sure that he could infer the alphabet by comparing the telegram to the note that Blackadder had gleaned from it, and if necessary, he could change some of the words he'd used.

Going over to sit at Alister's desk, Rat reviewed the original telegram in Morse code and the paper that Alister had translated it to. He quickly determined what the Morse code alphabet was, minus a few letters that he felt he would be able to work around. It took him a little time, but finally, Rat ended up with a note in Morse code quickly enough that he allowed himself to feel proud of this accomplishment.

Glancing at a pile of papers on the right side of the desk, Rat suddenly noticed his name on one that was partially hidden under a book. Normally, Rat loathed the idea of prying through other people's things, but in his new role for the Bureau, he'd made his peace with the possibility that he might have to overcome this qualm. Apart from anything else, if it was about him or a telegram for him, Rat felt he had a right to know what the message said. Gingerly pulling out the paper, Rat read what seemed to be an encrypted telegram for him that had been decoded from Morse code. He wondered why Alister Blackadder hadn't sent word to him this morning about the telegram. Even as he thought this, Rat realised that Blackadder might have done that and that a servant could be on his way to the riad at that very moment.

It didn't take long for Rat to decrypt the decoded telegram. Once he had, Rat sat back in Alister's desk chair and considered the implications of what he'd read. As the full import of the telegram from Lord Langley sank in, Rat considered if he even needed to send the message he had intended. Finally, deciding to amend it somewhat, he quickly wrote out what he wanted to say, encrypted it, and then again puzzled out what the correct Morse code would be. Finally, crossing back to the telegram machine, he considered how he could send the message.

Just as he was about to hit the first key, he heard a noise behind him. Turning around and seeing who had entered the office, all he saw was the hulking manservant. It seemed as if there was someone else standing behind him. Rat's first thought was to explain his presence there. He had just started to explain himself when the huge man crossed the room quickly, and before Rat could say much more, he found himself punched in the face. While the punch might have done no more than give him a black eye, Rat lost his balance, fell back, hit his head on the corner of the table that the telegram machine was on, and lost consciousness.

The last hazy words he heard were from a voice that sounded vaguely familiar, "Nosey, nosey, Mr Sandworth. Rifling through papers. What am I going to do with you now?"

As Rat lost consciousness, the voice said irritably, "Kacem, why on earth did you let him in here?" The only reply was a grunt.

When Rat finally came around, he found that he was in the dark and that he couldn't move. After a moment, he realised that his hands and feet were bound, his mouth gagged, and he had something over his head which explained the darkness. Where was he? The last thing he remembered was being in Alister Blackadder's office and trying to use the telegram machine. What had happened after that? It was all a little fuzzy, and he had a terrible, throbbing headache. Rat had no idea how long it had been since he first entered the office. Had he been unconscious for a few minutes or a few hours?

Rat tried to remember how he had come to fall, but those last few seconds were a blur. He did remember finding the still encrypted telegram and the shocking news it had relayed. Now, as he sat unable to do much more than think, Rat reflected on what it must mean. Timothy Shandling had been protected, helped to escape, and had continued to work for the Foreign Office in an unofficial, more shadowy role. The British Foreign Office!

While Lord Langley's telegram had been short on details and brief in its explanation, Rat had read enough to glean that various government entities might have somewhat different aims in North Africa. However, perhaps the most shocking part of the telegram had been the name of the person in the Foreign Office who had facilitated Shandling's escape: Somerset. That one word had shaken Rat almost more than anything. Somerset in the Foreign Office, the same man who had asked to call on Melody, was likely the duplicitous mastermind behind everything they had been investigating in Morocco: Brett Rothnie's disappearance, maybe murder; the attempt on Alessandro's life; and finally, Shandling's murder and Alessandro's arrest. And now, instead of being able to rush to Melody's side and protect her from whatever nefarious part of the plot Captain Somerset intended to implicate her in, Rat was bound and gagged, presumably by Somerset.

Lord Langley had implied that while the Secret Service Bureau worried that France's actions in Morocco might be a threat to British interests in North Africa and seek to curb French ambitions, the Foreign Office wanted to maintain Britain's neutrality in the Moroccan crisis. How far might the Foreign Office, or at least some men within it, go in their support of France's occupation of Fez? More to the point, what lengths might they go to in order to shore up their French allies in the region?

As Rat considered this question, he heard a door open and close, low voices speaking, though not in English. In fact, he thought they were speaking in Arabic. Rat wasn't sure what was happening, but he knew one thing: if anyone came looking for him, would there be any evidence that he had been violently taken from this room? Thinking quickly, he realised that while his hands were tied together, he could manipulate his fingers. He wore a pinkie ring that Lord Langley had given him on his sixteenth birthday. Before he had a chance to reconsider, Rat managed to get it off his finger. It landed on the floor next to him.

Rat realised that it was a good thing he had acted quickly because before he knew it, he was being picked up, thrown over someone's shoulder, and carried. A few moments later, Rat could hear another door opening, and then he felt that they were outside in the brutal heat of the middle of the day. If that was the case, then he had been gone for some hours. Rat was glad that Fatima at least knew where he had gone. How long before he was missed and someone came to discover what had happened to him?

This hope was shattered when he felt himself thrown into something, which was revealed to be some kind of cart. Then, he felt some kind of material thrown over him before the cart began to move. Where was he being taken, and what hope was there of his friends discovering him now? It felt like forever that he was bounced around in the cart. It wasn't moving quickly, from what Rat could tell, so he guessed that it was being pulled by a man, maybe a donkey, probably through the narrow, busy alleyways of the Medina.

Rat imagined that a cart, pulled by a donkey, with some nebulous lump covered in sacking wouldn't cause any comment in Fes. He tried to yell, but the gag was bound too tightly around his mouth. Finally, he felt the cart slow down and then come to a standstill. Before he knew it, strong arms had grabbed him out of the cart, thrown him over a shoulder again, and he was moving. And then, suddenly, he was put down.

Rat wondered whether he would be left as he was and was relieved when the sack was removed from his head and his hands and feet untied. It occurred to Rat that with his hands loose, he might fight back.

Just as he had this thought, a heavily accented voice said in broken English, "I hold a gun, so no funny business. Also, I take your gag off now. No people to hear you scream, so keep quiet," the man said before removing the material from Rat's mouth. "I put a ladder in hole and you climb down. Any of the funniest business, and I shoot."

Rat felt himself pushed down towards the ground where, after some scrabbling around, he felt the rung of a ladder. It wasn't easy climbing in the dark, but Rat had no choice and went down the ladder slowly until he reached the bottom. After a moment, there was a sound that indicated that the ladder was being pulled up. There was silence for a moment, then Rat heard movement, and the banging then the locking of a door. Rat looked around. Well, he could have looked around if it hadn't been so dark in whatever dank, uncomfortable hole he had been thrown into.

As Rat's eyes grew accustomed to the gloom, and realised with a start that he was not alone in the hole. "Nice to have company, finally," a voice said wearily. "I'm Brett. Who are you?" Rat realised with surprise that his new companion must be Brett Rothnie.

CHAPTER 25

When Melody had finally descended to the courtyard that morning, she was relieved to see Mustafa again serving breakfast. As he put a plate of fruit on the table not far from where she was sitting, Melody motioned for him to come closer. When he did, she whispered that she'd like him to come to her room when the meal was finished. The boy nodded.

Within twenty minutes, the group had finished eating, and Melody was able to escape to her room. She had been waiting for another ten minutes when there was a tap on the door. She quickly crossed the room to open it and waved Mustafa inside, indicating that he should be quiet until the door was properly closed. While there was no particular reason for caution, Melody was uncertain enough about the loyalties of the various members of the household hat she felt discretion was warranted.

Once Mustafa was safely in the room, Melody pulled him into an embrace. She had felt so guilty questioning the boy's true motives that it was a huge relief finally to put those worries aside. If Mustafa wondered about the hug, he said nothing. After Melody held him close for a few seconds, she released him and indicated that he should sit on her bed while she took the chair by her dressing table.

While she'd waited for Mustafa, Melody had considered how best to frame her question. Finally, she realised that it would be hard to explain away what she was asking if she was anything less than candid. "Mustafa, it was very helpful at the caravanserai when you told me what you had overheard the men discussing. So, I wonder, since we have been here, have you heard anything else that you believe might be helpful to Sidi Alessandro?"

The boy thought about the question carefully. "Do you believe that someone in Lalla Fatima's household is not what they seem to be?"

Well, the boy was undoubtedly astute. It was clear there was no point in beating around the bush. "I believe it is a possibility," Melody acknowledged. "That day when the man tried to attack Sidi Alessandro, and you stopped him, I wonder how that man knew we would be in the Medina. Someone must have been watching us ever since we entered Casablanca."

Even as she said these words, it occurred to Melody that Shandling might have been following them from Tangier. She cast her mind back. Surely, they would have noticed. Wouldn't they? Perhaps she wouldn't have noticed, but she was sure that Alessandro would have. The dusty road between Tangier and Casablanca had been busy with merchants, often travelling in long caravans. Then she considered whether they would have noticed a solo traveller, perhaps dressed in local costume, riding a horse or a mule, who had perhaps attached himself to one of these caravans. No, they wouldn't have noticed.

Despite this new consideration, Melody was still curious about what, if anything, Mustafa might have overheard. "I have heard nothing that would worry you or Sidi Matthew," the boy assured her.

Melody phrased her next question very carefully. She wanted to trust Omar; she really did. However, having been burned by Xander Ashby's betrayal, Melody was acutely aware that someone's apparent friendship might not be all it seemed.

"That is very good to know, Mustafa," Melody said before adding, "And Omar? Do you have any reason to believe that he is not the good friend that Sidi Alessandro believes him to be?"

The boy shook his head vehemently. "Omar is a very good man. He has been very kind to me."

Melody wasn't as comforted by these words as Mustafa intended. Again, reflecting on how hoodwinked she'd been by Xander, she wasn't prepared to accept that Omar's kindness towards Mustafa naturally translated to him being entirely honourable in every other regard.

Even so, she didn't want to prejudice the boy toward Omar unduly, so she said nothing more than, "Please let me know if you hear anything you believe I should know about."

"Of course, Lalla Melody. I would do anything to help Monsieur."

"I do not doubt that, Mustafa." And with that, she let the boy return to his duties.

Melody sat for a while, thinking. In some ways, they had quite a bit of information now, but it didn't feel like it led to anything that they could use to win Alessandro's freedom. In hindsight, she wished that she hadn't allowed her attention to be so monopolised by the charming Captain Somerset. As delightful as the flirtation had been, it had distracted her from talking to anyone else at the dinner party. Given the high-level French officials in attendance, Melody was sure she might have used her time more productively, although she wasn't even sure how much English they spoke. While it might have made more sense to have Fatima lead those conversations, she had been unable to extricate herself from Consul MacLeod.

Another tap on the door interrupted her despondent thoughts. When she opened it, she found one of Lahcen's household staff. He bowed and then handed her an envelope. Instead of leaving, the man stood there, evidently waiting to receive a reply. Melody was too curious about who the note was from to wait until she was back in the room, so she ripped it open as she stood in the doorway.

Melody pulled out of the envelope a folded light blue sheet of notepaper covered with an elegant script.

My dearest Miss Chesterton,

I wish that I could have sent a bouquet this morning, but alas, Fes is not London, and such things are not commonplace here. Instead, I will just have to relay my deep appreciation of you with mere words. I am not a poet and so cannot hope to convey my sentiments sufficiently. However, if you will do me the honour of accompanying me on a carriage ride to the most perfect picnic spot in all of Fes, I will at least try to put my admiration into practice. My man has brought this note and will wait for a reply.

Yours Eternally

William Somerset

Melody reread the note with great pleasure. There was no doubt that Captain Somerset's attentions were very flattering. While Melody's first thought was to write immediately to accept the invitation, this was quickly followed up by a wave of guilt; how could she think about gallivanting with a handsome man for the afternoon when every moment not spent working to free Alessandro meant another night he would spend in prison?

Of course, Alessandro wasn't in a actual prison but in a nice enough room in a palace. Nevertheless, he was under arrest, and that couldn't be pleasant. They had no idea what the Sultan's plans were for a trial, but presumably, that would happen at some point. Or did they not bother with trials in Morocco? Perhaps, as far as the Sultan was concerned, Alessandro's guilt was self-evident, and judgement had already been passed.

Certainly, Melody could only imagine what Fatima would say about her spending precious time so frivolously. Then, she considered Captain Somerset's position in the Foreign Office. She didn't know precisely what he did, but was it possible he could be helpful? While Sir Reginald had been unwilling to cross the Moroccan authorities on Alessandro's behalf, did that mean no British official would?

As she reflected on this question, it was not lost on Melody that they had no other plans for how they might more productively spend their day. The investigation seemed to be at a standstill, and so perhaps there was no good reason to refuse Captain Somerset's invitation, regardless of whether he could help.

Finally, deciding that she didn't care what nasty comment Fatima was likely to make, Melody took a sheet of paper and replied to Captain Somerset's note. She would be delighted to join him for a picnic. Would noon be a convenient time?

Melody found the manservant still waiting outside her door for whatever reply she was sending. She handed him the note she had put in an envelope. The man nodded and left. Now, she had some time to deal with the question of what to wear. Her caftans seemed far too much for a picnic, but the split skirts and blouses she had with her seemed to go too far in the opposite direction. Finally, she decided that a silk robe just spoke of trying far too hard to impress, and she changed into the least worn split skirt and the smartest of the blouses she had with her.

At noon on the dot, Captain Somerset presented himself at the riad. Melody had been waiting on tenterhooks in the courtyard. She stood to greet him with her stomach full of butterflies. Mustafa stood as well. As the captain approached her, he glanced at the boy, unsure what was going on.

Seeing his confusion, Melody explained, "While I am delighted to accept your invitation, it would hardly be appropriate for me to be out with an unmarried man alone. I can only imagine what Granny, the Dowager Countess of Pembroke, would have to say about such a dereliction of etiquette. This is Mustafa. He will be joining us as a chaperone." Privately, she was unsure that the dowager would consider an eight-year-old boy to be an appropriate guardian of a young woman's virtue, but needs must. The alternative was to have Rat or Fatima join them and neither option was particularly palatable.

Captain Somerset raised his eyebrows at her words but was wise enough to say nothing. Instead, he offered Melody his arm and then led her, with Mustafa following close behind, through the alleys back to where they had first arrived in Fes. There, where there was sufficient room for one, a carriage was waiting.

CHAPTER 26

The carriage left the fortified walls of Fes behind and quickly climbed into the hills behind the city. Melody had insisted that Mustafa ride in the carriage with them. Captain Somerset seemed a little put out by this unexpected impediment to his wooing. However, deciding to make the most of the time he had with Melody, he regaled her with more stories of his childhood and the trouble that he and his mischievous brothers used to cause.

When the captain asked about her childhood, she was a little vague. It wasn't that she meant to hide her working-class roots in the East End, but she also felt that she needed to know the captain better before revealing all her secrets. Instead, she said merely that she and her brother were orphaned and were taken in by the Earl and Countess of Pembroke.

Melody had been correct in her assumption that the captain was from an upper-class family. It turned out that his father was a baron. "With five older brothers, my father had his heir and more than enough spares and I was left to my own devices. I kicked around a little when I was younger but found my way to the army, and it was the making of me."

William Somerset was easy company. Unlike Alessandro when she first met him, the captain was very open and happily talked about his family and life back in England. Her time with Alessandro in Venice had made Melody all aflutter, unsure of herself. She had felt unsophisticated and immature. But her time with Captain Somerset couldn't be more different. He made her feel that she was the most beautiful, witty, fascinating woman in the world.

William gazed at her with adoring eyes, but not the puppy dog eyes that Xander Ashby had looked at her with. Or at least he had done an excellent job of pretending to look at her with adoration. Xander's infatuation, or supposed infatuation, had never felt serious to Melody. And now she knew why; it hadn't been. However, in Captain William Somerset, she felt she had met a man who saw her for who she really was; not as an idealised woman on a pedestal, and not as a silly girl, but instead, as an independent, strong-willed young woman who was ready to find her place in the world. Melody couldn't even put her finger on why she felt this way, but she did.

By the time the carriage came to a standstill high above Fes, she felt as if she had known William, as he now insisted she call him, for far longer than even less than twenty-four hours. Mustafa hopped out of the carriage, and William handed Melody down. Strapped to the back of the carriage was a hamper, which he retrieved, as well as a blanket. He spread the blanket down under an olive tree and offered Melody his hand as an aid while she sat.

It was fascinating seeing Fes from above. The warren of alleyways that made up so much of the Medina appeared from above as a dense expanse of earth-toned rooftops punctuated by the tall, tiled minarets of mosques.

"Why don't you sit, Mustafa?" Melody suggested. Instead of doing so, the boy hopped up and down and seemed too full of energy to relax on the blanket. Looking at him, Melody was reminded that he was a child and one who didn't have many opportunities to run around in the fresh air. "Would you like to explore a little?" she asked gently. The boy nodded his head enthusiastically. With a warning to not stray too far, Melody gave him permission to leave her side.

"I thought he was supposed to be your chaperone," William said in a gently mocking voice. "Do you now feel safe enough with me?"

Melody laughed, acknowledging the seeming inconsistency. "Is there a reason that I should not feel safe?" she asked coyly.

At this, William sat on the blanket, perhaps a little closer than he ought, and said in a solemn voice, all teasing gone, "If I have anything to say about it, you will always feel safe, Miss Chesterton."

Melody blushed deeply at the allusion. This was all moving quite fast. "If I am to call you William, then you must call me Melody," she said if only to cover her embarrassment.

The captain opened the hamper, which was positively bursting with scrumptious goodies. He also brought out a flask of mint-infused water, which was very refreshing on that hot day. He laid some of the food out on the blanket, and Melody took a sampling onto a plate. She called Mustafa to come and eat something. The boy ran over, plucked an orange out of the basket, and then skipped away.

"How did the boy come into your service?" William asked.

Melody couldn't have asked for a better opening for the conversation she hoped to have with the captain. She had been considering how she could tell the story while omitting the part where Alessandro and Rat were Secret Service Bureau operatives. Even though William worked for the Foreign Office, it was not her place to share that secret.

Instead, she spoke of Alessandro being called to Morocco on business. She said that she and her brother had asked if they might join him, and Alessandro agreed. Melody wasn't sure how credible that story really was, and she hoped that William wouldn't question the rather apparent holes in the narrative.

Instead, he said, "Yes, I remember your brother mentioning that you had both met Conte Foscari in Venice and then travelled here with him. You mentioned last night that the conte has been falsely arrested for murder."

Melody then explained how they had first met Mustafa and the role the boy had played in alerting Alessandro to his would-be attacker. They had then taken the orphan into their employ.

"You must have identified strongly with the idea of taking in an orphan and providing a safe harbour," William observed.

"Exactly!" Melody exclaimed, happy that he so immediately understood. She then told the rest of the story: the vice-consul's party, Mustafa recognising the man who had tried to attack Alessandro and finally the discovery of the dead body.

"And so, the conte was discovered by the Pasha's men, leaning over the dead body and was arrested?" William asked. "And the vice-consul and consul did not step in to help?"

Now, they were getting to the crux of what she wanted to discuss. "No! They said that the Pasha was adamant about taking Alessandro, I mean Conte Foscari, into custody, and the French consul was concerned about further inflaming local tensions and insisted that the Pasha be allowed to do as he wished. Then, the next morning, we heard that the conte had been brought to Fes, and we followed. It seems that he is being held in the palace. We were able to get an audience with the Sultan and spoke with the conte briefly."

William looked surprised and impressed at this news. "How did you manage to get an audience with the Sultan?"

"Fatima is related to one of his wives." Melody took a deep breath before making her request. "Captain Somerset, William, while the British vice-consul and consul in Casablanca were unwilling to lift a finger to help the conte, is there anything you might be able to do to help given your role in the Foreign Office."

There was a pause. A long pause. So long that Melody was worried that she had angered William with her request. Finally, he answered, "Perhaps." Then, seeing Melody's eyes light up, he added, "Though probably not. As you may know, the situation is very tense in Morocco now. The Foreign Secretary, Sir Edward Grey, wants to do everything he can to bolster the French claims in the region at the expense of the Germans. If the Moroccan authorities want to hold your friend and make an example of him, there may be little that the British Government is prepared to do. Particularly if the French consul refused to step in."

"But that's the thing, why does the Sultan want to make an example of the conte?"

"I doubt it is personal. I think that an opportunity presented itself to make a show of independence from the French, and he seized it. Though, why were the Pasha's men there so quickly?" William asked.

"Exactly!" Melody exclaimed. "That was the question we asked."

In the end, all William could promise was that he would send a telegram back to Whitehall to see if the Foreign Secretary were at all inclined to get involved. "But I would not get your hopes up," he cautioned.

Melody expressed how grateful she was that he was even prepared to try. This was the first glimmer of real hope she had felt in days. Laying a hand on his arm, she said warmly, "Thank you, William. It means a lot that you would even try." The smile he flashed her in return said more than any words could about why he was prepared to extend himself in this way.

The rest of the afternoon was delightful. Melody and William relaxed in the shade of the olive trees, eating dates and pastries while Mustafa played in the grass near them. For the first time since they had left Venice, Melody felt happy. For a few hours, she was able to forget about the difficult situation she and Rat had found themselves in and enjoy being in the company of a handsome, charming man who was obviously smitten with her.

Too soon, William suggested that perhaps they should pack up the remnants of the picnic and head back into Fes. Melody knew he was right. She had left word for Rat that she was going out for a ride with Captain Somerset, but if she were gone much longer, he would start to worry. He was probably already worried, in fact.

Less than thirty minutes later, the carriage had dropped them back in Fes, and William had escorted her and Mustafa to the riad's door. He declined to come in, saying that he had work to get back to. Melody dismissed Mustafa and wandered into the riad's courtyard, feeling as if nothing could ruin her good mood.

"Well, finally! And where have you been with the oh-so-charming Captain Somerset?" Fatima demanded. "Wasting time, I presume, when we should be dedicating every waking hour to securing Sandro's release."

Melody was irritated beyond belief. "And how have you spent the day more productively?" she challenged. The look on the other woman's face was all the answer she needed. So, Melody continued, "As it happens, I used the outing to request that Captain Somerset try to use his connections within the Foreign Office to assert influence with the Sultan!" She said this last sentence more gleefully than she had intended. In truth, William had promised to try but also had little faith that the Foreign

Office would be prepared to intervene. However, Melody decided to omit this detail for now; she had no desire to dilute her triumph. She was rewarded with a sulky look from Fatima who huffed but said no more about the outing.

Melody was about to retire to her room when Omar and Lahcen entered the courtyard. "Have you seen my brother?" she asked.

Lahcen and Omar shook their heads, but Fatima said, "I believe that he had returned to the vice-consul's home sometime this morning. It seems that there was something in the telegram he received yesterday that led him to believe that there might be an additional one today. Or maybe he wanted to send one. Perhaps both."

Melody wondered what Rat was expecting or wanted to send. Rat hadn't mentioned anything when he relayed the telegram's contents the previous evening. Had he omitted to tell them something? Why would he do that? Curious but not worried, Melody excused herself and returned to her room. She hadn't written in her diary in days and felt the need to commit her thoughts about William to paper while they were fresh in her mind. She found that writing things out usually helped her to work them out in her head.

In her bedroom, Melody took out her diary and sat at the dressing table, but the words didn't come as easily as they usually did. Chewing on the end of her pen, Melody wondered what was preventing the words from flowing. She tried again.

Dear Diary, Captain Somerset, William seems to be such a wonderful man.

Then she crossed that out and tried again.

William seems to be everything I've ever looked for in a man.

She paused again. Was he everything she'd looked for in a man? This wasn't so much a question about William but more about the idea that she had ever previously thought very deeply about what she wanted in a romantic partner. Trying one more time, she crossed out that line as well and wrote.

I had a lovely afternoon with William. His evident admiration was a true salve to my bruised ego. However, even as I say that, I second-guess myself. I thought that Xander's admiration was evident. I believed that he was quite infatuated with me, and yet I couldn't have been more wrong.

Putting down the pen, she considered her flirtation with Xander Ashby from the first time she had met him at Lady Bainbridge's party to that last, final encounter when he had laughed in her face and mocked the very idea that he had ever admired her. As she thought about that last conversation, Melody realised something that hadn't really penetrated through her shock and fear at the time: while it had seemed then that all of Xander's infatuation had been playacting, on reflection, she didn't entirely believe Xander's protestation that he had never felt anything for her. While there was no doubt that he had put on quite a performance, Melody didn't think that he was a good enough actor to have so thoroughly convinced her of feelings he hadn't truly felt.

Even as she thought this Melody told herself, what did it matter if there was a small kernel of genuine admiration? There was no doubt that Xander would have killed her or at least let Martha kill her and Rat.

Then, Melody's thoughts inevitably turned to the other romantic entanglement in Venice that hadn't been all that it seemed: Alessandro. It was a far more uncomfortable experience to revisit this, and it made Melody squirm just to remember the very amorous gondola ride that she had shared with the conte. Had there been anything true in his feelings for her? At the time, Alessandro had pointed out that she was a maiden, not a woman of the world, and that it would not be right to go any further despite his desire for her.

Now, as she remembered his words, Melody blushed at the memory of her rather wanton behaviour that evening. Alessandro had pushed her away from him and told her that despite his attraction to and desire for Melody, he couldn't overlook her naiveté and lack of understanding of what she was agreeing to when she seemed to be encouraging him to go further than merely kissing.

Was there any truth to any of this? Not the bit about her naivety; Melody did not doubt that was both true and what Alessandro genuinely felt about her. But the rest? Had he totally feigned desire for her? Melody wanted to believe that he hadn't, but his ability to detach from her utterly after that moment and during their entire trip to Casablanca made her wonder.

So, now she let her mind wander back to Captain William Somerset.

Diary, I am unsure that I trust my judgement about men after Venice. I will proceed cautiously with William and guard my heart carefully until I can be sure that there is no artifice in his professed admiration.

Satisfied that she had finally articulated what she truly felt, Melody decided to rest until dinner. It had been a challenging few weeks, physically, intellectually, and emotionally demanding.

CHAPTER 27

Melody thought little of it when Rat still had not returned by the time she had got back to the riad. However, when he still wasn't back by the time she descended to the courtyard for their evening meal, Melody started to worry. Then she chastised herself for being such a mother hen. Perhaps Rat had got caught up in something and hadn't arrived at the consul's home as early as he planned. Maybe he and the consul had fallen into conversation, and the hours had slipped away from them. Melody could well imagine that the garrulous Consul MacLeod had pressed him to stay for dinner. Morocco wasn't like London, with easy access to telephones. She might wish that Rat had sent a servant with word, but she could imagine her polite brother not wanting to make the request of a new acquaintance.

Lahcen's household ate dinner quite early by Moroccan standards, and so Melody wasn't even concerned when Rat hadn't returned by nine o'clock; it was possible that the consul took his evening meal somewhat later and then Rat had to make his way back to the riad. Over lamb tagine and couscous, Fatima had mentioned that Rat hadn't planned to take a mule or a servant with him. On hearing this, Melody was a little anxious that he might have got lost in the Medina, which was difficult enough to navigate during the day, let alone at night. She hoped that the consul would insist on sending a servant to guide Rat back.

When her brother had not returned by ten o'clock, Melody was worried. Omar, Lahcen, and Fatima were sitting with her in the courtyard, drinking mint tea, seemingly unconcerned about her brother's continued absence.

Her mint tea sat untouched on the table in front of her as Melody nervously nibbled at her nails. Finally, she interrupted the conversation to ask, "What do you think is keeping my brother?"

"Matthew is a grown man," Fatima answered dismissively. "Surely he does not have to answer to his little sister for his whereabouts."

Melody was so worried that she didn't even bother to feel irritation at the other woman's harsh and unfair words. Omar smiled kindly and answered, "It is possible that Consul MacLeod offered your brother a bed for the night. His home is some distance from here, and it would take a servant almost an hour to see Sidi Matthew home and then return. I am sure that he will be here by the time you come down to break your fast."

The words were well meant, and Melody tried to receive them as they were intended, but she was just too plagued by anxiety at this point and snapped, "And if he isn't? What if something has happened to him? Are we to all go to our beds and rest our heads on our pillows as if we do not have a care in the world?"

It was now Lahcen's turn to attempt to placate her. "Lalla Melody, what would you have me do? If it will soothe you, I am happy to rouse my men from their beds and send them out to walk the streets and alleys between here and the Batha district looking for your brother."

Melody would have liked to take him up on this offer and suggest that if his men were going to do this, they might not go all the way to the consul's home and inquire about Rat. However, even as she thought this, Melody realised how unreasonable such a request might be. She knew that Lahcen's servants rose early and worked a long day to ensure the comfort of her and the rest of the household. It seemed quite outrageous to expect them to spend hours looking for her brother, only to crawl back to their beds to grab some rest before rising early.

Instead, Melody said, "Thank you, Lahcen. I will not ask your servants to do that. However, if my brother is not home by tomorrow morning, I will ask that someone escort me to the consul's home to inquire about him."

Melody wasn't sure how she was going to sleep for worrying about Rat, but somehow, she fell into a slumber eventually. When Melody woke the following morning, she was so impatient to find out if her brother had returned that she didn't even bother to pin up her hair properly before rushing to knock on his door. When there was no reply, she opened his door and saw that his bed looked as if it had not been slept in. Melody then went down to the courtyard where Lahcen was sitting drinking mint tea. It seemed that Melody had slept later than she had intended, and it was almost ten o'clock.

When she told Lahcen that her brother was not in his room and he acknowledged that he had not seen him that morning, Melody burst into tears. "Lalla Melody, do not cry," Lahcen said in a kind, concerned voice. "All will be well. I will have some of my men go to the consul's home."

"I will be going," Melody asserted. "But I would appreciate if one of your men could accompany me."

Whatever Lahcen might have said in response was pre-empted by a servant who announced that there was a guest in the vestibule. While Melody didn't understand what the servant said, she did catch the name Somerset. Had William come to make a morning call?

Melody's guess was confirmed when Lahcen turned from the servant and said, "Lalla Melody, it appears you have a morning caller. Would you like my man to turn him away?"

While her first instinct was to say yes, Melody considered her proposed trip to the consul's home. Surely, her concerns would be taken more seriously if Captain Somerset accompanied her than if she, a young woman, turned up with only a servant for a companion.

"Please have him shown through," Melody said to Lahcen, who then said something to the servant.

A few moments later, Captain Somerset was shown into the courtyard. He came towards Melody, his hat in one hand, a bunch of roses in the other, and a broad smile on his face. "Miss Chesterton, please excuse the early call, but I came across a stall in the souq where flowers were being sold, and I had to bring you some. I meant merely to leave them, but I could not resist asking for you." At this, the man wore such an adorably sheepish look on his face that if Melody hadn't been as worried as she was, she would have smiled.

Instead of smiling, she approached him eagerly, ignoring the flowers in his hand. "Captain Somerset, William, your timing is perfect. I have need of your aid."

"I will do whatever is in my power to assist you; just say the word." Melody explained the situation and said she intended to visit the consul's home to discover what might have happened to Rat.

Without her even having to make the request, William said, "Then let me accompany you, though I would also be happy to make the trip myself." Melody assured him that she had no intention of being left behind. She ran back to her room to pin her hair up and get her hat, and a few minutes later, the riad door closed behind her and Captain Somerset.

"I left my carriage back towards the Bab Ftou," William explained. "The route it can take is a little circuitous, but if we use it, we can drive through the wider streets on the Medina's perimeter to get to the Batha district, where the streets are wide enough for my carriage."

Melody had noticed the day before that the captain's carriage was narrower and more lightweight than the ones traditionally used in Europe. She now realised that this was so it could navigate at least some parts of Fes. There was no doubt this would be quicker and certainly more comfortable than a mule, and Melody gratefully accepted the suggestion.

Neither Melody nor Captain Somerset said much for the journey; Melody was too distracted by her worries about Rat and William was too distracted by Melody. When they finally arrived at the consul's house, Melody didn't even wait for the captain to help her down but jumped out of the carriage and was halfway down the path to the front door before he closed the carriage door.

The same servant who opened the front door the night of the party opened it again. Melody inquired whether her brother was there, but the man looked blankly at her. William then asked in serviceable Arabic, but the man still shook his head.

"What did he say?" Melody asked impatiently after the servant had replied.

"He said that he has not seen your brother since the night of the consul's party." William then exchanged a few more words in Arabic with the servant. "He also says that he was away from the house yesterday, and another servant might have let Mr Sandworth in. However, he is sure that there were no guests for dinner, nor did anyone stay in one of the guest rooms."

William said a few more words, and the servant stepped back to let them into the house. "He said that the consul is not here. However, Mr Blackadder, the consul's secretary, is, and he suggests that we go through and talk to him. Follow me. I am here quite frequently and know the way."

The captain led the way down the corridor to the secretary's office and knocked on the door. A hale, "Enter," greeted them and they made their way into the office to find Alister Blackadder sitting behind his desk, buried in paperwork.

He didn't seem surprised to see Captain Somerset but was caught off-guard by Melody's presence. He had not met her the evening of the party and was very curious about the captain's charming companion. Introductions were made, and Alister offered them seats. Melody was far too anxious and impatient to sit, but after a glance at William, she realised that it would be insulting not to accept the invitation.

"How might I help you both this morning?" Alister asked.

"I believe that my brother came here sometime yesterday to send another telegram, and he never returned to the riad. I had assumed that he had stayed for dinner and then the night as Consul MacLeod's guest, but the manservant assured me that was not the case. As you can imagine, I am very concerned."

"Your brother?" Alister asked in a bemused tone. "I am not sure I know who your brother, Mr Chesterton, is."

Melody mentally kicked herself for not being clearer. "I apologise, Mr Blackadder. My brother and I have different surnames for reasons that are unimportant at the moment. His name is Mr Matthew Sandworth."

"Ah, Mr Sandworth. Yes, I had the pleasure of meeting him the night of the consul's party. He did receive a telegram that evening, which I decoded for him." Alister shook his head sadly, "However, I am sorry to have to inform you that I have not seen your brother since that night. I certainly did not see him yesterday. Of course, I wasn't here for most of the day. The consul had business in Fes, and I was with him most of the time."

Seeing Melody's crestfallen face at this news, Alister hurried to add, "It is certainly possible that your brother was here at some point; I just cannot vouch for that."

The servant who answered the door said that he had not been around most of yesterday. Do you have any idea who might have answered the door if my brother did visit?"

Alister rose. "Let me go and ask Ali, who opened the door for you today. He should know who might have done so yesterday." He left the room and a few minutes later re-entered with an enormous, scowling man whose thick, black beard almost came all the way to eyes which were so dark they were almost black.

"Now, Kacem, please tell Miss Chesterton what you told me."

Alister said this in English, and the man replied, "No visitors yesterday."

"And you are sure that no one else might have answered the door," Melody pressed, her anxiety rising. If Rat hadn't even arrived here, then what had happened to him? Suddenly, she had visions of her brother being set upon by some Moroccan equivalent of footpads. Had they left him wounded in an alleyway or worse?

"No visitors," was the large man's only terse answer. He then looked at Alister who nodded in dismissal.

Alister Blackadder retook his seat, clasped his hands together and said in a voice that mixed admiration with almost the tone of a supplicant, "I am so sorry that we have been unable to help, Miss Chesterton. Of course, both the consul and I will assist in any way we can to locate your brother. Not only is it part of our duties here in Fes, but it would be my personal pleasure to aid you in any way I can."

Melody noticed out of the corner of her eye that Captain Somerset seemed quite put out by Mr Blackadder's tone. Deciding that the last thing she needed at that moment was to manage two peacocks preening and vying for her attention, Melody was about to stand to leave when she noticed something. Out of the corner of her eye, she saw a glint of gold that looked awfully familiar. Standing and crossing to the side of the room, she stooped and picked up the object. Turning it over in her hand,

Melody was confident about what this was. She just wasn't sure what it meant.

"What do you have there, Miss Chesterton?" Alister asked.

Melody considered how she wished to answer. There was no doubt that the object now safe in her jacket pocket was Rat's ring. Embossed with the Langley crest, Melody would have recognised it anywhere. That his guardian and mentor had given him such a ring had meant the world to Rat. He knew what it signified: that while Rat could not inherit Lord Langley's title, he was considered in every way that counted the earl's son.

While tears threatened to well up in her eyes, Melody took control of her emotions. This was a time for cold, clear logic, not sentiment. It was evident that, despite assurances to the contrary, her brother had not only been in this house, but he had also been in this room.

Melody considered how to answer Alister's question. Finally, she said in as casual a voice as she could manage, "It is my brother's pinkie ring. He must have dropped it the night before last when he was in here during the consul's party."

While this was a plausible explanation, Melody was also sure that wasn't what had happened. She distinctly remembered seeing it on Rat's finger when they had stood in the riad's doorway discussing the telegram he had received from Lord Langley. Rat had a habit of turning the ring absentmindedly on his finger when he was anxious. And it was that evident anxiety that she remembered so clearly. Melody had thought at the time that there was more that Rat hadn't told her and Fatima and that it was obviously worrying him because he was twisting his ring as he spoke.

Alister Blackadder scrunched his face up for a moment as if he doubted Melody's words, but then quickly, he smoothed out his forehead, smiled and said, "Of course, that must be the case. I am glad that you spotted it there."

"Indeed. Well, we will take no more of your time." Melody crossed so quickly to the door that it took William a moment to realise that she was about to leave. He jumped up to follow her, and before Alister even had a chance to rise from his chair, they had bid farewell and exited the room.

CHAPTER 28

M elody walked out of the consul's house so quickly that Captain Somerset had to hurry to catch up with her. When they got to the carriage, she turned to him and said in a low voice, "William, I want you to tell your driver to take us just out of sight of the consul's house and then pull over."

Evidently burning to ask her what was going on, William nevertheless did as she commanded. By the time he returned from giving his driver the instructions, Melody had climbed into the carriage. He followed and sat opposite her with an inquiring look on his handsome face.

Taking the ring out of her jacket pocket, Melody showed it to him and explained, "I know, no, I am sure, that my brother was wearing this back at the riad after the party."

"So, what are you suggesting?"

"I am not suggesting anything. I am saying with absolute certainty that my brother was in that room yesterday and dropped his ring." She chose her words carefully. "I think it is possible that he didn't drop it by accident but instead left it as evidence that he had been there. If he was taken by force, he might have thought it the only way to indicate to someone who came looking for him that he had been there."

"And what if it hadn't been you who came? Or you hadn't noticed it?" William asked. Melody acknowledged that all those must have been possibilities, but perhaps Rat felt he had no choice but to try. "So, you think the manservant, Kacem, is lying?"

As the carriage started to move further up the street, Melody considered William's question. What did she think? "What do you know of Alister Blackadder?" she asked.

"Seems like a good chap, if a little young and green. He's quite new to the role. It seems he has quite an aptitude for foreign languages. Speaks fluent Arabic and some Berber. From what I understand, Consul MacLeod's previous secretary was recalled to London, and young Blackadder was sent in his stead. Actually, I believe that my brother recommended him."

"Your brother? Which one?" Melody asked, only vaguely interested.

"Adam. Seems Blackadder is the younger brother of one of Adam's close friends from Oxford." Melody was barely listening by this point. She knew that this kind of nepotism was the way that the upper classes ensured that key roles were manned by the "right kind of chap."

The carriage came to a standstill, and William asked, "Now what?"

It was an excellent question. Someone in the consul's house knew where her brother was, and if she was right about him dropping his ring on purpose, they had taken her brother prisoner. What had he found out that had caused him to be seen as such a threat? Of course, she had been concerned for a while that with Brett Rothnie and then Alessandro taken out of commission, her brother was the obvious next person to come for. It was doubtful that someone knew about Brett and Alessandro's work for the Secret Service Bureau but not about Rat. Perhaps his appearance at the consul's house merely provided the perfect opportunity to deal with the next person on the list.

As she thought this through, Melody realised that there was a good chance that whoever had taken her brother was now on high alert that Rat's disappearance was being investigated. Thinking through the events of the past hour, Melody said, "I am sure that Kacem is lying. After all, if my brother was in that house yesterday, then some servant let him in. Also, he hadn't sent a note ahead, so there was no reason for someone to be lying in wait, and it must have been a crime of opportunity."

She waited to see if William would ask why anyone would lie in wait for Rat, but he said nothing and so Melody continued. "If the basic facts of the domestic situation are as they were laid out, then the servant who opened the door for us today was not there, and Kacem took his place. There was something in how that man spoke to us that made me suspicious that he was telling the truth. And that was before I found the ring."

The captain nodded in agreement. "Yes, there was something a little off about him." He paused, "Do you imagine that he is the instigator behind taking your brother prisoner?"

"Not in the slightest. I do not doubt that whatever he did, it was at the behest of someone else. The question then becomes, is that someone in that house? Either way, I think that Kacem is going to leave the house soon to go and check on his prisoner. Isn't that human nature, after all?" In truth, Melody wasn't sure that she'd had enough life experience to declaim on human nature. Nevertheless, she could think of nothing more productive to do than to watch the consul's house and see if Kacem, or anyone else, left anytime soon.

Was there any merit in this plan? Melody wondered. She took some comfort from the fact that her brother had dropped his ring. Whatever else had happened, they hadn't killed him then and there. Or so she assumed.

Just as she was about to descend from the carriage, William said, "We might watch this house for a long time, and to what end? Just because someone leaves, it doesn't mean that they are guilty of anything. We could be following a totally innocent person through the streets of Fes. And how exactly do we do that without being observed? Neither one of us is inconspicuous."

Melody knew he was right, but inaction felt wrong. "What do you suggest instead?" she asked.

"Send the boy, Mustafa. One more child playing in the street won't attract anyone's attention. He strikes me as a smart, wily sort. Let him follow anyone who looks like they're acting suspiciously. We'll tell him to do no more than track them. If he believes he has discovered something, he can return, and we will take it from there."

It really was a very sensible plan, and yet every fibre in Melody's body rebelled against the idea of just sitting in the riad, waiting for Mustafa to discover something. She thought about what they had learned over the last twenty-four hours and decided that she had to presume that Omar was not implicated in any way. At some point, she had to take a leap of faith and trust someone.

"I think your idea is a good one, but it is more than one boy can do. Kacem aside, we have no idea who else in that house needs to be watched. Let us return to the riad and enlist the help of Omar and Lahcen. If they can send some young servants they trust with Mustafa, they can potentially follow multiple people at once."

Having decided on a course of action, Melody was anxious to return to the riad and implement it. William surprised her by saying, " While you return, I will stay here and watch the house. Something may happen in the time it takes for the boy to get here."

"What happened to not being able to be inconspicuous?"

"I keep a djellaba in a bag here, along with a turban. If I slip those on, I'll be inconspicuous enough. At least enough to keep an eye on the house."

Melody eyed him suspiciously. Why would he keep native clothes on hand? What was he expecting to happen?

Sensing her suspicions, William explained, "Much as it is often useful to make clear my status and rank as a British official, it has also proven to be helpful, on occasion, to blend into the crowd. After the first time, this necessity arose, and I was unprepared, I determined never to be caught flatfooted again."

This explanation did make sense. It certainly seemed far more practical for one of them to remain and watch the consul's house while the other went for reinforcement. While Melody would have loved to have made the case that she could be as effective a lookout as he could be, she knew that wasn't the case.

She briefly exited the carriage so the captain could change his clothes. It didn't take long, and before she knew it, a man who could have passed for Moroccan, complete with a perfectly wrapped turban, descended from the carriage. While many Moroccans were quite swarthy, there were enough with lighter complexions that, with his dark hair and eyes, Willam might have easily passed for a local.

"Do I pass muster?" he asked shyly.

"Very much so. Now that I see you in the djellaba, I realise that this is the far superior plan, William."

The young captain blushed with pleasure at her words. Moving towards Melody, he took both of her hands in his. "I promise we will find him. I will not rest until we do."

His words touched Melody. "I have no doubt that you will do everything you can, William."

Twenty-five minutes later, Melody was back at the riad. She rushed into the courtyard and was relieved to see Omar and Lahcen sitting and talking.

Both men looked up as the rather breathless young woman hurried up to them. "Lalla Melody, is everything alright? Did you find Sidi Matthew with Consul Macleod?" Omar asked in a concerned voice.

"No. I didn't. I believe my brother has been kidnapped." The men were shocked by her words. They persuaded the clearly overwrought woman to sit and catch her breath. Melody agreed to sit and then told them everything that had happened since she and the captain had entered the consul's home.

"Lalla Melody, I do not wish to cast aspersions on your story, but are you sure that you are drawing the right conclusion from finding your brother's ring on the floor?"

"What else can it mean?" she asked. "Everyone was adamant that Rat hadn't been there and yet he obviously had been, and someone in that house must have opened the door and admitted him."

"Is there no possibility that Sidi Sandworth dropped the ring the night of the party?" Lahcen asked, unable to disguise his scepticism at her conclusions.

"I have gone over and over that evening and I am more sure than ever that he was wearing it when we arrived back after the party. And there's something else; when we were small children, before I went to live with Lord and Lady Pembroke, my brother and I lived a very different life in a very dangerous part of London."

She could see the men's surprise at her words, but they let her continue. "Our parents died when I was very young, and Matthew had to look after me. Sometimes, he had to leave me alone to go and find work or food. He was always worried that someone would take me during those times. He used to tell me a story our mother had told him when he was my age about a little boy and girl who are in the woods and leave a trail of breadcrumbs to mark their way back home. He used to tell me that I should always try to leave him some kind of clue as to where I was going and that he would always find me."

Thinking back to those days, Melody had to shake her head at the young Rat's naivety in believing there was anything his four-year-old sister could have done to help him find her if she had been taken. Nevertheless, still a child himself, Rat had remembered his mother's story and thought it was possible.

"I believe that ring was him leaving a breadcrumb for me to find. He had to have known that I would come looking for him."

It wasn't clear whether this charming childhood anecdote won over Omar and Lahcen. Nevertheless, they both asked what they could do. Melody explained that Captain Somerset was watching the consul's home. Still, they needed more eyes watching it and, more importantly, small, nimble boys who could follow someone through the Medina without being noticed.

"I do not want any of the boys to put themselves in harm's way. If they feel they have been spotted, they should immediately leave off following the person and return here. But it will be invaluable if they can give us any information about who might have taken my brother and where."

CHAPTER 29

O mar and Lahcen were eager to help. They immediately rounded up Mustafa and two other boys who worked in the stables, looking after the mules. Omar explained what they were to do and told the other boys to listen to Mustafa and do whatever he said. Mustafa was bursting with pride to be entrusted with such an important job.

Coming up to Melody and putting his small hand on her arm, he said solemnly, "Lalla Melody, we will find Sidi Matthew, I promise."

While the boys were being given instructions, Fatima wafted down the stairs into the courtyard and demanded to be informed about the cause of the commotion. Melody told her what she and William had discovered and the role that Mustafa and the other boys were now going to play.

"This is ridiculous," Fatima proclaimed. "Who do you think you are, Melody, and what gruesome gothic novel do you believe you are living in the middle of?"

Finally, Melody could take no more of the woman's scorn and petty insults. "Fatima, I am not asking for your help in any way. Feel free to go about your day as if nothing was amiss." Fatima's response to this was a sniff worthy of the dowager. Even so, she took a seat on the couch, seemingly determined to observe the drama playing out in front of her.

The plan was for the boys to take the carriage back to the Batha district. Mustafa had experienced riding in a carriage, but the other boys were very excited at the prospect. Melody told the boys that once they had useful information about where her brother might be kept or by whom, they should make their way back to the riad, where she, Omar, and Lahcen would determine the next steps.

Although Mustafa was new to Fes, he assured her that the two other boys knew every alleyway in the city and that even he had gained some familiarity with the labyrinth of the Medina since they had arrived days before.

After the boys were sent off in the carriage, Melody returned inside and considered what she might do while she waited. She was surprised to see that Fatima was still on the couch in the courtyard.

"A package of new clothes arrived for you this morning," the woman said nonchalantly.

"I have bigger concerns than what I am wearing," Melody exclaimed with irritation.

"Indeed. However, if you are planning to follow those boys through the Medina without attracting attention to yourself, you might consider changing into the less formal djellaba I persuaded you to buy. With the hood up, your hair will be less obvious, and if you put a niqab over your face, you won't attract attention unless someone looks at you closely."

Melody had to admit that the woman had a point and now regretted her harsh tone. "Thank you, Fatima. I will do that."

"Do you have a gun? Because, if you do not, I have one you can borrow." Fatima said as casually as if she were offering to lend Melody a hairbrush.

"I have a Derringer pistol," Melody assured her.

"I assume you know how to use it. Would you like to take mine as well? These djellaba have the perfect deep pockets to carry such things in."

Melody considered the offer. Although Xander Ashby had disarmed Rat in Venice, the villain had not considered that Melody might also be carrying a gun. It had turned out to be very useful that he had never bothered disarming her. Thinking back on this, Melody realised that it was probably best to have as many options available to her as possible, so she gratefully accepted the offer of the second gun.

Thinking about weapons, Melody wondered whether Rat had carried his pocketknife with him when he visited the consul's home the day before. While he would have had no reason to imagine he was walking into danger, she knew that he often carried the knife with him and found that it was often useful for everyday activities. She hoped that yesterday hadn't been the exception to this normal behaviour. The knife had been an invaluable part of their escape from Xander and Martha in Venice, and Melody hoped it might be so again for her brother.

Returning to her room, Melody found the package of new clothes on her bed. She unpacked them, discarding the more formal caftans until, at the bottom of the pile, she came across the everyday djellaba that Fatima had convinced her to buy. Rather like the djellabas Rat had been wearing, it was a loose-fitting, ankle-length robe with long sleeves and a pointed hood. It was made of lightweight, beige material with a soft drape that would both keep her cool in the searing Moroccan heat but also allow for ease of motion.

When Fatima first suggested this material, Melody felt it was too drab. The other woman pointed out that Melody wanted a more everyday djellaba and that this was precisely the kind and colour of material that a typical Moroccan woman would choose. The one concession to Melody's desires was some pretty but subtle embroidery around the neckline and cuffs.

Melody quickly undressed and slipped the djellaba over her head. Pulling up the hood, she looked at herself in the mirror. She hadn't bothered to re-pin her hair but could see how, if she pinned it very carefully so that none of her auburn curls escaped, it would not be immediately apparent that she wasn't Moroccan.

While Melody and Fatima hadn't requested that the tailor make a niqab, it seemed that, fortuitously, he had assumed that one was necessary and had added it to the package. It was made of the same beige material. Melody quickly put it on and then turned back to the mirror. While her blue eyes were not a typical colour for the natives, she had seen some people, particularly Berbers, with colouring more commonly associated with Europeans. With only her eyes visible now, she believed she would not stand out and could pass as a local. While not all women who went out in public had their faces covered, many did, and it would not look at all out of place for Melody to do so.

Finally, satisfied with her disguise, Melody placed her Derringer in one of the djellaba's capacious pockets. On a whim, she wondered whether Rat had taken his lockpicks with him. He would have had no reason to suppose he needed them, and so there was a chance they were still in his room. Of course, not only did she have to find them — and she didn't feel comfortable rooting through Rat's belongings more than necessary — she had to be able to use them.

After discovering in Venice that her brother had this skillset, Melody had bothered him enough with pleas to teach her that he had shown her the picks and given some rudimentary guidance on their use. However, almost all this instruction had been on the ship to Tangier or during the carriage ride to Casablanca and there hadn't been many opportunities to learn using an actual locked door. Instead, Melody knew the theory of how lockpicking worked. Nevertheless, it couldn't hurt to take them with, if she could find them.

Melody made her way to Rat's bedroom and, not bothering to knock, went inside. Her brother had always been extremely tidy and organised, and his bedroom looked as she expected; not a book or a cravat out of place. She considered where he might keep the lockpicks if he didn't have them with him. Melody had no interest in rifling through her brother's more intimate attire. However, she knew that he usually kept some books, notepads, pens, and other practical items next to his bed.

Moving over there, she saw that the bedside table had a small drawer. Opening it, she found the items she would have expected, and there, at the very back, she found the lockpicks. Melody drew out the picks, feeling mixed emotions; on the one hand, she had come looking for them and was happy to have them with her in the hope she'd be able to use them if necessary. On the other hand, if they were here, then Rat didn't have them with him. Melody could only imagine Rat's frustration if he was presented with the possibility of escape and realised that he had left the picks behind.

Quickly pocketing them, Melody wondered if there was anything else she might need. Feeling around in the back of the drawer, she felt a small, cold, metal object and realised that it must be the torch that Lord Langley had given Rat as a gift. Small and nickel-plated, the electric torch had an adjustable aperture to make the beam of light wider or narrower. Again, it had come in very handy in Venice, and Melody saw no reason not to take it with her.

Leaving Rat's room, Melody closed the door behind her. A great wave of anxiety washed over her; would this plan work? What if it didn't? Melody realised that it was of no help to Rat if she succumbed to worry and second-guessed the scheme they had put into place. While it may not be perfect, it was a start. Something else she had learned from watching and listening to Wolfie and Tabby Cat conduct investigations over the years was that one started with a supposition and pivoted and adjusted as new information became available. It was neither likely nor necessary that a theory or plan was perfectly correct from the start. What was necessary was that one not become too wedded to an initial idea and, instead, were open to modifications.

By the time she returned to the courtyard, Omar and Lahcen had changed into more appropriate clothes and were joined by some of Fatima's men. This gave Melody pause. Despite all they had learned, she was not totally convinced that an enemy informant hadn't infiltrated their group. Sighing, she realised that she had no proof that this was the case and even less idea which of the men it might be. They needed all the hands they could muster to find Rat, so she would just have to hope that she was wrong. Certainly, she could think of no good reason to give not to accept the men's help.

"Lalla Melody, the men are willing to fan out through the Medina if you have any idea where they should start looking," Omar offered.

Melody spread her hands out and shrugged her shoulders in helpless resignation. She had no idea where they might start to look. "Lahcen and his people must have far more idea where our villain might be holding my brother."

Lahcen replied, "As you know, the Medina is a labyrinth of narrow streets, crumbling buildings, and hidden spaces. Any abandoned or partially used structure could serve such a purpose. It is even possible that they transported him out of the Medina. There are various places beyond the walls of Fes that might be secluded enough to serve as a prison."

As depressing as the thought was that they might be unable to narrow their search, Melody tried to be as logical as possible. "Let us assume, for the time being, that they have taken him somewhere close by, or at least somewhat close by. While I assume the consul has use of a carriage, surely it isn't used by other people in his household. Or at least if it is, wouldn't that be cause for comment?"

For a moment, it crossed Melody's mind that it might be the consul himself who was involved, but she quickly dismissed that idea. Why would the highest-ranking British official in the region be involved in kidnapping anyone, let alone a fellow British citizen? This was just too outlandish a theory even to consider. Instead, it made much more sense that one of his servants, perhaps a Berber, was in the employ of the French Government and involved in whatever intrigue Brett Rothnie had uncovered.

Following this thought, Melody continued, "So, let us work on the assumption that my brother is being held in the Medina and within a reasonably short walk from the consul's home." While she didn't explain her reasoning, no one challenged her theory.

Lahcen considered her words. "There are various warehouses that have fallen into disuse because the buildings are in bad shape. Since the French took so much control a few years ago, Fes' utility as a major trade hub has declined. Many of the warehouses that once stored goods for the caravan trade routes have fallen into disuse. Maritime trade has become the preferred method as the Europeans favour cities like Casablanca for their ports. The smart merchants have adapted by moving their warehouses nearer these major ports."

Finally, Melody thought, they had a place to start!

CHAPTER 30

L ahcen explained that most of the abandoned warehouses had been used by weavers or tanneries. He suggested that they split the men into two groups to search for the warehouses of the two groups of artisans. Omar would lead one group to the tanneries, and Lahcen would lead the other to the weaver's warehouses. They suggested that Melody wait at the riad in case the boys returned.

While she was initially reluctant to be left behind, Melody knew that it made sense. As the men left, Melody took a seat on the couch next to Fatima, who had watched the proceedings with interest. The woman seemed disinclined to be involved in the plan, and so her continued presence was irritating. Melody hadn't put on the niqab yet and now fidgeted with it to distract herself.

"For heaven's sake, Melody, do stop playing with that. Have a cup of tea or something."

"Some of us are concerned," Melody replied caustically.

"And how will tying that niqab into knots help your brother?" Then, adopting a gentler tone, Fatima said, "I know that you are worried about Matthew. We all are." Melody wasn't sure she believed that statement. Nevertheless, she let the woman continue uninterrupted. "It seems that you might have been correct, or at least more so than I gave you credit for in your theories of what might be going on."

Fatima said no more, and Melody realised that was as close to an apology as she was likely to get. She inclined her head in acknowledgement. A servant brought mint tea and some aniseed pastries, which, if nothing else, gave Melody something to do with her hands instead of fidgeting.

She didn't know how long it had been since the men had left. Initially, Melody had been checking the clock anxiously every few minutes. Fatima had become irritated by that as well and had insisted that Melody swap seats with her so that her back was to the grandfather clock in the corner of the courtyard.

Just as Melody thought she could no longer endure the waiting, Mustafa came running into the riad. "Lalla Melody," he said excitedly, "the large, scary man left, and I followed him to the tanneries. I saw where he went, and then I came here straight away. I ran all the way back," the young boy said with pride.

Melody had jumped up when Mustafa had entered the room and now embraced him gratefully. But what now? "The captain said that he would take the carriage and come here and meet me," the boy continued. "He said that I would be able to follow the man far more effectively than he could." Again, the boy's pride in the task he had been entrusted with was heartwarming.

As tempting as it was to leave then and there with Mustafa, Melody knew that wasn't the most sensible plan. If William was on his way, they should wait for him to arrive. While Omar and the men had headed off towards the tanneries, Melody had no idea how big the area was nor how likely it was that they'd run into each other. Even though she knew this all intellectually, the wait was excruciating.

Finally, after what seemed like forever but was likely less than ten minutes, William burst into the courtyard, still dressed in his Moroccan garb. Melody and Mustafa updated him on where the men had gone and where Mustafa had followed Kacem.

"Good job, lad," William said, slapping the boy on his back. Then, turning to Melody, he confirmed, "So, Omar and some men are somewhere in the tanneries? We don't know where exactly, but they are trying to identify an abandoned building where it is possible that your brother is being held?"

"Yes. We determined that the tanneries and the area of the weavers were the two most likely areas where there are a lot of abandoned warehouses, which seemed a likely place to hold someone."

"Good deduction," William said with a grin. "And it seems that you were correct."

Melody smiled shyly, "How do you know that this was my deduction? Actually, only a part of it was. Lahcen supplied the key information about where such abandoned buildings might be in and around the souq."

"Then, what are we waiting for?" William said. "Lead the way, boy."

In no time, they were weaving their way through the narrow, winding alleyways of the souq. Melody didn't want to show a lack of faith in Mustafa, but she was concerned that he might not know how to navigate through the Medina as well as he claimed. A couple of wrong turns didn't allay her worries. Mustafa stopped near where men were dying large bundles of cloth, turned around, and then said something in Arabic to one of the men, who pointed back the way they'd come.

They turned and retraced their steps, then took another route. Finally, Melody smelled the unmistakable odour that indicated they were nearing the tanneries. Mustafa seemed to have regained his confidence and led them down a particularly narrow alleyway between two shops selling all manner of leather products. At the end of the alleyway, they found themselves standing next to a raised structure containing deep vats filled with pungent chemicals.

Melody remembered seeing these vats from the upper window of one of the leather shops when they had gone on their shopping expedition with Hakima. Then, the shopkeeper had given them a sprig of mint to hold under their noses to try to mitigate the awful smells coming from the vats. Now, they had nothing to ward off the disgusting odours, and Melody was grateful that she at least had the niqab covering her mouth and nose.

Previously, Melody had seen the vats from above. Now, viewed from up close, she realised that the workers not only had to deal with the chemical fumes, which almost certainly burned their lungs, but they also had to be extremely careful as they balanced on the narrow ledges between the vats. Melody remembered Hakima telling them about the arduous and revolting process the leather hides had to undergo: washing, removing hair and fur in highly caustic limewater, cleaning, and finally, tanning and dying.

From this close distance, the sharp, acrid odour emitted from the lime vats and the reek of decomposition and dung from others was quite overwhelming, even through the niqab. Melody couldn't imagine spending all day, every day, in such an environment, to say nothing of the danger of walking the narrow ledges. Given what some of the vats did to animal hides, Melody could only imagine what a horrible death it would be to fall into such a vat.

Mustafa led them around the vats to a partially crumbling building with rusted iron gates and rotting wooden beams. He pointed to a large iron door and said, "The big man went in there." They had guessed that Rat was being held in an abandoned warehouse, and it seemed the supposition was correct.

The boy continued, "I think he brought food. He was carrying a bag with him."

Well, that was something, Melody thought. It meant that Rat was alive, probably. Moreover, his captors had been feeding him. Was Kacem still in the warehouse? Melody voiced this question.

William gestured for Melody and Mustafa to follow him as he went to the side of the warehouse, where a grimy window was located. Luckily, the noise of the tannery workers was so clangorous that there was no need to be particularly quiet. The window was too high for Melody to look through, but the captain found a large rock, which he stood on as he peeked through the small, greasy pane of glass.

Melody didn't want to rush him, but she could barely contain her impatience to know what he could see. Finally, after what felt like an age, he stepped off the rock.

"What did you see, William?"

"Well, it is dark in there and I wouldn't swear that Kacem isn't in there, but I couldn't see him. I didn't see anyone else either, though, but there is a large pit in the middle of the floor. I do wonder whether they've put your brother in that."

Melody's heart clenched; the thought that her beloved brother was being held as if he were livestock sickened her. They had to get into this warehouse and rescue him, no matter the risks. She couldn't bear the thought of leaving him there for a moment longer than necessary.

As if anticipating her words, William said to Mustafa, "I want you to see if you can locate the other men who came to search around here. We do not know what we are walking into, and it would be good to have them know where to find us as backup." Then, turning to Melody, he asked, "Is there any possibility that I can persuade you to go with the boy?"

"I have two guns with me, and I know how to use them," Melody said defiantly. "I also have lockpicks and a torch. I am breaking into this building to rescue my brother. Whether or not you join me is up to you."

William signed resignedly. He also looked quite surprised to hear that she was armed. "I have a revolver as well," he told her. "Do you know how to use those lockpicks?"

"Not as well as I should," Melody admitted reluctantly.

"Then, why don't you give them to me? I do have some experience." Melody raised her eyebrows but said nothing as she handed over the picks.

As they sent Mustafa off to find Omar and the other men, Melody considered the situation. "If the door is locked, then it's likely because Kacem has left. Why would he bother to lock the door after him?"

William wasn't sure the issue was as cut and dried as Melody wished it to be, but he conceded there was a chance she was right. After considering the possibility, he said, "Stay behind me but have your revolver at the ready. I am going to try the door handle gently. Whether or not your logic is unassailable, it is surely the case that if the door isn't locked then Kacem is still in there. If that's the case, he may be alerted when I try the door, and we will need to be ready to shoot. If the door is locked, then hopefully, I can open it with the picks. However, we should still proceed as if someone might be waiting for us on the other side of the door."

Melody nodded and retrieved her Derringer out of one of the djellaba's pockets. While she was glad to have Fatima's gun with her as well, Melody was used to her gun and would only use the other if she had no choice. Luckily, the warehouse was in the shadows of the vats. It was unlikely that any of the workers above could see them, and even if they could, would they care? They were far more likely to be concerned about their safety as they moved the hides in and out of the dangerous chemicals.

William moved towards the door and Melody stayed close behind him, her gun at the ready. He reached out for the door handle and gingerly tried it. With a sigh of relief, he turned to Melody. "It's locked. But even so, don't let your guard down." She nodded. He took the picks and made surprisingly quick work of the lock. "Let me go in first," he commanded. Melody was about to argue, then William continued, "If someone is waiting there, let him think that I've come alone before you spring your attack on him." It was a sensible plan, and there was no good reason not to agree.

Melody stood with her back flat against the warehouse wall just a little away from the door so that she would be out of sight when the door opened. Then, as quietly as possible, William opened the door and slipped into the building.

CHAPTER 31

Melody hadn't realised that she'd been holding her breath since William had turned the door handle of the now unlocked door. Now, as he slipped into the building, she exhaled. At what point could she be sure that he was safely inside and, more to the point, alone? She waited, and then she waited. There was no sound of a skirmish, but there was also no sound of anything else. Finally, she could contain her anxiety no longer and slowly and carefully slid through the door, trying to make as little noise as possible.

It was difficult to see much inside the warehouse. A few faint shafts of light pierced through cracks in the walls. In addition, the small window that William had climbed up to look through let in some light, though the combination of the gloominess where the building was located and the dinginess of the panes of glass meant that whatever illumination it provided was barely sufficient to see the figure up ahead, which she hoped was William.

Sticking close to the walls and tiptoeing, Melody approached whoever it was ahead of her, gun at the ready. It looked as if the man was standing by the pit that William had described. If this wasn't the captain, then had William been pushed in?

Just as Melody was seized by fear that this was indeed the case, the figure turned, and she saw with relief that it was William. He beckoned her over to the edge of the pit. As Melody looked over the edge, it was hard to see much in the pit's inky depth, but she thought that she saw two faint figures.

"Rat," Melody whispered. "Are you down there?"

"Melody?" a hopeful voice answered. "Is that you? How did you ever find me?"

This wasn't the time for an explanation. Instead, Melody turned to William and asked, "How do we get them out?"

"Are you alone?" Rat's voice wafted up. From the sound of his voice, the pit was deep.

"Captain Somerset is with me," Melody assured him.

"No! Not Somerset. Melody, Lord Langley warned me that he is the person responsible for Timothy Shandling escaping justice in Britain. He's behind this all."

Melody couldn't believe what she was hearing. It wasn't possible. Had a man's insincere regard fooled her again? From the outline of his figure, Melody thought that the captain was pointing his gun down. Without thinking twice, she covered the distance between them and pointed her Deringer at his head.

"You? It was you behind this all along?" she spat. "Did you create this charade of following Mustafa here just so that you could imprison me as well?"

"No, Melody, Miss Chesterton. I have no idea what your brother is talking about," Captain Somerset protested.

Rat's disembodied voice answered, "The telegram was very clear that Somerset in the Foreign Office had facilitated Shandling's escape. Are you going to believe that there are two men with the name Somerset at the Foreign Office?"

It wasn't such an unusual name that it was impossible. However, Melody realised that to believe so was to accept a more complicated, unlikely scenario.

Just as she thought this, William said in reply, "Melody, I told you that my brother Adam also works for the Foreign Office. He is Sir Edward Grey's private secretary. I have been worried for some time about where his loyalties truly lie, and this telegram that your brother received confirmed many of my fears. You must believe me, Melody. If there is a Somerset behind all this, it is Adam."

Melody stood, her arm still outstretched, her gun still aimed at William's head. She had never felt more conflicted in her life. She wanted to believe him, she really did. And she did remember him mentioning that his brother Adam had helped Alister Blackadder to get his position. Wait! Alister Blackadder. A lightbulb went off, and Melody lowered her gun.

Then, Melody said it out loud, "Alister Blackadder. You were abducted in his office, weren't you, Rat? Adam Somerset, the captain's brother, helped him get this post. Could he be the person who is somehow responsible for Brett Rothnie's murder?"

Suddenly, a different voice that wasn't Rat's piped up from deep in the pit, "Murder? I feel quite alive, if a little stiff from being kept down here so long."

"Meet Brett Rothnie," Rat called up.

There were so many questions that Melody wanted to ask Mr Rothnie but now didn't seem the most appropriate of times. Kacem or someone else might return at any minute. Their top priority had to be getting the two men out of the pit.

Just as she thought this, Rat yelled up, "There's a ladder up there somewhere. It's how they got us down here."

"Well, at least in my case, I fell part of the way," Brett complained. "I was bruised for days."

It didn't take William long to find the ladder and to lower it into the pit. Before Melody knew it, Rat had climbed the ladder and had her in his arms. She had never been so happy to see her brother. Brett Rothnie followed Rat up the ladder.

Again, there was no time to exchange pleasantries. While Rat was not entirely convinced that Captain Somerset was on their side, it seemed that the expeditious thing to do was to get out of the warehouse as quickly as they could.

Just as they were turning to leave, there was a sound by the door. "Stay behind me," William said to Melody.

"Who goes there?" asked a male voice. Suddenly, the room was illuminated as a torch shone in their direction. As the voice came towards them, Melody thought that it belonged to Alister Blackadder. As the torch shone on their faces, the man continued, "I came as soon as I learned of your capture, Mr Sandworth. It seems that Kacem, the consul's manservant, got a little carried away when he found you looking through papers in my office. The man is a buffoon, of course, and I will ensure that the consul dismisses him immediately." This was all said in a tone of such shock and concern that Melody immediately second-guessed her earlier seeming epiphany.

"I was not in my office because I had received word that Captain Somerset here is a traitor and was behind the attack on your friend in Casablanca," Alister explained.

"Melody, you know this isn't true," William said. "You just admitted yourself that you believed that it was my brother that Mr Sandworth's telegram referred to."

"Ha!" Alister sneered. "I have long suspected that your loyalties had been compromised, Somerset. Your brother had the same concern. You were working for the French, which is why you hired Mr Shandling to attack Conte Foscari."

"How do you know about Timothy Shandling?" Rat asked.

"You must have mentioned his name to me," Alister blustered.

"No, I am sure I didn't."

They hadn't realised that, as Alister had been talking, he had been slowly moving towards them. Now, in one smooth gesture, he dropped the torch he was holding, grabbed Melody and pulled her against him. While she had still been holding her gun at her side, the shock of the move caused her to drop it on the ground. The next thing she knew, there was a gun barrel being held against her head. Though the torch had fallen to the ground, it was still on and in the circle of light emanating from it, Alister could see that William was pointing a gun towards him.

"Drop the gun and kick it over, Somerset, or I will blow a hole in Miss Chesterton's pretty little head," Alister snarled.

William did as he was ordered. Now, noticing that Rat and Brett had been freed from the pit, Alister continued, "You think that you're so smart, Mr Sandworth, don't you? The new shiny operative from the Bureau. Yet you didn't even think that you had decoded your telegram at my desk. Did it not occur to you that your pen made an indentation in the blotter and that I could use that to recreate your decrypted message?

Thank you for doing that for me. When I saw that your Lord Langley had somehow made the connection with Somerset, I hoped that you would jump to just the conclusion that you did. If it hadn't been for this pretty little sister of yours, that is."

All Melody could do was think about how to keep Alister talking until the others managed to disarm him. He was a cornered man, and who knew what he might do to make his escape.

"But why, Mr Blackadder? Why are you in league with the French Government?" she said in an almost pleading voice.

"He's not acting on behalf of the French Government," Rat told the stunned group. "He's working for the British Government, or at least a faction within the Foreign Office."

"A faction?" Alister said mockingly. "Try the faction. Shandling and I both had our orders from on high."

"Then why kill Shandling if you were in league with him?" Melody asked, genuinely curious.

"Yes, well, that was a rather unfortunate deviation from the plan by the Grand Vizier. It seems that he was not pleased when Shandling failed to stop Conte Foscari. And the man was starting to be rather a loose cannon."

Melody couldn't believe all that she was hearing. Just when she didn't think it could get worse, Alister continued, "I was hoping not to have to kill Mr Rothnie and Mr Sandworth. We prefer not to eat our own if possible. However, now you all know too much, and I have no choice. I am sorry, but you are going to have to die. All of you. Even you, pretty Miss Chesterton."

As Alister was speaking, Melody was slowly and carefully moving her hand towards her pocket. Now, Alister suddenly pushed her ahead and said, "All walk back towards the pit. I think that's a perfect place to dump your bodies, and you might as well save me the trouble of dragging them over."

Once Alister's grip on her loosened, Melody put her hand in her pocket and pulled out her gun. She had only a split second to consider where to shoot him. She wanted to disarm the man but not necessarily to kill him. But it was dark, and she had no time to aim properly. Instead, she turned quickly and tried for his leg. As the bullet hit its mark, Alister screamed in pain, went to grab his thigh and dropped his gun. William took advantage of the moment and ran at the other man, shoving him to the ground.

"Grab the gun," William yelled at anyone close enough to act on the command.

Melody thought that the scene couldn't get more chaotic, but suddenly, there were more men in the room and lots of yelling. From what she could see, Rat had also rushed to tackle Alister Blackadder, who was writhing on the ground in agony from his bullet wound. Melody saw the torch still lying on the ground and went to pick it up. Shining it upwards, she saw that the new arrivals in the warehouse were Omar and Fatima's men. It seemed that Mustafa had managed to locate them and find his way back to the abandoned warehouse.

CHAPTER 32

It had been more than two weeks since the confrontation with Alister Blackadder in the abandoned warehouse in the tanneries, and Melody and Rat were still in Fes, still staying at Lahcen's riad. All in all, it had been quite a frustrating time. They had initially taken the wounded Alister Blackadder back to the riad to discuss what to do with him. Given that he did, in fact, seem to be acting on orders from the Foreign Office, or at least someone there, and that there had been some kind of unofficial partnership with the Grand Vizier, al-Muqri, it wasn't a simple matter to accuse the man of even kidnapping, let alone of being a possible co-conspirator in the death of Timothy Shandling. And, because none of this was simple, Alessandro was still being held in the Sultan's palace.

Finally, Consul MacLeod decided that he would send his secretary back to Britain to answer for any overzealousness in carrying out his Foreign Office orders. Even Blackadder's imprisonment of Brett and Rat wasn't viewed as entirely out of line with his mission. As frustrated as Rat and Melody were by this decision, William made clear that this was an injustice they would likely have to make their peace with.

In the immediate aftermath of the confrontation with Alister, Melody had found Captain William Somerset to be a rock of support. It had not been lost on Melody that he had partnered with her, in the truest sense of the word, to rescue Rat. Unlike so many of the men she seemed to encounter and be related to, he hadn't tried to wrap her in cotton wool but instead had welcomed her help, even as the plan became more dangerous.

William had visited the riad most days, and this second day of July was no different. Initially, Fatima had insisted on remaining in the courtyard when the captain had visited. However, her pleasure in thwarting Melody's blossoming romance had waned as the days passed, and soon enough, she went about her business and ignored the not-quite-official young lovers.

Rat had his own qualms about the romance. He was convinced that the Somerset that Lord Langley's telegram referred to was William's brother, Adam. Nevertheless, the entire incident had left a lingering sour taste regarding the captain. When challenged about his attitude by Melody, all Rat could do was shrug and say, "I'm trying to get over it." Rat acknowledged that his worries about Captain Somerset had no logical basis, and he tried to make himself scarce during the visits.

That morning, Melody was sitting in the courtyard with Rat, sipping mint tea and anticipating a morning visit from William. When, as expected, he was announced by a servant, Rat rose and made to leave as per usual. William put his hand out and said, "Mr Sandworth, I need you to remain, if you do not mind. I have news, and you should both hear it."

Well, that was quite ominous. Melody's first thought was that something untoward had happened to Alessandro. What she was not expecting were William's next words, "Germany has sent a gunboat to the Moroccan port of Agadir. They claim that it is to protect Germany's interests in the region, but I'm not sure anyone believes that."

A gunboat? That couldn't be good, Melody thought.

"What will this mean?" Rat asked.

William shook his head. "I am not sure, but it cannot bode well. I can only imagine that the French will interpret it as an aggressive manoeuvre designed to pressure them into giving Germany concessions that they would rather not give."

"Why would the Germans escalate the situation in Morocco like this?"

"Well, to be fair to our Teutonic friends, I imagine they would say that France escalated the situation by occupying Fes," William explained.

"Meanwhile, our Foreign Secretary has quickly and strongly voiced Britain's support for France and warned Germany against any further escalation of the situation. In particular, he has said publicly that any attempt by Germany to establish a naval base at Agadir would be unacceptable."

Rat nodded, and even Melody, who had finally found a reason to be interested in foreign affairs, understood the gravity of the situation.

William added somewhat bitterly, "Of course, one might say that the Germans have played into Grey's hands. From word that I received from Whitehall, it seems that this has strained Anglo-German relations, with many in Britain, including the press, finally agreeing with Sir Edward's position and viewing the incident as evidence of Germany's ambitions to challenge British interests overseas."

"Any word from the Sultan?"

"None that I have heard. However, this cannot help his efforts to seem independent of foreign influence. I can only imagine that this crisis will make it even more evident that Morocco is no longer an independent country."

Then Melody asked the question that was most personal to her, "And what will this mean for Conte Foscari?"

When the captain didn't answer immediately, Melody's thoughts went to the darkest of places. Her hands flew to her mouth, and she exclaimed, "No! Don't tell me this has made his situation worse?"

If William thought anything about her very apparent distress over the conte's dilemma, he made no comment. Instead, he replied, "Well, truly, I'm not sure. I know that in light of what we learned from Blackadder, the consul has visited the Grand Vizier and made a case for the conte's release, but so far, there has been no official response."

As he said these words, a servant entered the courtyard, followed by Brett and Olympia Rothnie. After his release from the warehouse, Brett had accompanied them back to the riad with Alister Blackadder. However, since then, he hadn't been heard from and had been somewhat forgotten in all the efforts to get Alessandro released.

Now, Brett and his wife were greeted warmly and joined everyone on the couches. Mint tea was brought out and some dates and fruit.

The group made small talk for some minutes until Olympia Rothnie cleared her throat. "I must tell you how very grateful I am to you for returning Brett to me. He has decided to retire from, well, from all his professions."

"Will you return to Britain?" Melody asked.

"Heavens, no!" Brett said fervently. "After what my government has put me through, I have no interest in returning. And anyway, I don't believe the weather will suit my dear Olympia. We will be returning to Greece, where I intend to photograph nothing more exciting than birds and the occasional fisherman."

Everyone gave their best wishes and assumed that expressing gratitude had been the primary reason for the social call. Thus, they were surprised when Brett continued, "But that is not the reason for our visit today. Olympia has informed me that you guessed that I had discovered evidence that the French Government might not want to be made public."

Now Brett had his audience's rapt attention as everyone leant forward a little in anticipation of his explanation. Melody couldn't help adding, "The Sultan's wife, Lalla Rabia also suggested that such a document exists."

"Did she now?" Brett said in surprise. "I always assumed that her father had known about the letter. It was only after my release from that pit that I discovered that Madani El Glaoui had been dismissed from his role as Grand Vizier and replaced with al-Muqri. I would imagine that Madani El Glaoui's knowledge of the letter only fortified his resistance to the French occupation."

"But what was this letter, and where is it now?" Rat asked, impatient with the winding explanation.

"It was from Justin de Selves, the French Minister of Foreign Affairs, to General Paul-Charles Moinier, who was the highest-ranking French official in Fes at the time. It instructed him to ensure that the Sultan formally requested French assistance to restore order in Fes. It was signed and had an official seal. I was alerted to its existence and was able to take a photograph of it."

"Who alerted you, and how on earth did you get access to it?" William asked in amazement. Brett's only answer was to tap the side of his nose with his forefinger. Realising he was not going to get an answer, William tried a different question, "I am assuming that you alerted the Bureau to the existence of this proof of French manipulation of the situation?"

"Indeed. The next thing I knew, that weasel Blackadder waylaid me in the street, demanding I hand over the photo. I told him that I didn't report to the Foreign Office and I certainly didn't report to him and that the photo was in a secure place. The Bureau had said I was to sit tight and that a secure courier was arriving in Fes and would contact me and transport the evidence back to Britain. After that encounter with Blackadder, I had a feeling I was being watched. Then, that Tuesday, I went out, and that hulk of a man, Kacem, I think his name is, snatched me."

Melody was confused, "If Alister Blackadder was working for the Foreign Office, why didn't they just wait until you had sent the photo to London to intercept it?"

Brett had no idea, but William could guess. "My brother, Adam, is fervently anti-German, much like his employer, Sir Edward. However, there are others in the Prime Minister's cabinet who are inclined to a more conciliatory approach to Germany and are wary of Britain being too overtly supportive of France's ambitions in Morocco. In particular, they are nervous about the unintended commitments towards the French and being drawn into an entanglement that might escalate tensions with Germany. I am sure that the Grey faction, spearheaded by my brother, considered that the safest option was to ensure that the photograph never arrived in Whitehall."

Picking up the thread of the conversation, Rat asked, "Isn't that all rather moot now that the Germans have sent a gunboat? It seems that the escalation has happened."

"Indeed," William agreed. "And as I said before Mr Rothnie arrived, I am sure that the Foreign Secretary is thrilled. Whatever voices of dissent there are in the government must find their opinions no longer carry weight either with the Prime Minister or the public; Germany is now seen as the aggressor."

As everyone reflected on William's words, there was a noise coming from the riad's vestibule. It seemed that someone else had arrived. Melody assumed it was Fatima back from whatever social call or shopping expedition she had been busy with that morning. She glanced up, expecting to see a servant laden with parcels following in Fatima's wake. To her amazement, the face she saw was Alessandro's. Looking perhaps a little wan but otherwise no worse for his weeks as a prisoner. Without considering her actions or audience, Melody leapt to her feet and threw herself into his arms.

"Alessandro. You're here? How? Why? What happened?" Melody cried as she hugged him tightly. Suddenly, aware of the impropriety of her behaviour, Melody pulled back, but she couldn't contain her amazement. "We just heard that the Sultan refused to release you. How did this happen?"

The conte shrugged his shoulders. "I have no idea. All I know is that a guard came into my room earlier and said that I was free to go."

"Hmm, well, I may have had something to do with that," Brett offered. "I am only sorry it took this long for me to act. Honestly, being stuck in that pit for weeks was quite traumatic."

"He wasn't himself when he first returned home," Olympia added. "He was so thin and had terrible dreams each night."

"It's true. At first, I never wanted to think about that damn photo again. But then, as I started to feel better, I began to think about the conversations I'd had in that pit with young Matthew here. He'd told me everything about what you were all doing to obtain the release of your friend. I had been tempted just to destroy the photo, but I hadn't done it yet. I talked it over with Olympia and we knew we wanted to do something to repay what you had done for me. Then, this morning, I heard about the German gunboat and the kerfuffle it's caused, and I knew just what to do."

Rat and Melody looked at each other in amazement. What on earth had Brett done that had managed to secure Alessandro's release after all their failed attempts over the past few weeks? And where had he managed to hide that photo that they had been unable to find it in his study? Rat gave a little shrug; it didn't really matter at this point.

"I went to visit the office of Colonel Henri Gouraud," Brett continued with a flourish, clearly enjoying the dramatic telling of his story. "I am now a private citizen again and do not feel myself beholden to the Bureau. I told the colonel that I believe that the British newspapers might be very interested to learn that the situation that Morocco now finds itself in with a German warship anchored off its coast was perhaps not quite as unavoidable as is now being claimed. I told him that all I wanted was for his government to ensure Conte Foscari's release. And hey presto! What do you know, here he is!"

Melody retook her seat, and Alessandro joined the group. He seemed a little dazed at his sudden freedom but otherwise happy to be back amongst friends. Melody had noticed that he looked at William with curiosity. Suddenly, she realised that, as much as the captain had become a fixture in their lives at the riad, the two men had never met. She made a mental note to introduce them when the group was a little less exuberant and to ensure that Alessandro knew what a pivotal role William had played in releasing Brett and Rat and, therefore, Alessandro himself.

It was only when a servant approached the couches with more pastries that Melody glanced up and saw that William had left the table and was slipping out of the courtyard. She jumped to her feet and rushed to follow him, calling out his name.

Finally catching up with him just as William was opening the door to the riad, Melody exclaimed, "Why did you not say goodbye before you left, William?"

He turned towards her with a look of sad longing in his eyes. "It seemed better if I just slipped away, Melody."

"What do you mean? I don't understand. Is something wrong?" she asked, closing the space between them.

William reached up and brushed a stray curl from Melody's face, then left his hand gently cupping her cheek. "These last few weeks with you have been magical, Melody," he said softly.

"For me as well. So why are you leaving like this?"

"What I feel for you, Melody... well, I have been hoping that you feel the same way. But I saw your face when Conte Foscari arrived, and I knew that my cause was a lost one."

"No, no. You have it all wrong. I was merely happy that a friend was now safe. That is all," Melody protested.

"I have been down this path before and know better than to attempt it again. Loving a woman who is in love with another man only leads to heartache." Then he removed his hand, turned and opened the door. Pausing with his hand on the doorknob, he looked back. "Be well Melody. Love well." And with that, William was gone.

Melody stood looking at the closing door, overwhelmed by confusion and sadness. She knew that a good man had just walked out of her life. A man she might have been happy sharing a life with. And she had lost him for what? A silly infatuation for a man who felt nothing in return. Melody wiped the tears from her cheeks as she whispered William's parting words, "Love well." Shaking her head, Melody took a deep breath and made a vow: she would no longer look or hope for love. Certainly, she would never expect it from Alessandro.

EPILOGUE

M elody looked out at the sea and pondered her time in Morocco. She had yearned for adventure, and that was indeed what she had found. Now, with the hardships of travelling back to Tangier via Casablanca, the terror of Rat's disappearance, and the fear for Alessandro's safety behind her, Melody's recollections of Morocco softened into images of vibrant designs and colours and memories of delicious smells and delectable bites. She remembered the good, kind people who helped her and the fascinating culture she had caught a glimpse of.

They had been on the ship for two days and had at least one more day ahead of them before they arrived at the French port of Marseille. From there, they would have a long train ride to Amsterdam. Despite the length of the journey, it was by ship and train and not by horse or mule and so Melody was unphased by the prospect. It was amazing how her appreciation of modern travel had grown after the arduous trips between Casablanca and Fes and then up to Tangier.

Dear Diary, where to begin? I know that I should be happy that I am being included in Rat and Alessandro's trip to Amsterdam, but I have not been entrusted with the reason for our journey. It seems that I haven't yet proven myself sufficiently, though it is hard for me to understand how that could be. What is most galling is that I am quite sure that Fatima knows more than I do. Can you believe it? She has joined us on our journey.

Having that woman with us is almost enough to drive me to abandon my European travels and return to London. Whatever respite I had from her petty insults and her preening during the trip to Fes, she reverted to form thoroughly once Alessandro was returned to us. And yes, then there is Alessandro. While Fatima was quick to take as much credit for his return as possible, Rat ensured that the conte was in no doubt as to where most of it lay: with me. Alessandro thanked me very politely, and then that was that. His behaviour has reverted to what it was once we left Venice: cool and distant. Why does this irritate me so much?

As Melody put down her pen and contemplated this last sentence, her reverie was interrupted.

"Lalla Melody," the sun is going down and so Miss Mary thought you might need your shawl."

Melody took the shawl from the young boy and smiled. "Thank you, Mustafa. How do you feel about leaving Morocco?"

Mustafa smiled broadly. "I am happy to serve Monsieur, you, and Sidi Matthew. I have a soft bed and regular meals. Mustafa is very happy." With that, the child bowed and left Melody to return to her thoughts.

It wasn't that long ago that she and Mary, accompanied by Rat, had set out for London. Now, their group had doubled in size. Between Mustafa, Alessandro and Fatima, there were new cultures, tensions, and, at least in Fatima's case, layers of ulterior motives to deal with. It all made Melody's head spin and made her view the backbiting of London society with far gentler eyes. She had thought she was escaping the drama of the Season by leaving London, but that now seemed like child's play compared to the vortex of political tension, international intrigue, and personal ambition that she now found herself caught up in.

Pulling her shawl a little more tightly about her, Melody closed her journal and sighed. She knew that she was not the same naive young woman who had set out for Europe barely three months prior with her head full of fictional heroines and their romantic adventures. Now, Melody carried with her the understanding and fear that Europe was hovering on the precipice of war and that the success or failure of Rat and Alessandro's missions could have a direct impact on whether or not the great powers were tipped into outright conflict. That was an enormous burden to carry and Melody only wished that the two men were more willing to trust her to shoulder it with them. Whatever their new mission was in Amsterdam, Melody anticipated it with a frisson of excitement but also with trepidation at the enormous stakes involved.

~

NOTE: TWO BOOKS THAT WERE INVALUABLE REFERENCES FOR the runup to the second Agadir Crisis in Morocco were: The Sleepwalkers: How Europe Went to War in 1914 by Christopher Clark and The Road to 1914: The War that Ended the Peace by Margaret MacMillan.

~

FOR SHORT STORIES, BONUS CHAPTERS, INSIDER INFO, AND more, **sign up for my newsletter** or find the link at **sarahfnoel.com.**

~

FOR A SNEAK PEEK BOOK 3 IN THE CONTINENTAL CAPERS of Melody Chesterton series, The Amsterdam Enigma, keep reading...

DESPITE THEIR BEST EFFORTS, MELODY AND RAT FOUND themselves powerless to prevent the crisis in Morocco from spiralling out of control, threatening to ignite the powder keg of tensions between Germany, France, and Britain.

WITH THE SPECTRE OF WAR LOOMING, BRITAIN IS DETERMINED to expand its influence across Europe. After the Agadir Crisis, the preservation of Dutch neutrality, crucial for Britain's access to Dutch ports, becomes an even more pressing concern. Rat, the new Secret Service Bureau operative, is dispatched to Amsterdam on a mission of the utmost importance- to untangle a puzzle that could decide the fate of Dutch neutrality.

DESPITE HER SIGNIFICANT CONTRIBUTIONS TO HER BROTHER'S previous cases, Melody is frustrated; Rat is still not convinced that she should continue to be involved and is even trying to persuade Melody to return to London. To add to her frustration, the handsome yet exasperating Conte Alessandro Foscari insists on travelling with them.

WILL THIS BE MELODY'S LAST CONTINENTAL CAPER, OR WILL she solve The Amsterdam Enigma?

Afterword

Thank you for reading Mischief In Morocco. I hope you enjoyed it. If you'd like to see what's coming next for Melody, here are some ways to stay in touch:

SarahFNoel.com
Facebook
@sarahfNoelAuthor on Bluesky
sfnoel on Instagram
@sfnoel on Threads

If you enjoyed this book, I'd very much **appreciate a review** (but, please no spoilers).

About Sarah F. Noel

Originally from London, Sarah F. Noel now spends most of her time in Grenada in the Caribbean. Sarah loves reading historical mysteries with strong female characters. The Tabitha & Wolf Mystery Series and its spin-off, The Continental Capers of Melody Chesterton, are exactly the kind of books she loves to curl up with on a lazy Sunday.

Visit Sarah's website (sarahfnoel.com/) to join her mailing list, connect with her on social media, and see what's coming next!

Printed in Great Britain
by Amazon

62973687R00137